FAMOUS

FAMOUS

HELLCAT RELEASED™ BOOK SIX

MICHAEL ANDERLE

DISRUPTIVE IMAGINATION®

Version 1.01, October 2022
ebook ISBN: 979-8-88541-471-5
Print ISBN: 979-8-88541-472-2

THE FAMOUS TEAM

Thanks to the JIT Readers

Christopher Gilliard
Dave Hicks
Diane L. Smith
Dorothy Lloyd
Jan Hunnicutt
Zacc Pelter
Jeff Goode

If I've missed anyone, please let me know!

Editor
The SkyFyre Editing Team

DEDICATION

To Family, Friends and
Those Who Love
to Read.
May We All Enjoy Grace
to Live the Life We Are
Called.

— Michael

CHAPTER ONE

A torrent of heavy autocannon rounds shredded the ground behind the running Dante and Nasreen. Each one dug a new crater and shot more dust into the smoke-filled air. The clear day had turned into a dust storm.

Dante was grateful for small favors. The rounds landed so close that had they been pulsecores, he and Nasreen would be lying on the ground crispy and dead. He'd sprung for better armor for the team's non-augmented members, but that didn't make him a strategic hard-cased soldier. Direct plasma explosions could burn their armor with far too much ease.

The dry, cracked dirt around them hadn't seen water for some time. Rock outcroppings increased in number toward nearby long-dry waterfalls. One tall cliff extended off a craggy area filled with rocks and the scattered remains of metal and concrete walls. The remnants of a factory lay spread all over. Portions of walls had crumbled, and disintegrated flooring that hadn't survived the decades covered the area. Half-buried machinery lay everywhere.

The area was the perfect site for a Plunderer job. It *wasn't* the ideal site for two competing groups of Plunderers.

"Yeah." Dante huffed as quick dashes and turns brought him

behind an overturned cargo container. "This could have gone better."

"That's putting it lightly," Nasreen replied.

The gunship made another pass. Bullets rained down, penetrating the weathered and ancient cargo container with ease. Dante ducked low, not liking how loud the *whizz* of a projectile sounded as it zoomed past his helmet.

"Hyde," Dante shouted, hoping all the running and shooting hadn't damaged his comms gear. "Our armor isn't going to survive a direct hit from that cannon. When I came up with the plan, the idea was you'd take the damned gunship down."

"I got you, *Papi*," Hyde replied. The comms static made him hard to hear. "It's not like Mugoi could have done this."

Dante sprinted and threw himself behind the remnants of a thick metal wall surrounding a forest of overturned metal columns. Nasreen jumped behind the wall, dissipating her momentum with an agile roll. The gunship firing at them screamed overhead again, the autocannon not letting up. Rounds blew holes in the nearby wall.

Another round blasted into a column. Purplish dust puffed out from inside.

"Don't breathe too deeply," Dante advised. He waited until the gunship finished its pass and hurried toward another wall and a series of twisted pitted cables.

The gunship banked hard. Chunks of metal and wire trailed it. Sparks flashed from the wing, highlighting a large, dark metallic form clinging to it—Eduardo H. Curtidor, better known to his friends and enemies as Hyde. Right now, the vicious cyborg was the team's only hope for survival.

His metal hands clawed at the gunship's wing and fuselage. He shredded and dug with a furious intensity. His efforts yielded a large panel that he flung to the ground. Dark smoke poured from the gunship's wound.

"I'm making progress," Hyde reported. A hollow, metallic growl followed the first transmission.

The gunship was too close. Dante's ability to make out so much detail proved that.

They'd not come equipped to deal with the level of resistance they encountered. This was supposed to be a straightforward job in an area with little Dirtwalker presence. Towering Nightmutt-filled mountains surrounded the valley containing the old factory and discouraged the Dirtwalkers from entering.

The gunship pilot pitched into another round of aggressive banking. He failed to dislodge their metal tormentor. Hyde had punched through the wing with his other arm and folded his arm back to grip the gunship.

He was right. Mugoi was an impressive cyborg, but he lacked Hyde's raw strength. Even without his original fully crafted hydraulic body, Hyde was a one-man tank.

"These other Plunderers are ruining my day," Braelin drawled over the comms. "We ain't got a good angle on 'em to fire back. These guys know what they're doing."

"We've lost sight of the fireteam detachment that broke away," Jolo reported. "Ambrose, be careful up there!"

Dante glanced at a craggy area in the distance. From the top of a cliff, hard-cased men and women rained bullets and pulsec-ores below where the apprentices had taken cover behind more half-destroyed buildings and machinery. The overlapping *crack* of rifle fire punctuated with high-pitched reports and rattling *booms* said as much as his words.

He'd ordered the apprentices to shelter there while he and Nasreen tried to distract the gunship until Hyde took care of it. The plan had been great until the ambush by ground troops and the missiles showed up.

The team's shuttle flew overhead, its cannon silent. Ambrose was too distracted by the two missiles roaring after him to provide ground support. He spun the shuttle to the side, dove toward a nearby hill, and pulled up at the last second. The bottom of the shuttle was so close to the ground that Dante's stomach clenched. Protective systems and fields could do only so much if a pilot slammed his ship into the ground.

Ambrose's boldness paid off. The missiles couldn't match his maneuver. Both exploded against the side of the hill and became massive fireballs.

"Nice flying," Dante offered.

Another enemy popped up from behind a wall with a missile launcher on his shoulder. He turned to track Ambrose before pulling the trigger. His missile shot into the air with a *hiss* and a massive plume of smoke and arced toward the fleeing shuttle. Another hard dive toward the surface took Ambrose behind a hill. The missile followed. Dante couldn't see anything but the flash of an explosion and the smoke plume.

Nasreen took the brief seconds of respite as an opportunity to reload her rifle. "This isn't sustainable, Dante."

Dante ignored her. "Ambrose, is the shuttle intact? We're not going to be able to find friendly Dirtwalkers around here if we have to walk out of this valley."

"You need to do something about the SAMs!" Ambrose shouted over the radio. "There's only so long I can pull off those kinds of maneuvers."

Dante smiled despite the situation. Ambrose was worthless on the ground, but the man was as dangerous as Hyde in the air.

"Dante!" Ambrose yelled. "Do you hear me? It's a miracle they haven't hit me yet."

"Yeah, yeah. Whatever." Dante and Nasreen were too far away to poke at the Plunderer fireteam with the missile launchers. "I'm working on it. We need that shuttle you're flying."

"Very funny. Work faster, please."

"Stay low and fast until we do something about the fire team. I—" Dante dropped flat to avoid a withering autocannon barrage. He sat upright as a jagged piece of metal plummeted from the gunship and pierced the ground beside his body. "Huh. You think my helmet could take that, Nasreen?"

Nasreen jerked her head back and forth, unsure whether to focus on the pinned apprentices or the aerobatics on display from Ambrose. "If you have to ask that, things are not going well. Can you take this more seriously, please?"

"I am. This is what happens when you double-book. I've told you again and again, 'whatever happens on the surface is fair game.' You're not one of the apprentices. I shouldn't have to tell you this. We shouldn't have come to an area where Plunderers were already operating. That's what caused this whole thing."

Nasreen scoffed. "I know it's hard for you not to be arrogant when you're Dante Shale, but how are you blaming me for this? You're the one who picked the job area. I checked the primary job sources. The area was clear.

"You were supposed to double-check using your other sources. You said, and I quote, 'There are people I can talk to that you don't know. Sometimes things slip through.' And you're the one who insisted we needed to do a job instead of remaining on standby until Firewall says they're ready for us."

"All this gear and equipment doesn't exactly pay for itself," Dante snapped. "All the new armor we bought wasn't cheap." He grunted and dropped low again to avoid an autocannon burst that knocked off a piece of the wall and covered his armor in rock and dust.

"Until Firewall gets their shit together, we have bills to pay. I thought we'd drop off those parts, and they'd be ready to go in a couple of days, not that we'd have to sit around waiting for them."

They need time to work on countermeasures, Midas offered.

"Not now, Midas."

Yes, sir. I'll restrict myself to target highlights.

"That'd be helpful. Now let's do something about that fireteam while we have a chance."

Dante chanced popping up to fire his pulsecore carbine at the missile team's hiding spot. Despite the far distance, he hit the wall he was aiming at and blew it open in a satisfying green explosion that added a touch of real color to the dark brown and gray of the ruins.

The wall collapsed. No one was hiding on the other side. The fireteam launched another missile at the shuttle from thirty-five feet away before rushing, crouched low between the maze-like wall ruins. Dealing with professionals was always annoying.

Dante ducked behind his hole-filled cover. "I know I said the job site was clear. You must have missed something. That would have led me elsewhere."

"If you were going to blame me anyway, why bother having me check?" Nasreen scoffed. "I checked, and my sources said it was clear. I told you during your little speech that it was fast-changing information. You were supposed to make sure."

Dante motioned at the missile streaming away. "Then why the hell are we now fighting the Khallabash Brothers' crew? I know you haven't been in the business as long as I have, but you don't know how these guys are. They're stand-up in most situations unless they think you're coming into their territory. In those cases, they might as well be Hyde when we first met him."

Nasreen glared at him. "You somehow can't make mistakes, but I can?"

"We're fighting another crew." Dante shrugged. "Mistakes were made."

"Oh, love the emphasis there." Nasreen rolled her eyes.

Sporadic gunfire in the craggy area became constant. Muzzles flashed in sequence from the cliff. The Plunderers were not letting up on the apprentices nor were they blindly firing. Courage and good tactics made a dangerous combination.

Hyde tore out a huge piece from the gunship's fuselage and hurled the metal toward the ground. Dante didn't understand how the gunship was still in the air and flying as well as it was with all its damage. Smoke streamed from so many places on the vehicle that the dark cloud obscured the back. Hyde's efforts had torn enough holes that Dante could make them out from the ground, even without Midas' highlights.

"You know what's not helpful in the middle of a firefight?" Nasreen continued.

"A razorfist?" Dante guessed. "You'd be surprised. If you're closer than ten feet, you can take a man down with a knife or razorfist faster than he can draw and shoot you."

"I'm talking about blame-game garbage," Nasreen retorted. "Setting aside, it sounds like you've dealt with the Khallabash Brothers before?"

Dante shrugged. "Once. It was less complicated than this situation. We ended on neutral terms. That time it was the opposite. They were coming into a job I was working. Once they realized that, they backed off. No shots fired."

"Then that's all the more reason to try something foreign to you, diplomacy. We can figure out who screwed up after we get out of here. Otherwise, it won't matter because we'll both be dead, along with everyone else."

Dante couldn't challenge the logic. Other than a brief radio transmission he'd received confirming his attackers were the Khallabash Brothers, he'd not bothered to talk to them. The missiles and explosions had pissed him off.

He tapped a control panel on his wrist vambrace to adjust his broadcast frequencies. "This is Dante Shale to the Khallabash Brothers. Please come in."

The response that came was blunt and to the point. "Die, die, die! Screw you, claim jumper! We're going to bury you Dirtside. In the future, a rich asshole will pay a Plunderer to dig your bones up."

"At least I know you can hear me," Dante replied. The opened transmissions added to the cacophony of the weapons fire, with

Dante now hearing the same shots amplified over his comms system. "This was an honest damned mistake."

"Die! You can pay with your honest damned life."

Nasreen winced. "This is what you call stand-up guys?"

Dante cut his open mic, changing back to his normal frequency. He nodded at the sky. "In a sense. They won't shoot you in the back for looking at them the wrong way."

"I see." Nasreen found a small hole in the wall. She poked her rifle barrel into it and sprayed a burst toward the walls hiding the fireteam. "At least you tried. What now?"

Dante waited. He'd been expecting another gunship run. When it didn't come, he peeked over the wall.

"His turns are wider now that Hyde's shredded half the ship. We're not getting out of here if Ambrose can't get to us without taking a missile up the ass." Dante gestured at the cliff, then the ruins where the SAM fireteam took cover. "The apprentices can smoke the fireteam out if we can free it up for them. They'd have a great angle if it weren't for the assholes on the cliff."

Nasreen glanced at her rifle. After searching the area for a moment, she pointed her gun toward two half-melted piles of old bullet-riddled hovercars. They formed two curved semi-walls with a convenient makeshift ramp that could serve as a firing platform. "It's about two hundred yards over open ground before we get there. Once we're there, we should be able to pressure the cliff team."

"We'll move after the next pass," Dante advised after mentally working the firing angles in his mind. After their year together, he'd molded Nasreen from a spy to an effective Marauder. Most of the time, he was glad she was his second-in-command.

The gunship swept toward them again. Its latest volley sheared off the top of the wall, with the attack making their cover only useful if they laid down. That made the decision about Nasreen's plan easy.

Dante waited three seconds and shot to his feet. Trusting in

Hyde's damage and Nasreen's tactical awareness, he jumped over the wall and sprinted toward Nasreen's suggestion. She hurried after him.

He set a new record for clearing the distance between the walls and his new makeshift fort. When Dante arrived at the outer semi-wall, he vaulted over it. Nasreen joined him, her breathing ragged.

Neither stopped to recover. They didn't have long before the next pass. They scrambled up the ramp while keeping their weapons up.

Nasreen switched to full automatic and sprayed the top of the cliff. At this distance, they had little hope they would take down hard-cased Plunderers with standard bullets. A distraction would have to do. She ran out within seconds and slapped in a new magazine to continue the attack.

Dante laid down and steadied his pulsecore carbine, using the corroded roof of an old luxury hovercar to aid him. The cliff-positioned enemies had slowed their attacks on the apprentices under Nasreen's cover fire. The distraction had worked.

The Khallabash Plunderers moved closer to the cliff's edge. Two of them turned, aimed at Dante's and Nasreen's new redoubt, and fired back. Bullets thudded into their cover. Sparks danced all around.

There was no time to wait and no time for careful sniper shots. Dante fired his first pulsecore round, shifting and releasing his second shot before the first hit. He continued that, strafing the cliff's edge as close as possible to the enemy crew. Green blasts traveled the cliff's face like an eerie wave of fire.

A massive rumble filled the air. Dante frowned, trying to match the noise with a weapons system. Nasreen looked panicked.

"Is that artillery?" he asked. "The Khallabash Brothers don't use artillery."

I don't believe that is a weapons system, sir, Midas replied.

"Then wh—Oh."

Cracks shot through the side of the cliff. A huge chunk detached and fell toward the ground in a cloud of stone and dust.

"Oh, crap." Dante stared, unsure if he'd doomed his apprentices.

Beyond the massive dust plume launched by the collapse, rock and dirt smashed into the ground far away from the apprentices. The collision had produced the world's largest smoke grenade.

A chunk of the cliff had collapsed, but it hadn't taken any enemies with it. The enemy Plunderers retreated farther from the edge, becoming mere outlines in the smoke.

"Please don't bury us, Captain," Mugoi transmitted. "I'm unsure how long I could survive in such conditions."

"I know how long I could, and it ain't long enough," Braelin complained.

Jolo offered a weary sigh over the comms. She didn't follow up with a voiced complaint.

"Burying you wasn't the plan," Dante replied. "But it made them back off. We'll keep up suppression." He blasted the cliff again with another pulsecore round. "You move on the fireteam, so Ambrose can get us out of here."

Braelin, Jolo, and Mugoi burst from their cover, darting between large outcroppings and chunks of metal and concrete strewn over the ground. Halfway away from their old cover, Braelin and Jolo brought up their pulsecore carbines and pelted the fireteam's current position. The new explosions blew apart the walls and machinery. Mugoi punctuated their fire with bursts from its rifle.

Unlike the men and women on the cliff, the fireteam wasn't wearing hard-cased armor. The first explosion sent them scrambling for cover, and one man dropped his missile launcher. Jolo half-melted it in her next attack.

"Ambrose, make sure you're close," Dante ordered. "I'm going to try more diplomacy."

"We're all going to die," Ambrose announced.

Dante switched back to wide-frequency broadcasting. "Listen, assholes. Both sides are hurt, but no one looks seriously hurt or dead. This doesn't have to end badly. We're willing to walk away if you're willing to stop shooting at us.

"You want to keep up the shooting? I guarantee we'll take people with us. You know my rep. You know what I can do. You had the upper hand, and you still haven't taken out a member of my team. That should prove something."

The gunfire slowed from both sides but didn't stop. The apprentices' staggered shots forced the fireteam to stay low. The men didn't dare try to risk moving from their cover. The cliff team had retreated far from the smoke-smothered edge and ceased fire. Dante and Nasreen stopped firing at them.

"You want this over, Shale?" a voice screamed over the comms.

Dante recognized it as Emil Khallabash, the older of the Khallabash Brothers. "Yeah. I do. That's why I'm calling you. This was an honest accident. We weren't trying to steal from you."

"I don't believe you," Emil snarled. "The great Dante Shale, the man so impressive he became a legend after death as Hellcat. You think you can come and steal our job. You figured you took out SSS, so you can take out anyone. Is that it?"

This was going about as well as he could expect. Once a man was killed, it'd be too late.

"No, you stubborn asshole. Listen to me. We got bad info. Ask yourself, Khallabash, if you've ever heard of me jumping someone else's claim or job. People have a big-ass list of my faults. Is that one on it?"

Gunfire marked the tense passage of seconds. The bursts joined Dante's pounding heart. The radio only offered silence. He had no doubt his team would win the battle if it came to that. As much as he didn't want to kill anyone not associated with Block 9X, he cared more about his team. He also had no doubt that he'd lose people should they continue.

Ambrose's shuttle rose over the hill. His flight pattern remained erratic. Dante admired the tactical instincts to not make it easy for the Khallabash Brothers.

"You want this to be over?" Emil asked. "Then get that psycho cyborg off my ship. He's trying to kill me."

"You heard the man, Hyde," Dante transmitted. "It's time for a show of good faith."

The rest of the gunfire petered out, leaving everyone to concentrate on the roar of the gunship and shuttle engines. Pieces of the gunship continued to fall from above.

"Hyde, do you hear me?" Dante shouted. "You take down that gunship, there's no way we can walk out of this with everyone."

Dante gritted his teeth and held his breath. He wasn't sure if the pieces were from earlier attacks or if Hyde was still ripping into the ship. A moment later, the gunship shed altitude with a lurching drive before turning into an aggressive bank that flung Hyde toward the ground. He bounced and rolled before digging his hand into the soil and carving a deep furrow before stopping.

"Hyde, you okay?" Dante asked. "It looks like he was trying to give you a chance to survive, but that fall would have killed most people."

"I'm not most people," Hyde scoffed. "That *pendejo* could have dropped me from higher up. I would have been fine. Don't give him too much credit."

The gunship flew overhead without firing.

"Okay, everyone on my position," Dante ordered. "Ambrose, don't land. Hover close enough with the door open so we can board."

"Are you sure?" Ambrose asked. "What if they're trying to get us all in one place for a missile?"

The thought had occurred to Dante. The next couple of

minutes would be a gamble.

"The Khallabash Brothers have a sense of honor," Dante replied. "They're not murderers. We're going to use that to get the hell out of here. Now, move your asses!"

The apprentices kept low and under cover for the first portion of the run. When they cleared the final wall, they sprinted flat-out to head to Dante and Nasreen's hovercar fort. Hyde jogged their way, not bothering to use any cover as if daring the Khallabash Brothers to attack.

Ambrose hesitated until the ground team had all made it to the fort. He cut speed and spiraled down toward the location, avoiding any straight line flying until he stopped next to the team, hovering a couple of yards off the ground, and opened the back of the shuttle.

Dante motioned the apprentices into the ship. Braelin hesitated, not budging until Jolo moved. She slung her weapon over her shoulder and jumped into the back of the shuttle, catching the edge of the cargo bay and pulling herself up. Braelin mirrored her. Mugoi charged and high-jumped into the bay with ease. Nasreen headed in next. Shaking his head, Hyde glared at Dante before leaping into the bay.

With the crew all safe, Dante sprinted and jumped into the bay. Ambrose flew forward immediately, not increasing altitude until the back door was closed and they'd put a couple of miles between the shuttle and the ruins.

Dante didn't like the looks of defeat on his team, but he understood how they felt. He'd been there before. He didn't say anything for a couple of minutes until Ambrose headed toward the high atmosphere.

"Any fight you can walk away from is a victory," Dante said. "I'm not going to say it doesn't burn having to turn tail, but we can't risk pissing off other Plunderers. Something went wrong on our end. We'll figure that out later. The important part is no one got hurt."

The apprentices all avoided looking directly at him. Nasreen pursed her lips and kept quiet.

"That's crap," Hyde snarled. "We just got our asses beat, and now we can't make any money. We shouldn't have run."

"What?" Dante frowned. "You questioning my call?"

"I almost had that gunship, *Papi*." The affectation always held a faint mockery, but Hyde injected concentrated disdain into the most recent use of the word before he slammed his fist hard against the wall, leaving a dent.

"Hey," Ambrose called from the front. "I see you on the cameras. Don't break my shuttle."

Hyde began, "Once the gunship was down, it would have been easy to finish off the fireteam. We almost had them even without that. That means the fight was almost over. You surrendered for no reason."

"We weren't there to pick a fight with the Khallabash Brothers." Dante narrowed his eyes. "It's a good thing we were able to talk them out of fighting, and we stopped it before we all did something we'd regret. If we had taken them out, we would have been the target of every Plunderer team in the Stations."

"Screw that," Hyde growled. "We should have finished them off. You're worried about other teams? If we killed them, the next assholes would know not to mess with us. What's wrong with you, Shale? You drop your *cojones* Dirtside? Did one of those cannibals eat them in Hungary?"

There was a whiff of irony to a man with an artificial body using that type of insult. Dante scratched his nose while looking around at his apprentices' weary and disappointed faces and Nasreen's annoyed expression.

Running around trying to avoid taking high-velocity auto-cannon rounds through the chest had left Dante exhausted. That was not the only thing. Something clicked in the back of his mind. A flare of anger burned away his fatigue.

He was tired of Firewall. He was tired of the Omega Syndrome, and he was tired of being questioned.

Dante glared at Hyde. "*Shut up!* I don't want to hear it from you."

"You're hearing it from me because the rest of them won't stand up to you." Hyde slapped his chest. The metal on metal produced a dull *thud*. "Next time, don't start what you can't finish."

"I told you to shut up, Hyde. Don't make me give you a warning."

"And I—"

Dante snatched up his discarded pulsecore carbine and flipped off the safety in a smooth, practiced movement. He pointed it at Hyde's head. "Shut up, or I will end you. Consider this your last warning."

"Whoa," Braelin shouted and threw an arm in front of Jolo. She frowned at him and stepped out from behind him but backed up.

Mugoi's brow lifted. The smaller cyborg remained quiet but widened its stance and lifted its fists.

Nasreen sighed and spoke softly. "Dante, put down the gun. We don't need to threaten our team. This goes well beyond stupid brawls."

"It's not an idle threat. I want him to understand he's going to stop talking about this, or I'm going to end him. Consider it a promise."

Hyde stared at Dante. He shrugged and sat with his back against the bay wall.

Everyone stood there, frozen and unsure about what to do. Dante kept the gun trained on Hyde for a long, tense moment before flipping the safety back on and tossing the carbine to the bay floor with a resounding *clang*.

Dante tore his glare away from Hyde. "I'm going up front with Ambrose. Nobody bother me until we're back at HQ."

CHAPTER TWO

Tense minutes of silence ticked by while the crew rested in the shuttle. No one commented and only showed the briefest of reactions as they passed through the different gravitational fields between the transit from humanity's original home to their new home.

After passing into the Station, the quiet remained. No one did much until they closed in on their headquarters and Ambrose slowed the shuttle and prepared for a hangar landing. Everyone exchanged looks, except for Dante, who glared at the shuttle as if trying to burn through the hull using anger. Nasreen watched him from the corner of her eye the entire time, trying to plan what she would say to him when they landed.

The shuttle set down in the hangar. As everyone filed off, Nasreen kept close to Dante. Breaking the silence after so long would put him on the defensive. She couldn't let this go. They needed to talk soon about his aggressive display. There was no way they could go to their next job until she figured out how to handle him. The absurdity of pulling a gun on Hyde had left her shaken.

Ambrose exited the shuttle last, frowning at a dent in the

bulkhead from Hyde's earlier hit. He glared at the cyborg but didn't say anything as he headed for a door and stepped through while mumbling.

"It's not my fault Dante was a jerk."

Hyde's aggressive pettiness didn't surprise her in the slightest. The man liked to fight. They'd used the tendency to their advantage on countless adventures. He'd left behind his flesh-and-blood body decades before to become better at fighting. Not running away from a fight made perfect sense. He had no investment in saving other Plunderers he'd never met.

The more Nasreen thought about Hyde's reaction, the less she understood Dante's. The team had been through trouble before and the occasional job that went south, and he'd never reacted that way. He'd never come close to it. His previous threats against Hyde were always controlled and half-joking, not the crazed, aggressive display that might have ended with a close-range pulsecore explosion inflight in a shuttle. Dante had months to turn a gun on Hyde and plenty of good reasons, making the shuttle insanity much more perplexing.

Braelin, Jolo, and Mugoi walked over to a multi-tiered supply rack near the hangar's wall. They slammed their helmets and weapons onto it. Nasreen set her rifle and helmet there with a sigh. Dante took off his helmet and threw it in front of the rack where it clattered against the floor. His eyes blazed with fury.

Nasreen drew a deep breath. They weren't on the shuttle anymore. Waiting too much longer risked only allowing the festering emotional problem to worsen. She opened her mouth to question Dante. All her careful planning was interrupted by an unexpected voice.

Midas spoke through a nearby headquarters terminal. "It's unfortunate that this job will net zero income."

Dante stopped and turned toward the terminal. "Wow. Thanks for that, Midas. We wouldn't have known if you hadn't mentioned that. Did you need a special mission analysis upgrade module to figure that out?" He tapped the side of his head. "Did you spend my money on crap like that?"

The AI's effete upper-class English accent was more pronounced than usual. "With all due respect, sir, improvements to my capabilities were going to follow the payment for this job. The failure, therefore, will have lasting effects on my readiness and thus your readiness."

"Huh? What the hell are you saying?" Dante's brow lifted. "Are you talking about that ancient script translation module crap you mentioned the other day? I was mocking you when I said that I'd thought hieroglyphics would come in handy. We're Plunderers, but we stay more modern than that. That'd be a waste of my money, and like you pointed out, we aren't going to get paid, so too damned bad."

"There were other upgrades I mentioned," Midas replied with a hint of snippiness. "They included backup navigational upgrades, more resistance to local EM disruption, targeting aids, additional medical database information, and other practical areas. And the ancient script translation module doesn't solely focus on hieroglyphics. There are numerous ancient languages included in the package. It'd give me parity between my modern and ancient language capabilities. You can't guarantee it won't be useful."

Nasreen rubbed her temples. "Midas, Dante's right. The usefulness of that module is debatable. He's never been to those kinds of ruins. The others make more sense, and I understand where you're coming from. That said, maybe now isn't the best time."

"That's not the point. I've been waiting patiently for the upgrades. Promises were made to me. I don't understand why those promises would be made if they weren't going to happen, sir."

Nasreen marveled that an advanced AI, the product of the most up-to-date human technology, could sound so much like a petulant child and share about as much ability to read the room. She looked at Dante. He'd stopped glaring. Midas' whining might have snapped him out of his mood.

Dante sighed. He set his pulsecore carbine on the rack. After finishing that, he whipped his backup pistol out of its holster and put three rounds into the terminal. The sound echoed loudly, making Nasreen wince. Smoke poured out of the damaged terminal, and it sparked before dying.

Nasreen stared at the destroyed device, barely comprehending what she'd witnessed. She turned her head toward Dante, hoping he'd offer a logical explanation for his dangerous actions.

"Shut up, Midas," Dante growled. "That includes in my head. Was that stunt about trying to win people to your side? Poor damned choice. Keep talking, and I might remove half your modules just to teach you a lesson."

The apprentices stayed near Dante. Mugoi kept a hand near the weapons rack. Hyde smirked from his spot near the shuttle. Nasreen needed to defuse this situation before things got worse. The first, most obvious step was to reduce the number of variables involved.

She pointed at a door. "Everyone else out. Now."

Mugoi nodded and dropped its arm. It took a couple of steps away from the rack before it turned and walked straight toward the door. Braelin hesitated before heading out with Jolo not far behind. Both cast confused glances at Dante every few steps. Nasreen couldn't blame them.

Once the three apprentices had cleared, Nasreen turned to Hyde. "That includes you. This is going to be a two-way conversation."

"Ha-ha. Nah." Hyde shook his head. "I want to hear this. It's going to be the highlight of my month."

"Leave now, or I'll sneak in while you're sleeping, recharging, whatever you want to call it, and loosen every joint you have."

Nasreen narrowed her eyes. "Or I'll take your head off and stick it on a barely mobile tripod. It'll make your temp body seem like the ultimate augmentation in comparison."

"Is it threaten Hyde day, and nobody told me?" Hyde laughed. "You know, Nasreen, you might just do that. I'd love to know if you have it in you." He waved and sauntered to the door. "Have fun, *Papi*. Remember to be careful. You can't kill us all."

Dante's cold gaze followed the hulking cyborg through the exit. When the door closed, he set his pistol on the rack and stared at Nasreen expectantly, his arms folded.

"We need to talk about what happened now and earlier," Nasreen noted.

"Do we?" Dante shrugged. "What's to talk about?"

"You don't think any of that was over the line?"

"I'm establishing dominance." Dante nodded at the door. "Hyde's a killer. We know that. He's tried to kill us. We can use him, and I don't have a problem with that, but if he's not afraid of me, he won't listen to me. When we're on a job, he damned well needs to listen to me, or other people will die."

"He followed your orders and didn't complain until we were aboard the shuttle." Nasreen shook her head. "Hyde expressed an opinion. That shouldn't warrant being threatened with a pulsecore."

"An opinion?" Dante shouted. "He called my leadership into question." He slammed his armored boot into the weapons rack, causing the gear to rattle. "I needed to put him in his place."

"No." Nasreen folded her arms. "This is about more than dominance against Hyde. If you pulled a pulsecore on Hyde every time he smarted off, the apprentices would have long since quit rather than risk getting burned by a plasma explosion."

She flung her arm toward the smoking terminal. The acrid smell made her wrinkle her nose. "What's that about? Establishing dominance over an AI?"

"Why not? The chip in my brain should remember who's in charge."

Nasreen scoffed. "You insist we do dangerous jobs because we need money, then you shoot holes in our equipment. Terminals cost money, Dante."

He bared his teeth. "Midas needs to learn to shut up. Telling him wasn't working. I decided a more direct demonstration was necessary."

"He's a talkative AI who has his flaws. He was whining. I admit all that. That doesn't justify shooting a weapon into a terminal. You must have an idea of how insane that was.

"I've been working with you for over a year now. Despite everything we've been through, Dirtside and above, I've never seen you act like that. It's like you became a different man."

Dante scoffed. "Maybe I was acting like the man I've always been."

"I don't believe that." Nasreen locked eyes with him. "Stop pretending it was normal and start talking to me so I can help you. This also goes back to the planet where you blame me for the ambush."

"That's what this is? You're pissed about the planet?"

"No." Nasreen scrubbed a hand down her face. Throttling Dante wouldn't help, as satisfying as it might be. "It's another example of your unusual behavior. I'm not angry. I'm confused. All I want to do is help you as your friend and partner. Because if you think randomly brandishing weapons and shooting things for annoying you is reasonable, we're not going to survive long enough to take on Firewall."

Dante's feral angry expression had remained unchanged for the entire conversation until that point. He grimaced, and his glare softened. He looked away.

"I'm not apologizing to Hyde," he insisted. "That's the last thing I'll do."

"I'm not asking you to apologize to him." Nasreen let out a

quiet, dark chuckle. "Hyde has done enough to both of us that we could kill him and he'd still owe us an apology.

"This is less about you being angry at Hyde than completely losing it. I need to know that my partner is reliable and isn't going to freak out and gun us all down because he's pissed off. That means you'll have to be open and honest with me."

Dante braced himself against a nearby wall. He didn't speak for a long while. He turned his back and slid down the wall until he sat with his knees up. He laid an arm on them. When he spoke, disgruntled acceptance tinged his voice. "Did it come off that bad?"

"Yes." Nasreen knelt in front of Dante. "I'm not exaggerating when I say you were coming off unhinged. Didn't you notice the body language of the apprentices during both incidents? Those were trained people concerned they might have to take down their mentor and boss. They were ready to attack you because they couldn't trust that you wouldn't kill someone in a rage."

"Damn it. Okay. Understood." Dante scrubbed a hand down his face. "I'll admit things got out of hand. I'm not going to sit here and pretend that it was only a case of me trying to be a hardass and screwing up. Shit happens."

Nasreen inclined her head toward the destroyed terminal. "That destruction undercuts any case for it being about you as a hardass."

She smiled at him. "Come on, Dante. We've been through too much together. We took down SSS together, and we've faced death together. You can talk to me."

Dante shook his head. "I know I screwed up."

"By aiming the gun at Hyde? I want you to be very specific about this."

"I'm still not convinced that part was a mistake." Dante sucked in a breath. "But that's not the screw-up I mean."

"What then?" Nasreen shifted so her legs would be more

comfortable. "Because I'm having trouble translating your Dante-ese into plain English."

"I screwed up the job." Dante ran his hands through his dark hair. "You were right. I was supposed to check on everything.

"It's not sloppy that you missed the Khallabash Brothers working the job. They're known for keeping jobs close to the vest because of paranoia about people hitting their areas. Even before I had you doing that, I always checked right before and during mission deployment. Things change too rapidly for me not to do that."

"And those paranoid assholes are stand-up guys?" Nasreen arched a brow.

He shrugged. "They're okay. The point is, I know where to look and who to ask at the last moment to make sure that doesn't happen. I also knew that information wouldn't come up in the channels you check. More than that, I checked Station sensors and the instrument feeds before landing for other Plunderers. And nothing."

He punched the wall. "I don't make mistakes like that. I can't make mistakes like that." He stood with a grunt. "I'm Dante damned Shale. I'm the Hellcat, too. I'm the best damned Plunderer there is. That's why Slaine came to me. It's why Firewall was interested in our team."

"We all make mistakes." Nasreen shrugged. "I was one of the best freelance spies out there until I miscalculated one woman's paranoia, and it almost cost my life. I was lucky you were around. Otherwise, I'd be dead."

"It's not the same." Dante turned and slammed his other fist against the wall. "When I made the call to go against the o-harvesting on that job for Slaine, and when you screwed up on your job, the only people's lives on the line were our own. We made choices and mistakes, and we'd be the ones to pay."

"You don't think that's the case now?"

Dante shook his head. "This team's different than before,

different than the crew that betrayed me. Yes, Ambrose is still on the team, and this applies even to him. Everything's changed."

"Okay." Nasreen circled her hand before her. "I'm beginning to follow you. Please continue."

"I…" Dante growled. "I don't know. The team, the apprentices, you, even that damned bastard Hyde. They don't deserve to die because of my mistake."

"Most people don't deserve to die because of other people's mistakes. Everyone knows this is a dangerous job. They also understand taking on the Omega Syndrome is dangerous. If that's what you're worried about, you should stop. No one is deluded about what we're facing."

"No!" Dante shouted.

Nasreen stepped back. She kept quiet, watching him with a neutral expression, a product of years of experience as a free-lance spy. She didn't want to agitate him more than he was.

"Take your time," she said quietly. "It's not like we have anywhere else to be."

Dante curled his hand into a fist and glared at it. "I've never worked alone. I'm used to having a team. I'm used to leading teams. If my old team had my back during that o-harvest crap, we could have taken Hyde and the rest of them.

"Things are different with the new team. They're more my responsibility. It's like, I don't know… It's hard for me to find the words. It's going to sound stupid."

"If it doesn't end with you pulling a gun on me, it'll be okay."

Dante thought that over before offering a curt nod. "It's almost like being a dad."

"I understand the apprentices." Nasreen couldn't help the joke that slipped out next. "You're Hyde's and Ambrose's dad, too?"

"Eh. Uh? They're left over from my last marriage?" Dante chuckled. The anger eased off his face. "But they're included. If I wanted them dead, I would have killed them myself. Yeah, I'm keeping them around because they're useful, but I'm not Slaine. I don't spend time with people who think the only thing they've got going is being useful. I don't think about people that way."

"Okay. That makes sense." Nasreen patted his shoulder. She pulled back when he tensed at her touch. "I'm getting it now. You have a beyond mentor and parental feeling of responsibility for the team. You also worry that taking them down this path, especially against the Omega Syndrome, will get them all killed. Does that about sum it up?"

"What?" Dante frowned. There was pain in those striking green eyes that had been rage-filled not all that long ago. "How did you know about the Omega Syndrome? I didn't mention them. You're the one who brought them up earlier."

"You might not be that good at expressing your feelings. That's not the same thing as being hard to read." Nasreen patted her chest. "You've turned me into a Marauder, but don't forget where I came from.

"I had to read people to make it through my jobs. When I made mistakes about that, like I did the day I met you, that's when things got dangerous." She smiled. "When you've lived your life dedicated to blunt honesty, you're going to have trouble keeping the truth hidden because you're letting it come out in different ways."

"The blunt truth is that I need everyone on this team to pull off jobs and to take down the Omega Syndrome." Dante glanced at the door. "I've done my best to make sure they're the best. I've trained them the best I could.

"It's not so easy to talk about knowing what they're walking into. No one on the team, including Hyde and Ambrose, originally signed on to fight anything like the Omega Syndrome. It's my fault if any of them get killed…for making us the best."

Nasreen walked to the equipment rack. She gestured at a pulsecore carbine. "You can't protect everybody at all times."

"That doesn't mean I can't be careful."

"Of course, but that's not the same thing. You could give up on the Omega Syndrome. We both know that's not going to happen. Even if you could and you focused only on the job, it's dangerous. The only way to ensure nobody gets hurt is to stop them from being Plunderers.

"You might call the apprentices kids, but they aren't. They're adults, and they came to you to become Plunderers. They understood the risks from the beginning. As for Hyde and Ambrose, they know more than anyone about the risks of the job, and you've given them the chance to walk away without hard feelings. They chose to stay."

"Yeah." Staring at the floor, Dante leaned against the wall with one arm. "I keep telling myself that. I think I understand that. Somehow it doesn't make it feel any better."

"Feelings aren't something you can fight with pulsecores and a razorfist, Dante," Nasreen replied softly. "All you're responsible for doing is making sure that people have the skills they need when they're out on jobs, and the best way to do that is continuing to train them and me."

"That sounds about right." Dante shrugged.

"You can also help make Ambrose a better man and keep a rein on Hyde so his violence helps the innocent people rather than hurts them," Nasreen continued. "No one expects you to be in control of everything. The only thing we can ask is that you do your best. Everyone involved in any dangerous line of work understands how much pure chance can be involved."

Dante looked up. "Doing our best might get us killed."

Nasreen smiled. "According to Hyde, you still have lives left over, Hellcat."

"Yeah. That's what he tells himself to justify why he's the one taking orders from me." Dante glanced at the carbine. "Weren't you always trying to control things as a spy?"

Nasreen shook her head. "You don't get it. One of the reasons I spent so much time preparing for jobs was because I understood I couldn't control everything."

Dante drew a deep breath. He reflected in silence before offering, "Thanks."

"You're welcome."

"I'm not good at this…feelings crap."

"Oh? I hadn't noticed that *at all* since meeting you." Nasreen laughed. "There's no shame in reaching out to me. We took down a mega-corporation and elite conspiracy together. I think we can share the occasional secret."

Dante grimaced. "I'd prefer fighting crazed cyborgs."

"Excuse me, sir," Midas chimed in, this time from a shuttle intercom speaker. "I apologize for interrupting, but this is relevant to your overall mission and unrelated to my purchases. I do not intend to defy you nor is this an attempt to take advantage of your improvement in mood."

Dante chuckled. "You could have used the normal voice module. I'm not going to shoot myself."

"There's a message from Firewall on the encrypted channel," Midas reported. "To be clear, it came in right before I spoke. It hasn't been waiting."

"Okay. Good to know." Dante nodded. "We'll check it out. And Midas, I'm sorry for getting pissy and shooting at you." He glanced at the pistol, and uncertainty snuck into his voice. "If that makes sense."

"Technically, you shot a terminal. Although I find it curious and strange that a human is apologizing to an AI. I do, however, appreciate your apology as I understand it is coming from a sincere place and a desire to achieve self-improvement. On a fundamental level, I very much understand wanting to improve oneself and achieve better possibilities and control."

Nasreen fished out her sphere to retrieve the message. Her smile dimmed as she read the first few lines. She finished with an irritated hiss. "Damn it. This is what I was talking about when I mentioned not having control."

Dante looked at her. "What is it? Is Firewall threatening to kidnap me this time? Because they wouldn't like trying to interrogate me. There would be much more spit involved."

Nasreen shook her head. "That'd be easier to handle and half-expected at this point." She sighed and straightened her shoulders. "Not that their message is unexpected.

"They've confirmed active manipulation of the Station sensor grids, comms, and signaling networks related to Dirtside travel and activity. Firewall is confident the Omega Syndrome is involved. They're unclear on this manipulation's goal since the Omega Syndrome has not previously shown an interest in these systems. They're seeking our input as 'experienced Plunderers.'"

Dante narrowed his eyes. "You do know what this means, don't you?"

Nasreen stared at the message, willing it to be anything else, no matter how minor. The team might not be ready for the implications.

"The most likely explanation is that the Omega Syndrome is actively trying to sabotage our team," she replied. She tossed the sphere to Dante so he could read the full text of the message himself. "Being the most likely explanation isn't the same as being certain."

"Nothing's certain in this business, but it explains the Khallabash Brothers crap. I might be up my ass at times trying to figure things out. That's not the same thing as making such a rookie mistake."

He frowned. "The more I think about it, the more things now make sense. The Khallabash Brothers couldn't have ambushed us like that if they'd arrived after we did. The Station data should have let me know if there were Station teams in the same flight area. That means they were down on the ground before we were on our way."

Nasreen frowned. "You're suggesting that from down there, they would have been able to detect an incoming ship and take positions to hide from our instruments and spring their ambush."

Dante nodded. "Exactly. The only reason they didn't kill us within seconds is we're a damned good team, and Hyde is..." He shrugged. "Hyde."

"Do you think the Khallabash Brothers are working for the Omega Syndrome?" Nasreen mused.

"Nope." Dante shook his head. "Not at all. The Omega Syndrome might have messed with the systems to keep any evidence of us coming from them, too, just to make sure it looked more like we were showing up out of nowhere to cause trouble."

"What about that 'Die!' stuff? That sounded psychotic."

"That's how Emil is." Dante shrugged.

Nasreen rolled her eyes. "Again, stand-up guys?"

"Relatively speaking. There are no saints in the Plunderer business." Dante scanned the message and tossed the sphere back.

"If this was a weird Omega Syndrome infection-responsible assassination attempt, there was no reason for them to let us go when they had us pinned down. Even if we won the fight, we would have taken injuries or lost people. Disrupting the sensor feeds could have ended with us dead and it looking like nothing more than Plunderers scrapping over territory."

He shrugged. "The Omega Syndrome pulled that stunt with Midas last year, but they aren't going to be magic. There have to be limitations to their ability to mess with people Dirtside."

"That's more assumptions than I'm comfortable with." Nasreen groaned. "That's not the worst part of this. This new infiltration means there's no way to ensure we won't be diving on top of another operation or that another operation won't come down on us the next time we head Dirtside."

Dante nodded. "Yeah. Pretty much. We can tighten our belts, but we're going to bleed money for the time being. Now, I have even more reason to take them out."

"Besides the idea that the Omega Syndrome is a dangerous conspiracy that wants to take control of humanity?"

"Yeah. They shouldn't have messed with my bottom line."

The door opened. Ambrose barreled through, wide-eyed and panting. Hyde lumbered through after him with a dark scowl. He didn't have any new blood on him. That was a small comfort given his angry expression.

Nasreen put her hand out. "I've handled it. Don't expect any apologies, but there will be no more threats like that in the future."

Ambrose shook his head. "It's not that. We both received messages from a contact in the Terra Restoration Group. Their facility near the Commune of the Crescent-Marked was attacked, and they need help."

Hyde narrowed his eyes at Dante. "I don't know what crawled up your ass earlier, but we need to get Dirtside ASAP. This isn't about you and me anymore."

Nasreen didn't like the timing of the attack. At the minimum, it was inconvenient. She didn't want to undermine Dante, so she kept quiet, waiting for him to offer his opinion.

"We've got complications with the Omega Syndrome that might affect things." Dante nodded at the shuttle. "The shuttle's okay to fly, Ambrose?"

"Immediately," the pilot confirmed.

"Then we'll get to them soon enough. Get everyone to the briefing room. We've got things to talk over before we go anywhere. After that, we'll get ready to do what we do best."

CHAPTER THREE

"And that's where we're at," Dante finished from the head of the meeting room table. "We've got to assume that for the moment, the Omega Syndrome will monitor any move we make Dirtside. They can send Plunderer or Reaper teams at us indirectly that way."

"Who gives a shit?" Hyde rumbled. Unlike everyone else, he stood to the side of the table with his arms folded and a pensive expression. "They want to send more *pendejos*? We'll kill them. Dirtside, we don't have to hold back. It'll make it easier."

Dante shook his head. "The Khallabash Brothers weren't asshole killers like Block 9X. Other teams sent our way might be the same. We don't want to do the Omega Syndrome's work for them."

Ambrose sighed. "The TRG efforts are different. I'm not going back on what I said about wanting to help you, but everything you've told us means we can't do jobs for a while. That's all the more reason to go down there immediately to help them and the tribes."

"I'm not saying we won't help the TRG and the Dirtwalkers, but that's not true about the jobs. We have to be smart about it and figure out how to plan jobs without relying on the compromised networks."

Mugoi chuckled. "Captain, that'll be difficult, even for you."

Nasreen leaned forward. "Be that as it may, it might be better for you three apprentices to stay on Station for the foreseeable future until we can get this situation under control."

"Why is that?" Braelin asked. "You saying you don't think we can watch your backs? I ain't saying we didn't get caught with our pants down Dirtside, but once we got a chance to catch our breaths, we did what was needed."

Jolo nodded. "He's right."

"It's not about the team. It's our lack of intelligence that's killing us." Nasreen shook her head. "We don't know what the Omega Syndrome's end game is. That makes it harder to defend against. And this isn't a normal job."

"Exactly," Dante interjected. "Nasreen, Hyde, Ambrose, and I all have a relationship with the TRG and the tribes they're helping. I'm not going to ask anyone to risk their lives for no money after we just got done risking our lives for no money and almost dying."

"No." Jolo shook her head.

"Yeah. We're not going to go bankrupt right away. We can take more downtime from you all."

"You misunderstand, Dante." Jolo grabbed the table's edge and squeezed until her fingertips turned white. "We took this job for many reasons, including the compensation, but I'm insulted at your condescension. Every time I think we've proven ourselves, you go back to treating us like foolish children."

"What she said," Braelin offered, although he looked confused. He slapped his chest. "I'm no kid."

Dante scoffed. "How am I being condescending?"

Jolo raised an eyebrow. "You'll trust us to help you fight the Omega Syndrome, but you don't think we'd help you and your Dirtside friends? We understand the danger, and we understand your perspective. At risk of you pointing a pulsecore at me and telling me to shut up, I'd argue that your conclusions are flawed."

"There are no pulsecores in here, and I'm not going to tell anyone else to shut up today." Dante shrugged. "Lay it on me in all your infinite wisdom, Neburu."

"It's simple logic." Jolo motioned at Braelin and Mugoi. "Strength in numbers. We're a team that has spent a year training together.

"There are also zero reasons to believe the Omega Syndrome wouldn't attack us if they felt they had an opportunity, such as you spending significant time away from us on Earth. Similarly, you need us to watch your back. That's even more true with the verification of the compromised networks."

Mugoi nodded. "She's right, Captain. It seems obvious to me. Helping you, Hyde, and Ambrose with the TRG might not be a paying job. That doesn't mean it won't compensate me. Learning to deal with different types of Dirtwalkers will only enhance my future success as a Plunderer."

Dante looked at Nasreen. She nodded.

"You all say I'm crazy, but you're ready to go Dirtside again after we just got our asses kicked," Dante observed.

A grin replaced Hyde's scowl. "Ha-ha. This time it's different. We'll be ready for trouble, *Papi.* Before we go anywhere, I need to make sure you're not going to have a problem with me killing anyone who messed with the TRG and the Crescent-Marked. Are you?"

"No." Dante shook his head. "The TRG's doing good work, and the Crescent-Marked saved my life." He stood and pushed his chair back. "Everyone arm up and reload. We'll head down to the Crescent-Marked base and try to figure out what's going on. If the Omega Syndrome wants to drop Reapers on us, they'll regret it."

They'd landed at a permanent shuttle landing pad sitting in the center of the small slice of the TRG's location that had grown up near the Crescent-Marked settlement. The smooth surface stood out among the nearby rough terrain.

As Dante led the team off the shuttle, he searched the area for trouble. They'd not spotted any fighting right before landing, but they'd passed through clouds of dark smoke. Hyde and Ambrose didn't have insight into what had happened. There were no other details in the message asking for their help.

The Terra Restoration Group had expanded its facilities since Dante had last visited. Tents mixed with the squat gray semi-permanent prefab structures arranged in careful rows. Cabling ran between them and antennae sprang from many of the buildings.

He spotted more signs of trouble. Bullet and arrow holes riddled walls. Scorch marks marred the prefabs and the outer, older buildings the Crescent-Marked had repurposed before the TRG's arrival.

Crescent-Marked men and women carried bodies, both Dirt-walker and Station dwellers, away into a building they had converted into a makeshift morgue. Dante had seen enough violence in his career to sort the injuries in his head—blade wounds, bullet wounds, and burns. Everything one would expect from a hostile Dirtwalker raid.

A tall figure emerged from the morgue, the Crescent-Marked leader Urshielle. The warrior woman had helped save Dante's life during the fateful job that set him against his old team and SSS. She'd helped him understand how wrong he'd been about Dirt-walkers and changed the course of his life.

Urshielle's gaze rested on Hyde for a moment before she jogged toward the group. The Amazon of a woman wrinkled her nose. The crescent-shaped scars on her face moved with the expression like they were alive. A hint of surprise lingered in her eyes.

"Dante Shale," she greeted in accented English, most likely for the benefit of the others, before nodding at Hyde. "We're pleased to have more than Ambrose Igento and our brave metal warrior. When I asked the TRG's man to send a message, I didn't think any of you would come so quickly, let alone so many. I'm grateful."

Hyde stepped forward. His expression was angrier than before. "What happened here and who do we need to kill?"

Dante nodded. "We'd all like to know. Although we need to know the first part before the second."

"A savage and strong group raided us." Urshielle followed the progress of another corpse being moved, a young Dirtwalker woman. "We put out the last of the fires just before your arrival. The TRG men and women took more injuries. That made it harder."

"Who were the raiders?" Dante pressed. "What tribe would dare to launch an attack on a facility working so closely with the Crescent-Marked?"

"That remains unknown to us," Urshielle replied. "We didn't recognize their tribal markings or any of their members. They can't be a tribe from anywhere in this area." She frowned. "That's what confuses me. They approached with great force yet achieved an ambush despite your people's machines that are to warn of such things."

"In other words, a group of tribal raiders somehow beat Station sensors, and nobody knows who they are?"

Urshielle nodded. "They used rifles, spears, and torches that burned with a thick liquid that spread more when we put water on it." She growled. "Is this something Moonfolk let them capture? That weapon is dangerous."

Nasreen shook her head. "Had they taken supplies from Reapers or Plunderers, they would have been grenades, not any type of oil."

"There's more." Urshielle pointed at a body another team

carried, a middle-aged woman with her throat cut. She wore a jumpsuit marked with the TRG logo. "The raid occurred when we had many members of the elders of the TRG visiting. She's the only elder who died. I can't say the same for the rest of your people."

"Elders?" Dante frowned. "I don't understand."

"Higher-ranking TRG officials," Hyde explained. "Bigwigs. Normally, you have techs and scientists Dirtside doing their thing and working with the Dirtwalkers. All the administrators and officials don't want to touch Dirtside any more than they have to. Every few months, the assholes would come down so they could see what was going on, approve new projects and spending. Crap like that."

"That's convenient timing," Dante replied. "Way too convenient timing."

Urshielle gestured at the prefab village. "They were here to inspect their gray village. Their great cause has grown. They were here to judge the success of a true settlement of Moonwalkers on the surface, living in peaceful permanent relationships with the tribes."

"Really?" Dante looked between Ambrose and Hyde. "Either of you know about this?"

He'd not paid that much attention to TRG efforts. Their projects didn't influence his work outside of specific locales.

Ambrose nodded. "They were talking about this right before you roped us back in, Dante. You see what they've set up in a short time. It's a grand plan. They understand they aren't going to get a bunch of volunteers to want to live Dirtside when they could live on the Stations."

He chuckled nervously, and his gaze darted to Urshielle. "We Station people can't even stay on the planet without our oxygen inhalers. But this was the first real step, a town where both sides of humanity could interact outside of TRG special projects. It was the beginning of the first true, long-term reclamation project."

"Yeah." Hyde's scowl had disappeared. He kept sneaking glances at Urshielle. "This planet might never be what it once was, but the *jefes* think they can build a network of stable communities. They'd use them to gather resources without sending assholes like us down, trade with the tribes, mutual benefit, all that crap. Civilization comes back." He pounded his chest with his metal fist. "The other big point was to stop monsters like me from ruling the future."

Dante asked, "How are small Station settlements down here supposed to stop cyborgs? Let alone monster combat cyborgs."

"He's not a monster," Urshielle offered in a stern tone. "He has helped your people and the tribes. He is not the metal man you once knew."

"Nah." Hyde shook his head. "We both know I'm a monster. I'm just you guys' monster." He nodded at Mugoi. "Same for Pretty Face. That's why these TRG guys are ready to take this to the next level. They look at the future, and they see me grinning back at them. It makes them want to piss themselves, *Papi.*"

"I don't understand." Dante stared at Hyde. "You're saying, what, they want to bring everybody back from the Stations? What does this have to do with cyborgs?"

Hyde looked at Ambrose and shrugged. "You explain it better. You always paid better attention when they were talking about it."

Ambrose shook his head. "Not exactly, Dante. They have many researchers working for the TRG. They've been studying volunteers in genetic studies with an eye toward something other than transplant."

He shrugged. "It's slow-going work since it's taken a while to earn the tribes' trust. You can imagine that after years of o- and t-harvesting, Dir...many people down here don't want to give anything to our scientists. They're suspicious and worry it's a prelude to a wide-scale return to harvesting."

"Sure. What's the point of the research?"

"We all know how humanity is splitting into different subspecies." Ambrose rubbed his shoulder. "And we know what's happening Station-side with children. I've had more than one doctor tell me they believe if we don't start interacting more down here and even…"

He averted his eyes. "Interbreeding, then it won't be long before we're sterile or completely reliant on technology. We're all destined to be Hyde and Mugoi."

Dante offered a shallow nod but didn't respond. Beyond helping him understand Mugoi better, his prior trip to an orphanage on behalf of Firewall had been eye-opening about the state of children and fertility among the Stations.

"I don't want my kid becoming a cyborg," Braelin drawled. He shrugged at Mugoi. "No offense. Just seems expensive."

"None taken," Mugoi replied. "It is expensive. I'm not sure this is the path I would have followed had my childhood been different."

Hyde offered him a confused look. "I like being able to kick ass. But, yeah, most people can't handle this. They're too weak."

Urshielle flared her nostrils. "The wicked men who conspired to take from the tribes before will come again if that happens. You might have chosen to be a metal warrior. I know enough to know that most of your people would choose to steal that which is more precious from us instead of becoming metal."

Dante had fought hard to end o- and t-harvesting from the Stations. He harbored no delusions that he'd stamped it out everywhere, but taking down Slaine and SSS helped bolster the TRG and cut down considerably on the practice. Urshielle was right to be worried.

"You think this project is that important?" he asked.

"It's as they say, Dante Shale," she continued. "This new settlement was the beginning of a new relationship between we of this land and you of the stars. The raiders must know that. Almost all the targeted were your kind."

"What did the raiders take? Tech?" Dante asked.

"They burned and slew," she replied. "You misunderstand. It confused even us when we understood what we were seeing. The raiders took no spoils, but they did take people, all of whom were your people, all elders."

"Damn." Braelin kicked the dirt. "They took slaves? That's messed up."

Urshielle looked insulted. "What good would Moonfolk slaves be? Your kind can't breathe here without machines." She shook her head. "The only Moonfolk they took were the elders. If the raiders sought slaves, they would have taken our people. We are strong."

"Ransom?" Jolo suggested.

Dante shook his head. "I doubt it."

Hyde growled. "This is crap. These *pendejos* show up out of nowhere one of the few times the high-ranking officials are here, kill a bunch of people, but grab only the *jefes* and run off?"

Dante walked over to a wall and crouched. He poked a gloved finger in a hole. "There are a hell of a lot of bullet holes around here. These weren't men who were worried about using up their ammo." He looked at Urshielle. "What type of rifles did they use?"

"Your kind."

"I've seen the occasional tribe who could make ammo for more primitive guns, but not ammo that works with Station rifles. That's why they tend to be careful about using it."

"They fired with abandon and a plan hard to understand." Urshielle gestured at a wall. "They attacked people with malice and cruelty. Others, they ignored. They fired more into the buildings than the people, although they shot many people, too."

Dante stood. "You're both right. This is all too convenient and suspicious. Why would tribal raiders care about TRG officials?

How would they know about them if they weren't from this area?"

"What if they didn't want more Station folks down here?" Braelin shrugged.

Jolo nodded. "If they understood what this represented, they might have worried about our people taking over the planet again."

"A tribe that no one recognizes?" Dante shook his head. "They would have attacked other TRG projects farther from here." He pointed into the sky. "It's weird, but it smells like somebody up there was using locals for their dirty work."

Urshielle frowned. "You slew your great enemy, Cormac Slaine, did you not? Has his tribe returned for vengeance?"

"Yeah, I finished him off and his…tribe." Dante stood and dusted off his kneepads. "That doesn't mean I've taken out every bastard in the Stations."

"What's the benefit to disrupting the TRG's work?" Nasreen asked. "There are plenty of corrupt individuals on the Stations, but there's almost no upside to destroying these projects."

Jolo frowned. "Unless someone thinks the TRG can stave off extinction and they'd prefer the opposite."

A shiver ran up Dante's spine. Something about that last part sounded far too plausible. They could go around all day. There was no point in debating anything when they had a much more straightforward solution available.

"Who the hell knows?" Dante replied. "We can ask a raider when we interrogate one."

Urshielle offered a curt nod. "Then you will lend your weapons to defend us?"

"Damned right. I owe you. We all owe you." Dante nodded at the shuttle. "We'll arm up, and you can help us track these bastards down. We can interrogate them and figure out if somebody Station-side put them up to it. After that, if we need to clean up there, you can leave it to us, Urshielle."

CHAPTER FOUR

"You can't be serious, Dante," Ambrose complained.

The pilot's folded arms and stuck-out lip reminded Dante far too much of a pouting child. Ambrose might want to run from most confrontations, but his bravery swelled for anything involving his piloting skills and helping the TRG. Dante didn't want to waste that, but he had to consider the larger tactical situation and related risk factors.

Dante nodded. "I'm damned serious." He jerked his thumb at the shuttle. "We don't know what's happening. The best play is to keep the shuttle here in case another raider group shows up. You can provide air support in that case. Strafe the bastards with the cannon, and they'll run."

"It didn't stop the cannibal cultists," Ambrose muttered.

"Yeah." Dante scoffed. "I think they're a little more fanatical than your average Dirtside raider."

The original plan had been to take the shuttle to follow the raiders. When Dante looked around at the damage and carnage right before boarding, he changed his mind. His Marauder instincts were telling him not to make too many assumptions. They could get people killed.

"How are we supposed to find them, then?" Ambrose asked.

Urshielle nodded at some three-toed tracks in the dirt. "On foot. If we use your machine, they will see us from farther off, and we might not be able to follow the tracks from the sky."

Ambrose sighed. "Okay. Fine. I'll stick around the area."

"Keep on comms," Dante ordered and patted his shoulder. "We still don't know what we'll find out there."

A dark haze passed for the current clouds above the wastelands in the outskirts of the former Old Atlantica territory. They framed the mission in a somber atmosphere before they'd started. Everything else around them didn't help.

Shells of long-abandoned buildings filled the area and surrounded the team. The structures had long since been stripped of their contents, and holes from reclaimed metal, concrete, and glass covered them. Other buildings lay over-turned. The decades and unstable weather had proved unkind to what had been part of one of the grandest urban jewels of Old Earth.

Dante and Urshielle led the formation, trudging through the hard-packed dirt crying out for moisture. After countless missions Dirtside in hostile environments, Dante could never quell the small flicker of wonder that anyone had managed to survive in such hostile conditions, but the alternative was often worse. Better conditions meant more life, as it had in rural Hungary, and that meant Nightmutts and trouble.

The Terran Restoration Group claimed they could retake Earth. Ambrose had suggested the TRG was arguing the bulk of humanity needed to accomplish that mission for survival. Even if they were right, the question remained if they were more likely buying time for the species rather than saving it. Dante wasn't so sure.

He also didn't need to solve all of humanity's problems. He had far more manageable ones sitting right in front of him. Those problems lent themselves to solutions involving his lethal skillset.

First, he needed to find the raiders and save the kidnapped TRG officials. Second, he needed to take down the Station-wide conspiracy that could be another threat to the future of humanity. It all sounded reasonable and easy in his head once he ended every thought with "add pulsecore blasts and suppression fire."

Dante snickered and vaulted over a weathered concrete slab. He had everything under control.

"What amuses you so much, Dante Shale?" A flicker of concern crossed Urshielle's face.

"Simple men have simple pleasures. Don't worry about it." He nodded at the tracks. "Looks like they started taking longer strides at this point."

"They didn't fear attack in this area," Urshielle replied. "They believed they'd fled far enough to focus on swiftness."

Nasreen frowned at the tracks. "Are they colluding with the tribe that controls this area? That'd explain how they managed the ambush."

"Maybe," Dante commented. Local tribes wouldn't be so effective at beating TRG sensors.

Urshielle shook her head. "Many of the tribes from this area have moved to areas where your people have set up farms and fences to protect from beasts. This place had little to offer and is now mostly abandoned by anyone but the most desperate."

Dante's gaze flicked to a crushed hovercar half-buried underneath the collapsed roof of what had once been a garage. "Good to know the locals are getting something out of all this TRG stuff beyond the facilities around your place. That makes this all more plausible."

Hyde lingered in the back of the group with a slight frown. Every once in a while, he glanced at Urshielle. Even a metal man had a heart. Dante had done his best to steer the Crescent-Marked warrior Hyde's way in the past. Her comments suggested she wanted someone more flesh-and-blood rather than metal and hydraulic fluid. He couldn't do more than that.

The apprentices and Nasreen walked in a diamond formation sandwiched between Urshielle and Dante in the front with Hyde in the rear. Although Urshielle walked with a spear in hand, the Station team's weapons remained slung over their shoulders. Other than highlighting suspicious shadows for Dante's follow-up, Midas kept quiet.

"These assholes didn't try to cover their tracks," Dante said. "That's arrogant."

"They won the fight, didn't they?" Hyde called from the back.

"They're assuming they'll win the next. That's the big mistake." Dante shook his head.

"They attacked and targeted TRG people. That means they had a reason to suspect a Station-backed response. You would have thought they would have done more to cover their tracks. Unless they figure there's nothing we can do about it, or for whatever reason thought the Stations wouldn't care."

Urshielle shook her head. "The word of the TRG has spread through the tribes, as have your efforts in defeating those who would harvest from the tribes. There is no one who would come into this territory and think them acceptable as raiding targets."

"You said you didn't recognize the raider tribe," Dante countered.

"That's true." Urshielle frowned. "There's always something one can do, Dante Shale. You, of all Moonfolk, have proven that. We can rescue these people with your help. The other TRG men said warriors would come, but we are glad you came so quickly."

"Yeah. I'm faster than any security forces who might bother to show up." Dante squinted into the distance. "If I can't find these people, there's always revenge. I'm great at that."

Dante had started to regret not taking the shuttle until they reached the outskirts of the ruins. The widely spaced tracks had bunched up single file with less spacing to follow a narrow path between buildings and overhangs. The previous arrogance that had annoyed him had vanished. His prey had shifted to being more careful. He needed to reply in kind.

A stone-faced Urshielle strode forward, following the tracks. Her expression hadn't changed in a while.

Nasreen jogged up to the front. "Doesn't it bother you, Dante?"

Urshielle frowned her way. She didn't speak.

"Yeah." Dante motioned toward the tracks. "Our raiders went from sprinting in a huge group to going out of their way to hide." He lifted his head. "These tracks aren't that hard to follow from the ground."

"No." Urshielle grunted. Her small frown turned into a deeper scowl. "They mock us. It's as you said. They are arrogant."

Dante shook his head. "You deal with us all the time, but you don't think like us Moonfolk." He pointed up. "This confirms these raiders understood what they hit and the implications. They've gone out of their way to hide from aircraft. They were more worried about a Station response than we thought."

"Our people have long since learned of the dangers of your flying machines. They are symbols of harvesting and death to many tribes."

"Sure, but this isn't about hiding or attacking o-harvesters." Dante slowed at a narrowing alley. Whoever had gone through could barely fit. A speck of yellow and green caught his eye. He knelt, found a feather, and rubbed it between his fingers. "Just what are these guys riding?"

"All tribes have different names for them," Urshielle replied. "Most haven't tamed them. Your people at the camp spoke of them being ostriches and horses combined. I don't know what an ostrich is and have only heard legends of the horses that once roamed this world."

"We'll call them ostorses then." Dante stood and squinted into the distance. Patches of brown and green pressed against the grays and blacks of the ruins. "It looks like they ran into grasslands."

Braelin cracked his knuckles. "That doesn't sound so bad."

Dante stared at him. "We're chasing, on foot, a group of raiders who ride Nightmutts into an area where there will be more Nightmutts, and you don't think that's so bad."

"Oh."

Jolo and Mugoi chuckled. Hyde didn't take the opportunity for the easy insult.

Dante unslung his pulsecore. "Let's keep more alert from here on out." He nodded forward. "Tall grass means cover for Nightmutts and whatever raiders want to take a shot at us. There were too many bullet holes and fires at the site. These guys aren't sticking to spears and arrows."

The apprentices readied their weapons. This time Mugoi and Hyde both were armed with pulsecore carbines, but Hyde kept his locked onto his back, using a built-in weapons rack he'd installed.

Dante advanced through the alleys and narrow streets. The ruins held almost no plant life. The materials and conditions of the fallen cities had poisoned the land enough to keep it an open-air museum in places not aided by Dirtwalker and TRG help.

As the team moved forward, patches of greenery poked through the decayed concrete with increasing frequency. The tall grass that worried Dante so much swayed at the touch of the wind in the distance. It was as if nature decided to reclaim the land but leave what remained of a city as a reminder of humanity's arrogance.

Bright spots of color joined the green and brown. They were

flowers, not raider ostorses, but flowers could only exist with more life. They provided another reminder that not everything left on Earth was a horrible Nightmutt or struggling Dirtwalker.

More greenery ate the gray the farther they traveled. Following Urshielle, Dante stepped into the undergrowth and grasses running up to the border of the wastelands.

She stayed low and gestured with her spear at bent stalks and barely perceptible tracks. "They remain single file."

"Can you tell us more about these raiders?" Nasreen asked. "I'm not surprised at such a group existing, but we've been here many times and not seen them."

Urshielle shook her head. "You wouldn't have. The Long Riders were a distant concern until more recent days. Their main territories lay farther to the west. They've only come closer this last year."

"Nomadic raiders have always been around throughout history," Nasreen mused. "It was inevitable more would spread across what's left of Earth. They just had to find a replacement for horses."

"Rumors say they were more limited in the past years," Urshielle replied. "They feared the Ancient Great Paths as cursed. Then a newer chief among them spread a different thought, that the Ancient Great Paths had survived to lead them to new lands. While he doesn't lead the tribes, many believed his ideas."

"What's an Ancient Great Path?" Nasreen asked.

"The remains of a highway," Hyde chipped in from the back.

"He's right." Urshielle nodded. "The people at the camp taught us how they were left behind from when your kind lived proper lives on the ground and used wheeled carts that moved themselves. The tribes of our area didn't believe them cursed, but they are cracked and broken. They offered little hope, so we didn't follow them, not believing they would lead to anything great."

The team waded deeper into the grasslands. Dante stepped past the cracked skull of something large and feline. Much like

Hungary, squinting at the dull sky and ignoring the risk of Nightmutts made the area seem nice.

"You were wrong about one thing, Nasreen Joelle," Urshielle began. "You called them nomadic raiders."

She shrugged. "Back in ancient Earth history, there were always groups of hostile mounted raiders who liked to attack towns. The mounts look different, but this is an old story."

Urshielle shook her head. "Long Riders are often as willing to trade as they are to rob and steal. We didn't recognize any of these Riders. They might come from a tribe that only knows fighting. They should be called the raiders, not Riders."

"I'm not here to figure out all the Dirtside diplomacy." Dante lifted his carbine. "I'm here to help recover TRG personnel and convince those raiders they should leave your new village alone. If I have to do that by killing them all, I will."

"We'll do what is necessary." Urshielle hefted her spear. "They have harmed my people and those who would aid all the tribes. They will pay."

Dante slowed and frowned. He motioned at trampled grass and deep tracks flaring out in wide arcs in different directions. "What am I seeing?"

Urshielle crouched low and poked at the tracks. "Many of these tracks are old." She pointed with her spear. "But those are fresher. There's a camp nearby."

"I'm not seeing anything on the horizon," Dante replied. "Which means more walking. The longer we walk, the more we risk losing our daylight."

"You wish to stop?" Surprise tinged Urshielle's voice.

"Nah." Dante shook his head. "Short rest, then we pick it up. If we surprise them at a camp, we'll have the advantage."

Dante laid low, along with the rest of his team. Smoke drifting into the sky announced the camp long before the flickering lights of the distant fires danced across the open plain. He narrowed his eyes at the magnified view through his new helmet's visor, surveying the crude grass and wood huts marking the Long Rider camp.

Ostorses stood in a wooden pen. Most were lying in a heap with their large black eyes closed on the edge of their elongated heads. Their bright feathers offered a splash of color. Dante didn't like the look of their sharp beaks. Unlike the avian features marking most of their body, their four legs ended in single dark hooves.

Long Riders sat cross-legged around a large campfire roasting large lizard-like creatures on spits. Nightmutt fur and pelts dominated their clothing, but they left their faces exposed, unlike the sinister cannibal tribe the team had dealt with on their last Dirtside trip. Elaborate tattoos of red, blue, and yellow covered their faces. Both the men and women wore their hair long and unkempt. Two women had sleeping babies strapped to their backs as they laughed and turned their dinner over the fire.

Weapons lay near the Riders, spears, bows, and arrows mostly. Dante spotted fewer rifles but far more than he would have liked.

Sir, Midas greeted. He flashed a green outline over the ostorses in rapid sequence. *Please note the quantity relative to the observed population.*

"This doesn't look like the same group," Dante said. "No sign of the victims. And there aren't enough ostorses for the dozens of people here. They'd have to triple stack to handle that entire group, and I don't think those things look that strong."

Urshielle squinted into the distance. "Your Moonfolk vision is grand."

Dante tapped his helmet. "I'm cheating with a machine."

Nasreen crept forward. "We can't open fire on them without proof they were involved. There are children there."

Hyde waddled forward, the *clank* of his body making Dante wince. "It's a trap. This is their camp guard, leftover old people and mothers. We make a move, and they swarm us."

Mugoi peered into the camp. "There are many strong adults of younger age."

"How would they trap us?" Dante asked. "There are no real trees or buildings to hide a major force in. Most of their huts are open, and there's nothing in there but their pelt beds. These people are a different group."

He turned to Urshielle. "These Long Riders don't all serve someone like a khan, do they?"

"A khan?" Urshielle cocked her head and mouthed the word.

"A single great warrior who unites all the nomadic tribes," Dante explained.

Urshielle shook her head. "Not that I've heard. They share respect for their lifestyle, but all value their freedom."

"Then we'll try this a different way." Dante stood and slung his rifle over his shoulder. "We're going to try talking."

Hyde scoffed. "People tend to shoot at you when you start talking, *Papi*. I think it's your face."

"It's the one I was born with." Dante shrugged. "Nothing I can do about that."

"Nah, there's always something you can do about your face."

Nasreen put her hand to her mouth. She turned away to laugh into it.

Dante led the team toward the encampment. He kept his hands up, and his weapon slung over his shoulder. The Long Riders snatched up their weapons and rushed to take cover behind the sad huts. Dante wouldn't have bothered if he were them. One good pulsecore round would vaporize their cover.

Staring down rifles and arrows was part of the job. Wearing armor didn't make it any easier. He had no idea what ammo they had loaded into the rifles, and rather than old rusty clunkers they were Reaver 235 rifles that looked so new they might have sparkled with enough light.

"I'm not here to fight you," Dante called in the trade tongue. His Plan B involved hoping Urshielle spoke a dialect they understood.

An older Long Rider with a craggy face advanced. He held one of the rifles. "You come in numbers and with armor and weapons," he replied in the trade tongue. "We have no reason to trust Moonfolk."

"You don't. But if this was about hurting you, I could have fired my weapon from far away."

The elder narrowed his eyes. "Are you threatening us, Moonfolk?"

"He comes to offer trade," Urshielle shouted.

The apprentices and Hyde all tensed, unsure about what was happening. Nasreen sighed. Between upgrades to her language implant and her direct work, she understood enough about how the situation was unfolding.

Although the elder didn't drop his rifle, something flashed in his eyes, weakening the hostility. Dirtwalker, Station-born, it didn't make a difference. Dante recognized the new look, something universal to all men, greed.

"What could we have to offer you great Moonfolk in trade?" the elder asked. All the hostility drained from his voice. He hadn't made it to a polite tone, but he was getting there. He wrinkled his nose and waved toward the corral of ostorses. "The beasts' flesh is tough and unpleasant. It's a waste to eat them. We could trade them if you wish to ride."

Dante chuckled. "I'm not interested in eating your animals,

and we don't need a ride yet. We have questions about a tribe of Long Riders who might have come this way."

The elder narrowed his eyes. "Why should we help you hunt our kind?"

"Because they attacked our people and the community of the Crescent-Marked." Dante lowered his arms. "That causes trouble for all the tribes in the area."

"When there's trouble, we move." The elder lowered his rifle. "Men weren't meant to stay in one place. You Moonfolk understand this. You come from the moon to here because the wanderlust cries in your blood."

Dante didn't see a reason to contradict the man's belief. "Dealing with these raiders will make it safer for your people. Other tribes might think they are you the next time they attack someone."

"You say so many things." The elder sniffed and rubbed his nose. "None have to do with trade."

"We've got Moonfolk food," Dante said. "And medicines. The food is made to last a long time. You can save it and travel with it. Useful for people like your tribe."

"You'll give us your moon food and medicine? In exchange for words about the others?"

Dante nodded. "I'll give you supplies as a sign of good faith. You give us good information, and I'll give you more. We brought plenty with us in our flying machine."

The elder raised his hand and motioned toward the fire. "Then come and let us talk. We have no need to protect those causing trouble."

"Thank you." Dante opened his channel to Ambrose and switched back to English. "Any trouble there, Ambrose?"

"It's been quiet here. I've been sticking close to the shuttle."

"Good. Bring the shuttle over to our coordinates. We've got a trade to make."

An hour later, half the encampment had raised their voices in song. A Long Rider had pulled out a bowed instrument somewhere between a fiddle and a Chinese erhu. He moved his bow with skillful precision producing a wavering but jaunty tune. The Dirtwalker shouted their lyrics in a language that defied Dante's understanding. It wasn't close to the trade tongue he knew.

The tribe had formed a circle. Men and women broke off in movements to clap and spin around each other. Jolo and Braelin had joined in the fun, mimicking their hosts. Mugoi sat near the cookfires, smiling at children admiring its metal body.

Ambrose danced with a Long Rider woman who kept offering him sly winks. He grinned like a drunken fool. Hyde stood aloof with his arms folded while Nasreen, Urshielle, and Dante chatted with the elder in a tent away from the dancing.

The elder finished spooning down the final bite of chocolate pudding. His eyes half-closed, and he shuddered as a quiet moan escaped. "You Moonfolk die like any man, yet you eat such magical things. This is truly the food of the gods. Did you slay the gods on the moon to get it?"

"We have machines that make it." Dante held up another circular pudding container and pulled off the disposable spoon. He held it and didn't speak until the elder took the offering. "Getting back to what we were discussing, you said you've talked to them twice?"

The elder opened his new pudding. He frowned. "We talked once. They came the day before last. We didn't know them. They spoke only the trade tongue. Their accents sounded strange. They didn't come from the west like the other Riders and didn't sound like the tribes from this area who don't ride. We didn't speak to them the second time. We saw them riding through the fields with their prisoners."

"You didn't try to stop them?" Nasreen asked.

"Why should we?" The elder shrugged. "We don't value slaves, but it's not our place. We will trade with those who will trade with us. We fight those who fight us."

Loud claps joined the singing. Another Rider had pulled out a hide-bound drum from one of the huts and smacked away with a skillful rhythm to join the claps and the pseudo-fiddler. Dante could appreciate a group that liked to party.

"But you traded with them the first time?" Dante asked.

The elder nodded. He stroked the rifle. "They wanted mounts. They told us they had Moonfolk weapons they'd taken from your warriors, but they'd lost their mounts in the battle."

Dante inclined his head toward the rifle. "They traded those guns for...those." He gestured at an ostorse staring at him unblinkingly from the enclosure.

"Yes, Moonman Shale," the elder replied. "The hatching season comes soon. We could afford to spare most of them for such a trade. We have those precious weapons. Enough to fight even you."

The tribe had never seen explosives if they had that attitude. Dante didn't need to go that far. The man's blissful look with each bite of pudding proved that not all trades needed to be about weapons.

"We aren't surprised your raiders came this way," the elder replied. "We've used the same methods to conceal our numbers in the past and our directions." He grabbed the rifle and watched Dante. After the lack of reaction, the elder pointed the weapon off in the distance.

"They traveled that way with their new Moonfolk slaves. There are no other Rider tribes in that direction, and my tribe rarely goes there. You should have little trouble following them."

He set down his rifle and stood with his pudding. "Night comes soon. You may stay with us if you wish." He headed toward his whooping tribesmen. "I should join the merriment." He disappeared with a final nod.

Urshielle frowned at the rifle. "These are the same weapons that the raiders used. The men he speaks of must be the same."

"This is a new model of Station rifle." Dante motioned at the weapon. "It's been out for less than three months."

"More evidence that someone from the Stations might be manipulating the situation down here," Nasreen replied. "And supplying weapons to groups to do their dirty work. It's a good method to not have it traced back to them."

Dante glared out of the camp. "We can't wait around here."

"We won't be able to catch the raiders on foot," Urshielle replied. "They were only going slower to avoid your people. Now that they've come this far and used the overlapping tracks, they will have felt free to run faster and bolder. They are many hours ahead of us."

Nasreen inclined her head toward the shuttle. "We've got that. Why not use it?"

Dante shook his head. "Same problem as before. We use the shuttle and they'll hear us coming long before they see us. We stay on the ground and we keep the chance of surprising them. It could be the element that keeps the hostages alive."

"Then how are we going to catch up, especially when we're getting closer and closer to night?"

"I've got an idea." Dante grinned. "How many more rations do we have?"

Braelin shuddered as he slipped his boots into the stirrups of the colorful mount. He cast a nervous glance at Jolo, who smiled. "This is a bad idea."

Dante rolled his shoulders and tugged on the reins. "Nope. This won't be so bad."

Mugoi hopped into a saddle. The ostorse hissed and bucked

the cyborg off. Mugoi landed on its palm and pushed off into a springing jump that brought it back to its feet.

"That's the third time, Captain." Mugoi frowned. "This creature despises me."

Hyde shook his head. "I'm not getting on this. I'd crush it."

Nasreen shuddered and furiously punched the armor controls on her forearm. She almost fell off her mount.

"What's wrong?" Dante asked.

"I'm shifting to full NBC filtration mode," Nasreen explained.

"Huh?" Dante looked around, trying to fight against the instinct to hold his breath. "You think there's a chemical weapon in use?"

"No. These things smelled bad from far away. On top, they smell like something that died." Nasreen shivered. "That's wrong. They smell worse than something that died."

Dante sniffed. Pungent and sulfuric notes flowed together in an interesting bouquet. It wasn't the most pleasant thing he'd ever smelled, but he'd run into far, far worse Dirtside. He'd barely noticed until she pointed it out.

Mugoi leapt on his mount only for it to fling it off again. It jumped back up. "This is becoming untenable. This creature is annoying me."

Hyde scoffed. "Ha-ha. I agree with Pretty Face. Just no, *Papi.*"

Urshielle pulled back on her reins. "Your elders were wounded during the battle. Waiting gives the raiders more time to escape and your people more time to die. We shouldn't wait."

Dante patted his ostorse on the back of his head before scratching him on the back of his neck. The animal let out a quiet hiss. "She's right. You two need to figure it out."

"No." Mugoi shook its head and stepped back. "This won't work. But I have another solution."

"What? No shuttle."

A deep grinding noise and whirring sounded. The music died. The curious tribe rushed over to watch. Mugoi's legs lengthened, and the angle of connection to the lower body widened. Its hips shifted, rotating forward.

The cyborg motioned to its legs. "This is less efficient and hard on my parts. I'll be able to keep up now. Readjustment will be necessary before any fights."

"Huh." Dante nodded. "Sure. Yeah. Whatever. That works."

Hyde grunted and leaned over. His leg and hip transformation was even louder and included sparks that the tribe cheerfully clapped about. "I hate this crap. I'm going to kill all those *pendejos* when we find them."

CHAPTER FIVE

Although it wasn't needed yet, night vision mode on the helmets and Midas' aid would make it easy for Dante to lead his band of riders through the twilight and night of the Dirtside wilderness. While the occasional hill broke the monotony of the surface, endless grasslands stretched out in front of them. The occasional hint of an old road poked up through the ground or made the plants uneven, but this far away from the ruins of Old Atlantica, nature had taken full control.

The long, effortless strides of the ostorses kept the team barreling over the land fast enough that Dante could have challenged a vehicle. Despite being new to the beast, he needed only the slightest tugs on the reins to change the animal's direction. Other than their disdain for the cyborgs, they didn't show any distress at Dante's armored, backpack-equipped team riding on their backs. He could easily imagine these creatures being mass bred on the surface for the use of all tribes and TRG project members. A return of Station-born humanity might mean taking advantage of old, proven ways.

Nasreen had been quiet for a long while. That's why the sound of her breath catching came off louder than normal.

"Something wrong?" Dante asked.

"We're nowhere near an old highway," Nasreen replied.

"Yeah. With all the changes on the surface, there are no guarantees they will be everywhere. The Riders might use the highways to head toward the ruins of old cities, but we've seen that these guys are different."

"I hope that's all it is." Nasreen shook her head. "There's something about all this that still bothers me. I feel like we're missing something."

A flutter from a lone tree surged into a horde of tiny, winged lizards with reflective red eyes. They spiraled into the sky before flowing over the team and their mounts like a river of wings.

"We're Dirtside." Dante spoke slowly as he watched the lizards. "There's always something we're missing Dirtside. For now, we proceed with the idea that the raiders wouldn't have bothered with the trouble of taking people this far only to kill them. They wanted those officials for whatever reasons. I don't even know if I care why as long as we get them back."

"Destroying this tribe will ensure peace between our peoples," Urshielle said.

"Yeah. Sometimes diplomacy starts with an explosion."

An hour later, Dante pulled on the reins to slow his mount. He was glad he rode at the front of the formation and had a helmet on. Nobody could see his gaping mouth. The wonder came out in his voice. "Would you look at that?"

A massive herd of shaggy, dark bovine-like Nightmutts with four twisting horns wandered and frolicked in the expanse of grasslands, munching on the plants and paying little attention to the humans riding the ostorses. The horned bison-like creatures clustered along a large stream of fresh water, alternating drinks between their mouthfuls of lunch.

Braelin whistled. "That many stampeding could crush a shuttle."

"That's a sobering thought," Jolo replied.

"They couldn't crush me," Hyde offered.

Mugoi laughed. "You don't have to threaten a massive herd to prove your strength."

"I'm not threatening them, *pendejo*. I'm explaining what would happen."

Dante laughed. Of all the conversations he'd imagined he might have throughout his life, he never anticipated hearing a combat cyborg brag about his ability to survive a massive stampede Dirtside.

"It's not funny." Hyde growled.

Urshielle stared at the herd, wide-eyed. "There are so many."

Hyde's expression softened at her voice. "You haven't seen this many before?"

"No. This is the farthest I've been away from my home. I've heard tales of these creatures before, but I haven't seen them. I've never seen so many of any kinds of beasts together."

Between their foot and ostorse travel, they'd put a lot of miles between them and the Crescent-Marked community. Dante had lived his whole life descending from orbit to all over Earth. He had trouble putting himself into the mind of a woman who'd stayed so close to where she'd been born, even after leaving her original tribe and joining the Crescent-Marked. That didn't mean they had no common ground.

"It's the largest group of animals I've ever seen Dirtside," Dante noted. "If that makes you feel any better."

"Should we be worried?" Mugoi asked. "Hyde's protestations don't mean the rest of us would survive a confrontation with the entire herd."

"Midas, you noticing anything I'm not?" Dante asked.

No, sir. I've performed individual analyses on every animal visible in your line of sight. The overall group is barely paying attention to your team.

"We'll go around them," Dante decided. "They're prey animals, and humans aren't hunting them. They have no reason to fear or attack us unless we give them one."

Braelin walked his ostorse forward, smiling at the herd. "The TRG might be onto something."

"What do you mean?" asked Dante. "They're not onto great security. They've proven that much."

Jolo jogged her mount forward. Her piercing gaze took in the sight. She looked at Braelin. "It's like you always tell us, Dante. The Earth isn't dead. There is life."

"Sure." Dante chuckled. "I usually follow it up by talking about how that life will try to eat you, so make sure your safety's off."

"Back in the day, people said we needed to go into space because the Earth wouldn't recover," Braelin continued. "Everything we've seen and heard makes it seem like that ain't right." He patted his chest. "We're the ones who needed to recover and adapt." He gestured at the herd. "The Earth ain't dying if it can have that many weird creatures wandering around eating grass and not dying."

Hyde lumbered up to the front with the others. "You should spend more time down here." His voice was quiet and subdued. "You'd learn how much you don't know. That includes you, *Papi.*"

Dante squinted. The wide tracks led toward the stream before moving off to follow the water. Given the size of the herd, they might have been there when the raiders came through. Attacking thousands of animals, even with firearms, would have been idiotic. Men on the run with hostages would have less reason to create more trouble for themselves.

He urged his mount forward. "Let's follow the stream. These things need a drink anyway."

The minutes flowed together until the herd turned into a dark blob on the horizon. They stopped farther up the stream to let their ostorses lap up water with their long, flexible tongues.

The raider's tracks hadn't disappeared. Deeper, fresher tracks told him exactly what he wanted to know. They were getting closer.

Most of the day, sunlight had peeked through the dark clouds over their long trip. The sun had dropped lower in the sky. Twilight was giving way to true darkness, and they would soon have to rely on night vision. A spare set of night vision goggles would help Urshielle, but Dante had no idea how well the raiders operated at night.

This wasn't like a normal job. He was used to hitting locations and traveling in the wilderness, but there was always a discrete target location, even if the goods remained elusive. Wandering so far away across Dirtside left him unsettled.

It wasn't the danger. They'd run into nothing dangerous for most of their ride.

Braelin had been right. Station-born humanity had been told from the day they were born that there was no choice but to abandon Earth. Now, they struggled to conceive and had become parasites on the humans who'd stayed behind.

Dante wasn't ready to settle Dirtside. That didn't mean it wasn't as much humanity's future as it was their past. The TRG was the first step in saving the species. If they'd been living on the surface, they'd be less vulnerable to the Omega Syndrome. He planned to handle that problem long before anyone in the future had to make hard decisions about abandoning the Station.

"Is something wrong?" Nasreen asked.

"Yeah," Dante replied. "Raiders have hostages, and the raiders are still breathing. Let's give these things fifteen minutes to rest and get going. We might have all night. We can't be sure the kidnapped victims do."

What started as a soft and steady rumble grew in volume as the team followed the twisting and turning stream. The gently flowing water became a white-churning river. More trees appeared, the occasional lone sentry becoming a group, then the makings of a genuine living forest that lacked the gnarled appearance Dante had seen so often on Earth.

That left him questioning himself even more than before. Until the harvesting and betrayal incident, Dante viewed Dirtside as nothing more than a place to make money. There was no reason for him to concern himself with whether the Earth was recovering. He could have missed countless signs of the planet's health throughout the years. It wasn't as if it had all popped into existence in the last year.

The retreating sun had spread deepening shadows over the land. The faint stars shone through the slim parts in the cloud. Even the atmosphere didn't look poisoned and dying as he was used to. There was a stillness to the experience that left him calm despite the immediate goal of their ride.

All during these thoughts, Dante and Urshielle continued to follow the tracks. The frowning Crescent-Marked warrior reached up often to adjust the goggles Dante had loaned her.

He trusted her superior Earth-adapted senses, but that didn't make her a super-woman who could see in the dark unaided. Using flashlights, lanterns, or torches was too risky. They didn't need to scream their arrival to the raiders.

"These feel strange." Urshielle tugged on the goggles.

"You've never used this type of gear?" Dante asked. "You must have been involved in nighttime missions to help the TRG."

"We have torches and your Station torches back at the village. We don't fear your machines and devices, but we also don't want to depend on things we can't make or scavenge ourselves."

Dante slowed his mount as they trekked through the forest. "I figured. You're worried about the TRG giving up on Earth?"

"A wise woman plans for many possibilities," Urshielle replied. "If we fail today, your people might end the pacts they've made with mine. Your Stations can go back to picking from the carcass of the past."

Dante wanted to be insulted by the description. He also wanted to point out that the Dirtwalkers did the same thing without the benefit of full knowledge of what they found.

Despite that, he let the comment slide. Nothing she'd said was inaccurate, and she was right to be worried about what would happen if they couldn't recover the hostages.

The rumble became a resounding roar. The burgeoning stream fed a cascading waterfall plummeting into an ample pond. Raider tracks went up to the cliff before disappearing on one side and reappearing on the other side of the water.

Dante looked between the water and the far shore. Despite the width and current, the shallow depth would make it easy to cross. The raiders hadn't pulled off any impressive ostorse equestrian stunts.

A growl cut through the roar of the waterfall. Dante snapped his head in that direction, reaching up for his gun.

A Nightmutt crouched near a bush, blending in with the deep shadows. Powerful muscles marked the long, slender body covered with dark scales. The creature was between a panther and a lizard. The Nightmutt's sharp, curved claws looked far too perfect for tearing flesh. Slitted yellow eyes reflected the light, and huge fangs gleamed green in the night vision goggles.

Soft mewling sounded from the bushes, and tiny heads poked out.

Hyde flexed his fingers. "This will be easy."

Dante lowered his hand from his gun and put out his palm toward Hyde. He shook his head. "Yeah, but we don't need to mess up a mother protecting her cubs."

"You serious now?" Hyde asked.

"Yeah." Dante tapped the sides of his mount with his heels. "She leaves us alone. We'll leave her alone. Sounds fair enough."

Hyde looked like he was going to object until Urshielle nodded her agreement. The cyborg shrugged.

Dante's wary ostorse kept his head to the side and eyes on the panther-lizard as he splashed through the stream and emerged on the opposite side. Dante tugged on the reins to direct his mount to hug the cliff face.

"Everyone follow me single file," he ordered. "No fast movements."

"You think that's what the raiders did?" Nasreen asked.

Dante motioned at the ground. Ostorse tracks lay everywhere.

"Nope," he replied. "But that's what we're doing."

Urshielle fell in behind Dante. Nasreen walked her mount through the stream but watched the Nightmutt the entire time. Jolo led Braelin next. Mugoi scoffed before trudging through the water. Hyde growled and stomped through. The Nightmutt growled in return and reared back.

"Come on," Dante replied. "We're almost through. We're going to have to kill plenty of people today. No reason to waste ammo on an animal who doesn't have it in for us."

He jogged his ostorse along the path marked out by the earlier tracks. With each yard, the Nightmutt grew quieter and calmer until lowering herself to the ground and letting out a rattling sound from her throat that elicited more mewling from inside the bush.

"The damned planet really is starting to recover," Dante whispered and shook his head.

"What was that?" asked Nasreen.

"Nothing. Just thinking that getting these TRG officials back might be more important than I thought. I hope the raiders didn't feed them to any Nightmutts along the way."

Darkness had taken over completely, accompanied by a night choir of chirping and buzzing. The team had long since left the cliff and waterfall behind to follow a sloping forested path. It narrowed into a barren ravine in the shadow of a craggy peak.

Deep tracks and more dried dung than Dante had ever encountered since an ill-fated raid near old Iceland warned they were closing on the raiders. With luck, finding them would prove the most difficult part of the mission.

He pulled the reins to stop his ostorse and craned his head upward. He sniffed the air. "I smell smoke." He pointed at a dark cloud obscuring the rising moon. "That looks like smoke."

"I don't see any fire," Urshielle commented. "And no rising smoke."

"Whoever was here killed the fire recently." Dante frowned. "Ambrose, you better be awake."

"I am!" Ambrose complained over the scratchy radio link. "I'm back at the main TRG camp."

"I want you in the pilot's seat and heading our way," Dante ordered. "Stay low and wide, at least ten miles out until further orders. I have a feeling we'll need you soon."

"Roger. On my way."

The narrowing ravine left far too many blind spots where enemies could hide, such as a large overhang hovering over a circle of boulders that formed a natural fortress guarding the front of a cave. Ostorse tracks continued past the rock formation before heading off in opposite directions. The team's night vision gear would help, but it was no substitute for normal light.

Dante dismounted with a grunt. "We don't know this area. They could have caves down there or have their camp hidden by the rock. We've made good time, but we can't be sure we've caught up with them."

Urshielle dropped off her mount with a grace that made Dante think she'd ridden such a beast her entire life. "It could be another trick to throw us off their trail. These raiders are clever."

"You think they'd pull one this far away from the raid site?" Dante shook his head. "I don't want to think it. They might be trying to throw anyone who stumbled on them off, but my gut tells me they are close by."

"Then we need to hurry the hell up," Hyde grumbled. "Before they decide the victims they've got aren't worth much." He smacked his fist into a palm. "This isn't a problem that's complicated to solve. No politics to worry about here. They broke the rules for everybody. They pay the price."

Nasreen peered into the darkened ravine with a frown. "That doesn't mean we shouldn't be careful. They might be Long Riders, but we know they have Station-supplied weapons. If they have the right ammo, it could get messy for us."

Dante's ostorse bobbed its head a couple of times before clawing the ground, turning in circles, and letting out a quiet hiss of impatience.

Braelin pointed his thumb at his mount. "We going ancient calvary on them?"

Dante shook his head. "We can't fight on these things."

Braelin patted his mount's side. "Why not? The Long Riders do. They have guns too. That means these things are used to the sound of firearms."

"I'm sure the Riders are born in the saddle and all that crap," Dante replied. "Don't make the mistake of thinking these are biological cars. These are living creatures who can respond with fear and panic in a battle, just like a human. Without extensive training together, they don't make good mounts."

Braelin's shoulders slumped. "I thought it'd look cool."

Dante chuckled. "These guys are well-trained, and I'm surprised at how well they responded to a bunch of people in armor sitting on them, but trying to rush in there like ancient Mongols would get us and these things killed." He patted his backpack. "We have spikes in the packs and rope. We'll tie them up here and go investigate the ravine on foot. It won't matter if they panic then. If we get killed, the raiders will take them and give them a new home."

"How damned generous." Hyde ground away an old track with his foot. "What's the plan?"

"We'll go in with three teams," Dante explained. He motioned at the left side of the ridge. "We'll have one team follow the ridge line there. Another team will take the opposite side. One team down the center."

Nasreen's brow lifted. "Decoys?"

Dante shrugged. "Sometimes you have to poke the nest to see if anything's inside. If this is their territory, they could be hiding, and we might never spot them without giving them a reason to pop their heads up."

Hyde's scowl twitched into a smile. "Whoever's in the center is going to get action."

"Yeah. I'll lead that team since it's my idea."

"Nah." Hyde shook his head. "You should have me as my own team. I can take the shots better. They start shooting. I start killing. Then everyone else joins in."

Dante eyed the cyborg, worry building despite his earlier comfort with his plan. This wasn't a situation where diplomacy would help. The raiders had killed people and attacked a group considered neutral by most tribes in the area. Despite that, sending the fighting-obsessed cyborg ahead by himself might escalate things too quickly. Hyde might forget why they were there and who needed to die. The Khallabash Brothers incident remained fresh in Dante's memory.

Urshielle put her hand on Dante's shoulder. "I will accompany him, Dante Shale. We've fought many times side-by-side. I can see the worry in your eyes."

Hyde snorted. "Let me do what I do."

Dante wondered if his concern was showing that much on his face. Instead of asking, he shrugged. "Okay, then. If we play it that way, let's make the center team the strongest. Urshielle, Hyde, and Neburu down the center."

Braelin opened his mouth to say something before shutting it. He tapped his foot impatiently, muttering underneath his breath.

"Nasreen and Klement will take the right ridge," Dante continued. "Mugoi and I will hit the left. Everyone go in weapons hot and stay on comms, but remember the mission." He stared at Hyde. "This has become a hostage recovery first and foremost. If we can scare away the raiders, that'll work. We can't let them use those kidnapped people against us."

Hyde's legs whirred, and his hips tilted back into his standard configuration. "Killing all the kidnappers solves the problem, and it also solves future problems. Everyone needs to get the message about messing with the TRG."

"We can't guarantee we'll have all eyes on target right away." Dante sliced the air with his hand. "If we have any chance of saving those people, we will. One wrong move and they'll kill the hostages. That'll send the wrong message about the TRG."

Hyde snorted. "These assholes see a small team, and they'll get cocky. They won't kill the hostages. They'll charge out thinking they can kill or capture us. I'll make them regret that right before I kill them. The hostages won't be any worse off than before we showed up."

"Yeah. I don't think it's going to be that easy." Dante pulled down his carbine and flipped off the safety. "I'm not going to complain if it is." He turned and looked each apprentice in the eye. "I want to be clear about this. These raiders attacked the Crescent-Marked and their people. This isn't them defending their territory. They don't deserve the restraint that goes with my regular Dirtwalker rules."

"No mercy then, Captain?" Mugoi asked. "Do what we need to?"

"They can always surrender or run." Dante shrugged. He looked at Hyde. "If they live that long."

CHAPTER SIX

Nasreen followed the edge of the ravine, but not too close. A false step would send her tumbling into the darkness below. Her higher view only confirmed how far the ravine stretched down. The striated bands in the rock reminded her of a ladder. Large, dark cave mouths lay everywhere, both at ground level and above. Outcroppings bordered on creating an earthen maze with a taller mound in the center blocking her view.

Braelin crept behind her. He kept a tight grip on his rifle, ready to take out anyone who surprised them.

Nasreen wasn't worried. She couldn't make out what lay directly below their ridgeline. Only a handful of outcroppings lay on top. There was almost nowhere to hide.

"I can see caves," she transmitted. "I don't see any raiders."

"Same here," Dante replied. "Hyde, your team should use those rocks to keep from being spotted."

"We know what we're doing." Hyde sounded annoyed.

Something flashed in the darkness in the ravine. Nasreen dropped to her stomach. Braelin followed her without question. She squinted and crawled farther up the ridgeline. Her new position let her see past the mound, the circle of flickering torches, and the outlines of people and ostorses.

Rows of blankets with elaborate patterns lay beyond the mound. Nasreen didn't remember seeing anything like that in the other camp. Spears, bows, and rifles lay beside the blankets, although most of the Riders sat together in circles. Some chatted quietly, but one man gesticulated wildly as a circle of rapt raiders listened to him. The group had roped their mounts to wooden spikes driven into the hard ground.

"I have eyes on the camp," Nasreen reported. "They're using that central mound as a wall. I don't see any of the TRG staff yet."

"Hyde, hold position," Dante ordered. "Nasreen, you and Klement move up until you have a clear view of the entire camp. My team will be in position soon."

Nasreen crawled farther up the ridgeline before rolling to pivot herself. She set up her rifle and adjusted the scope to survey the camp in more detail, including the blind spot previously created by her angle and the mound.

An older thin man in an expensive suit knelt with his back to the mound, his hands bound with rope behind his back and his legs tied together. Bruises covered his face. A jagged tear ran through the sleeve of his suit.

A Long Rider approached him. The Rider didn't look that much different than any of the tribes they'd traded with, including similar Nightmutt skin clothing and facial makeup. Nasreen adjusted the scope again, focusing on his fisted hand.

The Rider opened his hand, revealing an oxygen inhaler. He shoved it in the man's mouth.

Nasreen shifted the scope away from the man, finding other obvious Station-born hostages kneeling or sitting nearby, all with their hands and legs bound.

"It looks like most if not all the captured officials are here," she reported. "At least the Riders know enough to let them use oxygen inhalers."

"That's good," Dante replied. "It could mean the kidnappers knew from the beginning that us Moonfolk need inhalers or the hostages managed to convince them. Either way, it proves the Riders wanted them alive. It also means they understood they'd make poor slaves."

Nasreen shifted from target to target, keeping her scope to her face. With all the hostages near the mound rather than being spread around the camp, good tactics could save their lives.

The gesticulating man jumped to his feet. He stomped over to another circle and pounded his chest. A bearded Rider in the circle stood in front of the man and squared his shoulders. He shouted something, but the ravine ate the noise except for a faint, distant echo. Every Rider in the camp snatched up their weapons and scrambled to their feet, forming two masses facing one another with hostile glares. One group all held rifles. The second wielded spears, axes, and knives, although they easily outnumbered the first group by a substantial margin.

The first Rider shoved the bearded Rider. The other man shoved him back and spouted something, his face contorted in anger. Nasreen couldn't read lips through a scope at night, especially when dealing with someone speaking an exotic language.

She narrowed her eyes. That wasn't right. The mouth movements were difficult to read through the greenish tint of the night vision mode, but they were familiar. She could have sworn they weren't trade tongue.

"*Vereinbarung*," she whispered.

"What was that?" Dante asked.

"It's German for 'agreement.' The two arguing. The bearded Rider said something about an agreement. I'm trying to read their lips. The bearded Rider was speaking German, not a trade tongue."

"I don't have an angle to have Midas try to read their lips." Frustration tightened Dante's voice. "It looks like we've got factions, or maybe two tribes. I don't care what language they speak if they fight each other. Hyde, get your team as close to the mound as you can without being seen."

"Time to kill somebody," Hyde rumbled over comms.

"Yeah. Time to kill a bunch of people."

The first Rider stomped toward a hostage. He pulled the man to his feet and shook him. Trembling, the wide-eyed hostage stared at the ground.

Another Rider ran across from the other group and pushed the first man out of the way. He backhanded the man, sending him sprawling to the ground in front of the bearded Rider. The downed Rider sat up and wiped blood from his face. When he did, his face paint came off and revealed a small geometric tattoo representing stylized clouds surrounded by jagged lightning bolts.

Nasreen's eyes widened. She swept her scope to another man's face and a third. "It all makes sense."

"What?"

"At the other camp during the party, I saw men wiping their faces. Their face paint didn't come off that easily. The man down there who fell, he did, and it came off."

"I don't have a good angle on his face from up here," Dante said.

"I do, and he has another tattoo on his face." Nasreen lined up her scope to center the man's face in her sights. "It's a symbol for Eastern Lightning."

Dante grunted. "The old merc company?"

"Yes. It's too precise to be a coincidence."

"Eastern Lightning doesn't exist anymore."

"Then he used to work for them," Nasreen suggested. "Look at the faces of the Riders farther back, the ones led by the bearded man. Far fewer scars and smoother skin in general. They're not from Earth."

"Mercs pretending to be fake Riders." Dante scoffed. "They still needed locals to make it seem real. It was never only about supplying someone with weapons. They couldn't guarantee any Riders they bribed would carry out their job. But who are they? I doubt Eastern Lightning somehow came back together for one last job on Earth."

The bearded mercenary gestured at the roped ostorses and a hostage before motioning at all the prisoners and pointing over his shoulder with his thumb. He shook his head and rattled off something so rapid that Nasreen doubted she could have understood it if she was standing next to him, let alone trying to read lips through a scope.

"It looks like the mercs are trying to convince the Riders to keep moving," Nasreen suggested.

The Riders spread out behind their leader, surrounding the hostages. They puffed out their chests and glared at the mercenaries while shaking their weapons.

A mercenary pushed past a Rider to yank up a female prisoner. With her legs bound, she tripped and pitched forward. He grabbed her hair and dragged her across the ground while pointing his rifle with his other hand. Her shriek echoed through the ravine.

Torchlight flashed off an ax blade. A Rider flung the weapon toward the mercenary, not caring that a rifle pointed at him. The blade sank into the merc's shoulder.

His piercing scream broke through the night. He spun, dropped to one knee, and pulled the trigger. His muzzle flashed with a burst, and the Rider's head exploded, splattering his blood before his body toppled backward.

No one moved. Both sides exchanged scowls and glares, eyeballing each other.

A Rider launched his spear. The resounding howl of the Riders filled the air to join with the *crack* of rifles. A burst through the chest silenced one howl. The rest of the Riders had released their spears and drawn their secondary weapons.

Mercenaries fell to the ground with blood shooting from

their necks or spears deep in their chest. A good third of the Riders dropped with huge holes in their chests or heads. One man lost the front of his arm and charged forward with an ax. He was three feet away from a wide-eyed merc when the man squeezed off a round.

The shot zipped by the Rider's face and tore a gouge in his cheek before nailing a cowering prisoner in the shoulder. With a final shout, the Rider planted his ax into the merc's chest.

Something flashed from across the ravine. A greenish blast dug out a crater and rained dirt and rock around the combatants.

The Riders and mercenaries jumped back, ignoring their wounded and the enemy in front of them to reform their lines. The bearded mercenary leader pointed his rifle toward Dante's side of the ravine.

"What's going on?" Hyde demanded in a near growl. "Are we killing these *pendejos* or not?"

"I needed to intervene," Dante replied. "They were going to get the prisoners killed with their crap. This way they have something more to worry about than—"

A storm of bullets ripped from the mercenaries. Dante and Mugoi pulled back, the bullets thudding into the ravine edge and kicking up more dust.

The Riders screamed another echoing battle cry and charged again. The closest mercenaries turned toward them in time to get knives and axes in their heads. A Rider snatched his spear from the ground and threw it into the face of a mercenary.

A frenzied Rider threw himself into a trio of mercs, slashing with his knife. He slit the first man's throat, slashed the second's chest, and plunged his blade into the third's heart in a quick blur. He pulled out the blade and spun toward the nearest target, the cowering woman from before.

Nasreen lined up her shot. Braelin was faster. His bullet screamed from above and carved through the head of the murderous Rider.

This time, the death from above didn't concern either group. The Riders stabbed, slashed, and crushed to bathe the ground in blood. The mercenaries bashed away too-close enemies using their rifles as clubs.

A merc lined up a shot and fired. His burst tore through a Rider rushing him with two knives. The bullets continued into the back of another mercenary, who dropped beneath two Riders. They pounced on him with their knives.

Prisoners scrambled and wiggled, trying to make it away from the brawl. A running Rider stomped over a man to swing his ax at a distracted mercenary. While a handful of prisoners had managed to escape the melee, most remained trapped within the interlocking circles of violence.

Dante and Mugoi walked pulsecore rounds away from the prisoners. The powerful explosions lit up the area, but they kept so far away from the complicated melee they only knocked one man to the ground. To Nasreen's surprise, other than a glance, most of the mercenaries ignored the barrage.

"The prisoners are too wrapped up in the fight," Dante transmitted. "We can't thin out the raiders and mercs with pulsecores without risking collateral damage."

The bearded merc leader shouted something while parrying an ax with his rifle. He yanked out a knife and shoved it into his attacker before kicking the man back. His fellow mercenaries tried to back away from their opponents and form a rough wedge formation. The sheer volume of crazed Riders kept the mercenaries separated.

"Forward team, extract the prisoners," Dante barked. "Everyone without a pulsecore provides overwatch support. Ambrose, you close?"

"I'm here," the pilot replied.

"We need you for pickup. Get here ASAP. Prepare for extraction."

"Roger. ETA, two minutes."

Nasreen swept her rifle toward the closest armed man near a hostage. She switched to single-fire mode, angled her shot high to ensure any pass-through wouldn't hit a prisoner, and squeezed the trigger. Her target spun in a dance of death before tumbling over.

Hyde bellowed so loudly even Nasreen could hear it and charged forward with his arms spread. Jolo and Urshielle were on either side. Jolo snapped her rifle from target to target, her quick trigger pulls and great accuracy sending single rounds through the unarmored heads of the men. Urshielle's mighty toss sent her spear through the neck of a mercenary. She kicked up a Rider's spear from the ground and launched it into one of his allies.

The appearance of a bellowing cyborg caught the focus of the bearded mercenary. He finished jamming his knife into a Rider before shoving the man back and whipping up his gun to fire a burst at Hyde. The bullets sparked and bounced off the cyborg's body while leaving deep gouges.

"Armor-piercing ammo," Hyde announced. "Ha-ha. These bastards came prepared."

Another mercenary pulled down his trigger and held it. He bathed the advancing Hyde in a river of bullets. Metal chunks ripped off his body. Dark fluids leaked from deeper wounds. Even a metal man wasn't invulnerable.

Jolo finished picking off the nearest enemies. With Hyde blocking the bullets, Urshielle hurried to a prisoner and sliced through their ropes with a knife. She tugged on the man's arm and motioned him around the mound before rushing to the next prisoner.

Nasreen jumped from prisoner to prisoner, trying to down the men closest to them. Her angle and worry about friendly fire kept her shots more sporadic than she would have liked. Mugoi and Dante triangulated on a mercenary who'd backed up too far. The dual pulsecore explosions launched his crispy corpse high into the air and earned the attention of a nearby squad of mercs.

Hyde's metal body was larger than a normal man's, even a not-so-normal one, but that still meant he made only a passable wall and couldn't stop every bullet. Rounds whizzed past his body or through his legs, whining by Jolo and Urshielle as they continued their work.

Riders swarmed the team. Hyde crushed one man's head with a punch. He smashed two others and launched them into a line of fire from nearby mercs. His kick left a Rider bent in half.

Urshielle broke from freeing the hostages to knife a Rider bringing an ax down on her. She grabbed his ax and threw the weapon into another man's face. Jolo stayed in position despite the withering gunfire and screaming barbarians all around her. She only stopped firing for her lightning reload sequence.

The appearance of Hyde's team had split the Riders' attention, making it easier for the mercenaries to reform their battlelines. Small surviving squads fired up at Dante's and Nasreen's teams while a dedicated squad alternated fire and reloads as they attempted to wear down Hyde.

Nasreen grimaced as a round scraped Jolo's neck. Her neck armor would be vulnerable to an AP round. The apprentice ignored the near-miss, instead putting two quick bullets into a Rider trying to spear Hyde.

"There's a problem," Ambrose transmitted.

"We've got a crap ton of problems," Dante barked. He forced back the bearded mercenary's squad behind a huge boulder with a pulsecore blast. "Be more damned specific."

"I've got two other aircraft coming in fast," Ambrose reported. "They haven't angled for me. I don't know if they've noticed me."

"Shit. Pull back, keep on comms and keep ready. Everyone else get ready to pull back on the ravine. We'll provide overwatch for Hyde, Urshielle, and Jolo as they move the prisoners to that circle of rocks under the overhang farther back."

Hyde grunted, the sparks from bullets bouncing off his body almost like fireworks from Nasreen's position. "That's a long way to move with a bunch of wounded people, *Papi*."

"Yeah, it is. If our new friends are gunships, Ambrose could get blown away while trying to extract us." Dante punctuated the sentence with two rapid pulsecore rounds that tore off a piece of the bearded merc's boulder and kept the man from returning fire.

Mugoi spread his shots near Hyde's team. The sporadic blasts did their job, discouraging Riders and mercenaries alike from daring to move closer.

Urshielle finished freeing the final prisoner. She grabbed her original spear from a dead body and hurried after them. Jolo switched to burst fire, now freer to spray bullets into the night. Hyde backed up slowly to shield her and Urshielle.

"Ravine teams will run and gun," Dante ordered. "On my count, three, two, one."

Nasreen and Braelin rolled away from the edge. They hopped to their feet and sprinted away from their previous position, spraying bursts into the ravine every couple of yards. The Riders couldn't do much, but the mercenaries replied in kind with too many bursts whizzing close enough for Nasreen to hear.

The last of the prisoners disappeared behind the mound. Jolo, Urshielle, and Hyde followed soon after. The writhing mass of screaming Riders surrounding the mercenaries seemed more interested in killing the men in front of them than going after the captives fleeing into the night. They might have believed they could always run them down later after they finished off their orgy of violence.

Her breathing ragged, Nasreen's heart jumped at the familiar rumble of engines. She kept up her sprint, sending the occasional burst before her new angle made it a waste of ammo.

A gunship and a large shuttle with a turret beneath approached the ravine, their flight pattern a tightening spiral.

The back of the shuttle opened as it descended. Armored men filled the back.

Nasreen slowed and brought up her rifle. As she lined up a shot, she spotted a familiar face slipping on a helmet next to another man. Her window of opportunity vanished with the shuttle's turn.

"DeFrieze is on that shuttle." She pumped her legs, her muscles aching as she sprinted toward the rally point. "So is Sheer."

She'd not wanted to ever see the operations leader and company commander of the Block 9X mercenaries ever again. That wasn't the same thing as being surprised. Certain inconsistencies now made more sense.

"Yeah. Perfect. Good for the Eastern Lightning bastard that he found a new merc company." Dante grunted. "Don't engage. Let the mercs and Riders thin each other out while we pull back."

"We're not getting out of here with a gunship on our ass," Hyde replied.

"We'll figure it out. Nasreen, your team still under fire?"

"No." Nasreen glanced over her shoulder to make sure Braelin was right behind her.

"Hyde, you still have all the prisoners with you?"

"Yes," Hyde replied. "They won't shut up."

"Nobody's going to hear them in all the fighting," Dante replied. "Everyone get beneath that overhang with the rocks, keep your heads down, and don't attract attention from Block 9X."

CHAPTER SEVEN

Dante's lungs burned. He leaned on the wall near the cave entrance. Shouts, gunfire, and screams continued to fill the air, marking the ongoing fierce battle. The whole thing was absurd. For as much beauty as he'd witnessed on their trip, every time he hit Dirtside, he ended up fighting for his life.

"I picked the wrong career," he whispered.

Would you have preferred a different career, sir? Midas asked.

Dante snickered. "I should have been an AI programmer."

I don't think you'd be very good at it.

"Probably not."

The gunship circled overhead menacingly, but Dante no longer had eyes on the battle or the shuttle. With luck, the Riders would swarm the shuttle and kill the Block 9X leaders, ending that part of the threat. The more likely scenario was the mercenaries would soon finish off their technologically inferior enemies and sweep the area for the mysterious snipers with rifles and pulsecore carbines who'd freed their prisoners.

Belligerent as they were, the leaders of the mercenary outfit weren't idiots. They might have figured out Dante's crew was involved.

Nasreen and Braelin were applying nanosprays and bandages to the prisoners. They'd sealed the wound of the man shot in the shoulder and put his arm in a sling. Other than grateful words, the prisoners hadn't said much. The haunted look in their sunken eyes said enough. They'd survived the horror of the first attack only to end up caught in a brutal free-for-all.

"We're going to get you out of here," Dante said to no one in particular. "We need to wait for a good tactical opportunity."

"Are we going to die out here?" a woman asked, looking down at her swollen and chapped hands. "You can be honest with us. I'd prefer to know if it was coming. I can make my peace that way."

"I've died before." Dante half-smirked. "I didn't care for it and wouldn't recommend it. It ruins your day. So no, we're not dying here."

The woman cocked her head and gave Dante an odd look before she sighed and sat. She rested her hands on her lap.

Standing near the front of the rocks, Hyde poked at holes in his legs. The amount of dark fluid covering his limbs and chest proved he'd not escaped the barrage unscathed.

Dante sometimes let himself forget that Hyde wasn't invulnerable. A year ago, a common street gang had all but brought him down, and drug-addled scavengers had been minutes away from finishing the job. All that lived could die, even when it was mostly metal.

Jolo stood beside Hyde, her gaze steely as she pointed her rifle into the darkness. Her armor had taken a beating, with panels missing and too many holes. Dante was glad he'd invested in the upgrades. She might not have been able to survive even with Hyde as a wall without the armor.

Urshielle gripped her spear tightly. Her gaze darted back and forth. She inclined her head at one of his holes. "You will live, Hyde?"

"I've been way more messed up than this and survived." He grinned. "This is barely a scratch."

"There's much blood for a scratch."

"That's not blood." Hyde shrugged.

"I see. You never took so many wounds when we fought together before. It's hard for me to tell with a man who can change bodies like another can change clothes."

Hyde grinned. "It's the advantage of being me."

Dante peered into the cave. The narrow path curved sharply not that far inside.

He'd sent Mugoi in for a quick reconnaissance. There was no way they could make it to the ostorses with the Block 9X aircraft in the area. Fleeing into a cave might be old-fashioned, but sometimes the best tactics Dirtside were old-fashioned. Old idea prejudice could get a man killed.

Dante tapped his foot. The modest number of minutes the cyborg had been away felt like an eternity with the small armies fighting not that far away. Gunfire was growing more sporadic. The battle was drawing to a close.

He opened his mouth to make another suggestion when a rhythmic *thud* echoed inside the cave. He waited until Mugoi appeared around the corner at a fast jog and slowed to exit the cave.

Mugoi's beautiful face had become a dirty mess, covered with the grime of the chase, battle, and spelunking. It was a subtle but powerful reminder of what they'd all been through.

"Tell me you found something useful," Dante greeted.

"It's a honeycomb of narrow caves, Captain," Mugoi reported. "I didn't have time to explore all of it, obviously, but I did find a stream that winds through. At least one path led to the openings farther into the ravine we spotted earlier."

"Damn it." Dante sucked in a breath. "I hoped this might be the closest exit." He surveyed the hostages, half of whom watched him with wide-eyed hope. "When you first went in, you mentioned an okay-sized chamber you spotted?"

"It's not a luxury hotel, but it'll fit our group, and it's not directly visible from the cave mouth. There are too many exits to defend it thoroughly, but if we assume the enemy will come from this direction, it'd work for a short while."

"Anything that gets us more time is good enough for now." Dante motioned toward the cave. "Everyone get ready to move. We're going inside. We stay out here, and we'll be next when they finish off the Dirtwalkers. I can down a gunship with my pulsec-ore, but not before they kill somebody."

Braelin offered his shoulder to a limping man. "It's safe in there?"

"It's safer. This is Dirtside. Nowhere's safe. Now move."

The dense packing of stalactites and stalagmites in the narrow dark tunnels reminded Dante uncomfortably of the jaws of a giant twisted Nightmutt. Three different passages extended from their current chamber and connected to two close but smaller areas with a plethora of exits.

Dante and the prisoners rested using the rock formations as backrests. Their firmness made them surprisingly comfortable.

Braelin continued his first-aid work, joined by Jolo. Hyde had applied nanofoam over his damage and blocked the main entrance with Urshielle at his side. Mugoi and Nasreen stood near Dante, both looking far more pensive than before they'd entered the cave.

Nasreen folded her arms. "We need a plan other than stall and hope for the best."

"I'm working on it." Dante surveyed the room. "Any plan includes evacuating wounded, unarmed people who are exhausted and can't fight."

Nasreen tilted her head. "Do you hear that?"

Dante stopped to listen. Other than the steady *drip* of water onto the ground and the light murmur of conversation, he didn't hear anything else.

He jumped to his feet. "Damn it. The gunfire's stopped."

"Exactly." Nasreen's gaze ticked toward the passageway leading to the front of the cave. "They finished off all the Riders or convinced them to chase us. Either way, we're in for more pain."

"We'll find more options." Dante motioned for Mugoi to follow him. "We need to do more recon. Show me some more paths. We need to find a way out of here before we're fighting an entire damned merc company."

Mugoi nodded and jogged over to an opening. With a smile, it mock-bowed. "Follow me."

"Midas," Dante began.

Yes, sir?

"Make sure you're mapping all this crap. Our lives might depend on it. You don't want to be disabled before you've achieved every upgrade, do you?"

There would be a certain disappointing quality to that eventuality. I'll do my best.

Following Mugoi with his backup pistol in hand, Dante ducked under a low-hanging stalactite. His helmet headlamp gave his night vision something to work with. "This is farther than you went before?"

"Yes." Mugoi nodded over its shoulder. "I was trying to get a feel for things with limited time. I trust you understand."

"You did great to get this much."

With Midas providing helpful navigational arrows, Dante didn't need to worry about making his way back to the main chamber. Still, all the AI processing power in the world didn't help him solve his more serious and immediate problem.

"The only plan that makes sense is finding an evac point for Ambrose to come and pick us up." Dante looked around. "Somewhere we don't have to defend. There are too many mercs with good equipment for that to work."

"You don't want to try to recover the ostorses?" Mugoi asked.

Dante shook his head. "Even if we could get to them and Hyde carried people, we'd have to double stack to get out of here with all the staff. The Block 9X gunship would tear us apart before we made it a couple of miles." He kicked a pebble against a wall, frowning when it bounced back into a puddle at his feet. "The mercs have to be watching those Long Riders if they haven't killed them. We fly out of here, or we start digging our graves to save them time later."

Mugoi slowed, running its fingers along a wall covered with a blue lichen-like growth. "If we left the staff behind, we might be able to elude Block 9X."

"That's not an option. If I didn't want to complete the job, I wouldn't have agreed to it."

"I'm glad to hear you say that." Mugoi smiled. "I wanted to confirm where you stood."

"I'm not into screwing over people who haven't tried to kill me lately."

Mugoi laughed. "Lately?"

"It's how I justify working with Hyde and Ambrose." Dante stepped over a mushy-looking white pile. He didn't want to guess what it might be. "Block 9X's involvement means this all relates to the Omega Syndrome. They wanted those officials out of the way. There's no reason to give them an easy win."

Mugoi squeezed through a narrow passage. The cyborg stopped, turned to look at the armored Dante before rubbing its chin, then smacked its hand hard against the rock wall. The *thud* echoed throughout the tunnels.

"What are you doing?"

Mugoi ignored him, flattened a hand, and chopped with

blazing speed. Cracks shot up the wall until a chunk of rock sloughed off and fell to the moist floor. With Hyde around, Dante forgot how strong Mugoi was.

"You wouldn't fit otherwise," Mugoi explained. "The armor makes it more difficult for most of the team. Hyde would be hard-pressed to have come this far." It cupped its chin. "Knowing him, he'd tear through without concern about anyone else."

"We'll identify an escape route, then worry about clearing it out."

"Very well."

Dante lost track of time as passage after passage flowed together. All the rocks, plants, and mushrooms looked the same. Midas' arrows were the only thing convincing him they hadn't traveled in circles. Finally, Dante and Mugoi found a gently sloping tunnel that offered promise when they heard the rustle of wind.

The tunnel narrowed far past the point of easy cyborg breakage and Dante's bulky armor wouldn't allow him farther. He stepped back and motioned Mugoi forward.

"Check it out."

Mugoi wriggled through the tiny gap and scampered up the wall using slick handholds. Its leg disappeared, but the thud of metal hands on the rock drifted from above, joining the faint sound of wind and a dull rumble.

Dante reached for his pistol. Nightmutts lived in caves, too.

A blur dropped in front of him. Dante whipped out his pistol and lowered the weapon with a sigh. Mugoi had jumped from above.

The cyborg shook its head. "There's an opening to the top of the ravine. Ignoring the other practical issues with this escape route, a Block 9X squad is sweeping the area."

The dull rumble grew louder, then waned.

"That must be the gunship or the shuttle," Dante concluded. "Damn. It's only a matter of time at this point. They know they were being sniped and must have found the mounts by now. There's no way they won't figure out where we are."

Mugoi wriggled through the gap. "Invading this tunnel system would be difficult."

"Difficult doesn't mean impossible, and they've got plenty of guys to do it with."

"True."

"Midas, project a map onto my helmet faceplate," Dante ordered. "Mark our current location."

Yes, sir.

The gaggle of lines and shapes presented all together only frustrated Dante more. He and Mugoi didn't stand that far from the chamber with the rest of the team in terms of absolute distance. That twisting navigational mess would make it hard to guard all the entry and exit points while complicating any escape with the weakened TRG staff.

Dante shook his head. "Nasreen, what's your status?" he transmitted.

"We're fine here. The treatment effects have had time to kick in. The former prisoners aren't going to run for hours, but at least they won't be reduced to crawling along the ground."

"We're still exploring options here," Dante replied. "We confirmed Block 9X is now looking for us. Keep alert, and if you need to withdraw, do so. I'll have Midas send you our current map."

"Be careful, Dante."

"Yeah. If I were careful, I wouldn't end up in a Dirtside cave surrounded by mercenaries." Dante nodded at Mugoi. "All these damned holes. One of them has to be useful."

As they approached another tunnel branch, a *splash* caught Dante's attention. He slowed and glanced at the ground. Puddles lay all over the tunnels. His insulated boots would have protected him from near-frozen mud, so he'd not paid much attention to the earlier water.

"This is deeper than before." He lifted his boot and smashed it into the water for a satisfying splash.

Mugoi crouched. He surveyed the area before gesturing at one of the tunnels. "More water's flowing that way. It sounds louder in that direction."

Dante peered into the tunnel. More rock, mud, bugs, and fungi repaid his interest. Other than minor color variations, there was nothing different than anywhere else in the cave. Between Hungary and this current job, he was beginning to hate caves.

"It's flowing downward." He walked to the indicated tunnel. "It's also not backing up and overflowing. That means it's emptying somewhere else."

Mugoi hopped to its feet and followed Dante. "Yes. All the changes on Earth haven't negated basic physics."

"Tell that to Atlanticore tech." Dante scoffed. "Mostly. But, yeah, I get what you're saying. It could be like the waterfall on the way here."

Following the evidence of their ears and eyes, the pair picked up the pace to a steady jog. Tight quarters and inconvenient rock formations wouldn't allow either Marauder to move much faster.

They were running out of time. The Riders had doomed themselves when they tried to take on the mercenaries. With the reinforcements present and an inferior tactical position, including wounded non-combatants, any lengthy battle would end in Dante's team's slaughter without a miracle.

Dante had given up on miracles when his old team betrayed him to side with SSS and their o-harvest team. He'd survived through good reflexes, training, and smart diplomacy, not a miracle.

He gritted his teeth. Block 9X had complicated everything.

They'd also left Dante wondering what their endgame was Dirt-side and how it related to the Omega Syndrome.

The Khallabash Brothers' incident was a warning. The kidnapping provided solid proof of the nightmarish reach of his latest enemy. Watching his back was no longer optional, no matter how far he ran.

"We need an exit." Dante splashed through the modest stream filling the tunnel. "We didn't come all this way so those people could die in a cave." He ducked underneath a low-hanging stalactite covered in green fluorescent moss. That was new. "I'm not dying in a cave. We're going to find where all this water is going."

The water had carved a streambed into the center of the widening tunnel, granting drier but still slick banks for Mugoi and Dante to follow. Dante hadn't bothered mentioning the stream yet over comms. There was no reason to spin everyone up until he'd verified a useful and practical escape route.

An ominous, resounding roar overwhelmed the stream's soft burbling. Their waterway flowed out of the tunnel into a long, straight river. Water from different tunnels fed it.

Dante motioned toward the water. "This is too straight and perfect to be natural. It must have been an old canal that got covered when the area around shifted. Somebody might have even dug out these tunnels to feed the canal."

He craned his head up. Accreted rock and dirt made it hard to be sure, but the perfect arch of the vast cavernous space and the noticeable lack of outcroppings supported his theory.

Mugoi tilted its head and peered down the length of the canal. "It narrows ahead. We won't be able to follow the water unless we're in it."

Dante sprinted along the path on the canal's bank, slowing as it thinned until one careless step might send him into the cold water. He narrowed his eyes, having trouble seeing anything in the darkness ahead other than the illumination of his helmet lamp.

"Midas, you were talking up that new imagery analysis upgrade last week," he said. "Do you have useful info to give me right now?"

Fortunately, you're wearing your helmet, sir. The AI spoke with a smugness that irritated Dante despite everything else going on.

"What's that have to do with anything other than better-integrated oxygen and saving my mug from stray bullets?"

Access to your visual cortex leaves me constrained by your sad human limitations. The camera in your helmet offers more options.

Dante grunted. "Yeah, yeah. Whatever. I'm a soft pile of flesh who should get better eyes. Do you see something or not?"

There is a faint light at the end of the tunnel. My analysis of the optical characteristics suggests moonlight. Changes in refraction farther down strongly suggest the tunnel opens to the outside. Mugoi's earlier concerns remain valid. The river flows to the point of illumination. Traversing the water is the only way to get there.

Dante knelt and ran his gloved hand through the water. The armor was insulated, but it wasn't a spacesuit. Going into frigid underground water would shock the system, and the tired and wounded hostages didn't have anything other than torn clothes to protect them.

He stood. "If there's one exit to the surface, there has to be another one."

Comms crackled to life with Hyde's irritated voice. "Those *pendejos* found us."

"Damn it. Status?"

"The two that snuck in here and tried to surprise us are fungus food. We've covered the exits, but we don't know how much longer until more of them show up. They fire a pulsecore or toss a grenade in here, and half these people join them as fungus fertilizer."

"Midas will transmit the route to our current location. Use the pulsecore and grenades to seal the tunnel as you pull back." Dante kicked a pebble into the water, annoyed at the small splash. "Let everyone know to get ready for swimming."

"What the hell?" Hyde laughed. "Are you shitting me, *Papi?*"

"We're out of options and time. I don't have time for a damned debate. Get everyone here, now!"

A distant rumble echoed through the chamber, coming out of every tunnel like an overlapping chorus of low, ominous moaning. Dante shoved his pistol into his holster and unslung his carbine.

"Was that you, Hyde?" Dante said.

"I sealed the first tunnel they came from," Hyde replied. "We're getting ready to seal the rest. No reason to make it easy."

"Fine. Nasreen, help get people moving. Hyde can close the back doors in the meantime. I'll get hold of Ambrose. We'll need to time this just right. Midas, I'm going to need your help again."

Her arrival heralded by more echoing explosions over the minutes, Nasreen popped out of the feeder tunnel first with two limping men behind her. The rest of the group had arrived far quicker than it'd taken Dante and Mugoi to find the place thanks to Midas' careful mapping.

Dante waved from the far end of the chamber with Mugoi. Minimizing the time in the water was their best strategy. Nobody was in such dire straits they would die of shock from the water. There was no reason to up the risk.

Braelin and Jolo emerged with the bulk of the hostages. The man with the wounded arm would be the most vulnerable. Dante had told Mugoi to help him in the water.

There was only so much they could do for the rest. There were too many hostages and not enough team members.

Hyde didn't enter the canal chamber until a good minute after the hostages and team had made it to Dante. The cyborg brushed rock and dirt off his shoulders and jogged toward the gathering. Urshielle glanced his way with a flash of relief on her face.

Dante motioned at the water. "Everybody, we've got three choices." He held up one finger. "We dig out and throw ourselves at the mercy of a bunch of killers. Not really a choice." He held up a second finger. "We wait here without much to eat and hope they don't find us and give up. Again, not really a choice." He held up a third finger. "We follow this river outside. Ambrose is flying low and fast toward us. Once we're in the river, he'll head our way."

A TRG official with a black eye glanced at the river. His legs shook. "What about the mercenaries? We're going to wait outside for a shuttle pickup with them hunting for us?"

Dante tapped his head. "I've got an AI implant in here who can be helpful when he wants. He's calculated the water's average flow rate and the distance to what should be the exit. We'll use that to let my pilot know the timing of the pickup. It'll be tight, but as long as nobody drowns, we should be able to get on the shuttle and fly away before they know what's going on."

The man groaned. "That doesn't sound like a great plan."

Dante scoffed. "Then starve to death or hang out with the violent kidnappers."

Nasreen sighed. "Dante, please. These people are scared."

"Too bad." He shook his head. "They need to understand the stakes. I'm not happy about having to get out of here with a bunch of victims through some half-collapsed cave system in an old canal, but we weren't planning to take on Station-equipped mercenaries when we set out after these people."

He faced the man. "I'm sorry for what you went through, but this is the best we can do. We've retrieved you and kept you alive. We'll continue to keep you alive. My team members will help keep the worst off above water, but there are only so many of us.

Anyone who can swim needs to swim for themselves because right now this is your only chance of surviving this ordeal. We get to that shuttle, and we're free. Yes, my pilot's that good."

The hostage with the arm brace stepped forward. "I can swim with this on myself. My legs are fine."

A woman rubbed her shoulders, shuddering. "We can't see anything. Your lights are the only thing keeping us from being completely blind."

Dante pointed at his helmet. "My team will keep their lights on and above the water at all times. If you get disoriented, focus on that."

He gestured at the dark liquid instilling such terror in the hostages. "It's going to be cold. I'm not going to sit here and say it's going to be fun, but you can do this. I'm not asking you to swim. I'm asking you to float and let the water do all the hard work."

"I don't know." The woman wiped away a tear. "I don't understand why all this is happening. Before I thought it was rogue tribes who resented us. Why would anyone on the Stations hire mercenaries to kidnap us? Who are these Block 9X that you people have been talking about?"

"That's a long and complicated story. We don't have all the answers. It doesn't matter."

"How doesn't it matter?"

"Because if we don't get in that water, we'll all be dead before we know the answers."

Nasreen patted the woman's shoulder. "I know this is frightening and confusing. I also know your work is important."

She smiled at Dante. "This is Dante Shale, the Hellcat. The man who helped take down the corrupt SSS and devastate o- and t-harvesting when everyone else wanted to look the other way. This man has done a lot to help the TRG's mission and help the Earth tribes. If he says this is our best way to survive, it's our best way."

Urshielle eyed the water. "He's a man who doesn't know how to die. Listen to him if you want to live."

The TRG woman's nod was firm. Other TRG victims stepped to the canal's edge, their expressions a mixture of wide-eyed trepidation and stone-faced resolve. Dante didn't mind either. Both states kept people focused on survival.

He pointed at the most obviously wounded and waited for his team members to move behind them.

"Starting our swim now, Ambrose," Dante transmitted. "I'm counting on you."

"I hope you're right about this." The pilot dropped out.

Dante leapt into the water. Men and women splashed into the inky darkness behind him. One man shrieked. Most of the team and hostages jumped in the first few moments.

Adrift in the river current, Dante turned his head. A handful of people hadn't jumped. Hyde swept them up in his arms and grinned ear-to-ear before leaping into the water with them. His massive frame pushed out a small wave.

The swirling, churning water wrapped around everyone. The current dragged the frightened woman from before underneath. Urshielle dove and pulled her back up until the woman could spit out water, her mouth barely above the surface.

Dante floated close to the man in the brace. The poor wounded man's teeth chattered with the bone-chilling cold, but he kept himself on his back and his face above water, his uninjured arm folded over his chest. The water carried him, the current picking up with each passing yard.

Braelin and Jolo stayed with single hostages, holding their arms and staying on their outside and closer to the tunnel walls. Whenever they drifted too close to the wall, they kicked their legs, swimming back toward the center of the accelerating river.

The man with the brace cried out in pain and stopped flowing with the water. His wounded arm hung underneath the water. His brace had snagged on something underneath.

Mugoi gently pushed his two current charges toward Hyde and wriggled through the water with such ease that he was like a metal eel. Dante's headlamp glinted off the cyborg's knife as it cut through the brace, freed the wounded man, wrapped his arm around its shoulder, and allowed the fast-flowing current to propel them forward.

High-pitched squeals ripped through the air. Dark shapes fluttered above. Flying Nightmutts flittered near the ceiling, their beady eyes reflecting the headlamps. Dante rolled onto his back and reached for his pistol, but the Nightmutts squealed louder and shot away in the opposite direction.

"Scared of light?" Dante asked. "Okay."

Nasreen swam between two of the victims, helping steady them. While none handled themselves with grace in the torrential flow, the desperate paddling and kicking kept most of the TRG staff above the water, leaving the team to support the others in worse condition.

The deafening roar of the river blocked all external sounds. Midas' connections made communicating with Ambrose easier.

"Their gunship and shuttle aren't nearby," Ambrose reported. "I'm settling down on a riverbank where Midas says you'll spit out. I see the cave."

"Be ready to take off right away," Dante replied. "We're going to shove these people in the back and run. Keep the running lights off until we're in the sky."

"Roger. This is an interesting plan. Very…creative."

Dante didn't like the wavering notes in Ambrose's voice. Better to die in the shuttle than in the damned cave.

The thought had barely left his head when his night vision shifted from the dim, barely there illumination of the headlamps to a softer, wider light from the magnified slivers of moonlight piercing the clouds.

Dante opened his mouth to shout in victory before his stomach lurched, and he flew into the air. The river spat him out over a small waterfall reminiscent of the one they'd passed when dealing with the mother Nightmutt on their way to the ravine. He windmilled his arms and legs before smacking hard into the water below with a grunt.

The wounded man crashed down next to him. Dante grabbed him and kicked, pushing them both toward the shore and the most beautiful sight he'd seen in hours, the open back of the shuttle.

Dante helped the hostage to his feet on the shore as his team members and the other TRG staff splashed behind him. He swam back out to grab the hand of a shivering and sinking man. The TRG victims staggered toward the back of the shuttle, an annoyingly dry Ambrose beckoning them as the rest of the team helped ferry the tired and wounded to the shore.

Hyde waddled out of the pond with three men draped over his shoulders. He cast a suspicious look at a man with a bruised face who lay on the shore on his back, breathing heavily.

"Get up," Hyde barked. "We wait here too long, and a gunship's going to come and blow our asses away."

The man groaned and rolled onto his stomach. He pushed himself up on his hands and knees. Urshielle waded out of the water and offered her arm, shaking her head at Hyde.

He shrugged. "It's the truth."

Dante searched the sky for any sign of an approaching enemy. Nasreen and the apprentices helped shepherd the soaked hostages into the back of the shuttle. Hyde lurched into the shuttle with his charges. Urshielle was close behind.

Ambrose rushed to the front of the shuttle. Dante swept the horizon one last time before offering a grateful nod at the moon. He sprinted into the back of the shuttle.

"I'm in," he shouted. "Get us the hell out of here, Ambrose."

CHAPTER EIGHT

While Nasreen and the others tended to the hostages, Dante sat in the copilot's seat, watching the readouts for anything suspicious. The mere minutes taken to fly back toward the joint Crescent-Marked-TRG village mocked all the hours they'd spent traveling across the land.

Dante held no regrets about the overland trip. Now that he knew Block 9X was involved, he understood flying after the TRG staff would have ended with his shuttle shot down long before he could have saved anyone.

Ambrose tapped a display. "Someone's spotted us."

The radio crackled to life. "Attention unknown shuttle approaching Terran Restoration Group Project Site. This is Joint Station Security Detachment Four. Please identify yourself immediately, or our defensive array will target you."

Dante scoffed. "Better late than never." He drew a deep breath before responding. "This is Dante Shale. My team has recovered the kidnapped TRG personnel. They are aboard."

He didn't care if anyone considered it arrogant. At this point, he assumed everyone on the Stations knew who he was.

"Roger, Shale," came the response. "Land on the north side of the encampment. You are to exit your shuttle unarmed. We will have medical staff on hand to help evacuate and treat the wounded."

"Roger." Dante killed the line. "These assholes are acting like we're responsible."

Ambrose wrinkled his nose. "You don't think they believe that, do you?" He swallowed. "We could make a run for the Station."

"What's the point? That's a joint detachment down there. We risk pissing off everyone if we do." Dante shrugged. "We've got plenty of witnesses on our side." He nodded toward the back of the shuttle. "Including the victims."

"What do you think they'll do when the victims mention how we threw them into a dark river and basically told them to sink or swim?" Ambrose let out a nervous laugh.

"They're all alive, aren't they? Just get us on the ground. Let me worry about the rest of it."

***

Dante stood next to the shuttle with his team, his helmet off and his arms folded, as Station medics helped carry off the wounded TRG staff on hover stretchers. The apprentices had spread out to offer aid to the locals, leaving Dante, Nasreen, Urshielle, and Hyde to deal with the security forces.

The radio call had mentioned a detachment. That description didn't do justice to the small army deployed around the site.

Scores of armored troops, including squads of hard-cased soldiers with pulsecore carbines and portable surface-air-missile launchers stood stationed throughout the area, watching tribal workers and TRG staffers collect debris or work on repairs. A hover tank sat outside a large shuttle with the turret pointed out toward the horizon. Anti-air turrets ringed the tank. Bored-looking helmeted but unarmored troops waited atop thrustbikes parked near the edge of the camp with arms slumped over the handlebars.

Dante surveyed the gathered forces. He'd not seen so many flags of different Stations gathered together since the last time he watched the Unified Station Thrust Bike League finals. Atlantica Central Station personnel were prominently represented in the force, but he spotted flags for at least a dozen Stations, including larger contingents from New Paris, Londonburg, and El Dorado.

An older man with an Atlantica Security Force patch on his shoulders finished chatting with a small group of TRG staffers before motioning for two of the troops to follow them. He turned toward Dante with a scowl.

Streaks of gray ran through the man's jet-black hair. Piercing intelligence and a touch of anger shone in his deep brown eyes. When the dismissed group headed toward a supply tent, the man strode toward the shuttle, every step confident and sure. His nametape read Ishimura.

"I'm Chief Takashi Ishimura of the Atlantica Security Force." He nodded at Dante. "I'm in charge of this joint detachment's little Dirtside vacation." He narrowed his eyes at a lone TRG official who'd been less wounded than the others and had waited near the shuttle, unsure of what to do with himself.

"Thank you, Mr. Shale, for your assistance in recovering the kidnapped personnel." He frowned. "Although I'd think that a Marauder team being necessary down here proves the short-sightedness of this whole affair."

The TRG official frowned. "What are you saying, Chief Ishimura?"

Takashi rubbed his chin. After looking over the man, he asked, "You're Stephan Bauer, correct? You're from New Vienna?"

"Yes, that's accurate." Stephan shook his head. "I don't understand what you mean by shortsightedness."

Takashi motioned around to the shuttles and troops. "I'm

nothing more than an old detective, and my opinion doesn't count for much, but playing house with Dirtwalker savages doesn't make sense. This is what happens. People get hurt. I'm glad your group got saved, but there were casualties, not to mention damage. Somebody's got to pay for all that."

Urshielle narrowed her eyes at Takashi and bared her teeth. He ignored her. With a nod toward Dante, she walked away, staring at Takashi as if daring him to stop her. Hyde smirked at the chief and jogged after the Crescent-Marked warrior.

"This wasn't Dirtwalkers," Dante replied. "Not entirely."

Takashi's brow lifted. "What's that supposed to mean?"

"A mercenary group, Block 9X, was working with the raiders." Dante gestured forward at a half-burned building. "They pretended to be an all-tribal group, but they used Station-produced rifles when they kidnapped them. There was no way those raiders could have kidnapped so many people without those rifles."

"Block 9X?" Takashi's eye twitched. "I'm getting tired of hearing that name. Why should I believe you? You're a known Dirtwalker sympathizer."

Dante let that sink in before responding. He'd never thought much about someone distrusting him because he treated Dirtwalkers with a touch of dignity.

"I have recordings of people from their group," he replied. "They appeared right when we found the victims. Their company commander and operations leader were on site."

Takashi nodded. "What did they do?"

"There was a falling out." Dante mimed cutting his throat. "Block 9X fought the Dirtwalkers they'd hired over a disagreement about what to do with the victims. We escaped with the prisoners in the chaos."

Takashi sighed. "In other words, you have footage of Station-born mercs attacking a group of kidnapper Dirtwalkers. Many people up there might call them heroes."

"You're misunderstanding." Nasreen stepped forward. "The mercenaries had people disguised as raiders. We were too far away to hear them, but it was obvious they'd been working together."

Takashi pinched the bridge of his nose. His following words dripped with barely concealed annoyance. "Another conspiracy from Shale and Joelle that's going to rock the Stations to their core? Is that what you're telling me? Shale was famous enough before he started bringing down major corporations. Does he need more fame? Do you, Miss Joelle, especially considering your background?"

"We were right about SSS and Slaine. This isn't about fame." Nasreen narrowed her eyes. "Or do you think we were wrong to help take down SSS and Slaine?"

"We all have to follow our conscience." Takashi's gaze followed medics carrying wounded staffers. He nodded at Stephan. "None of it changes the fact that if they weren't here, this wouldn't have been a problem. This whole sordid affair would have never happened, and we wouldn't be leaving the Stations less safe for a day."

Stephan blinked. "Excuse me? You're saying we're at fault when we're trying to help reclaim the Earth for humanity?"

Takashi scoffed. "Reclaim the Earth? It's full of Dirtwalkers and Nightmutts. We can't breathe here without inhalers." He shook his head. "This planet is dying. They found out the hard way a long time ago." He pointed up. "That's why we're there now. This whole thing is a waste of time and money."

"No." Nasreen shook her head. "That's not true."

"Oh, it's not true?" Takashi asked. "Did I miss something in history class? You wouldn't be paid a premium for your work if that wasn't true." He tapped his forehead. "Call me an ignorant security chief, and maybe I don't understand all your Plunderer sophistication, but I thought the point of you people was that

Dirtside was too dangerous for normal people. Now you're telling me Dirtside is safe?"

Dante ground his jaw. Getting angry with the Chief of the Atlantica Security Force wouldn't help anyone. He'd leave it to Nasreen.

She motioned at a Crescent-Marked man carrying a box. "People live here. There are other things out there, not only fields of monsters but creatures that have adapted that are no different than the wild animals before. That is, of course, they're different, but they're not inherently dangerous."

"Oh?" Takashi looked at Nasreen like she'd been inhaling hallucinogens.

She smiled. "I used to think the same way you did. I wasn't a Plunderer for most of my life, and every time I came down to Earth, I wanted to leave. It was nothing more than a job for me."

Takashi folded his arms. "You're saying it's safe? That I should invite my grandson here for a vacation? At least it'll be cheap. There's so much space and not much interest."

"I'm saying it's not what we were taught to believe." Nasreen gestured toward Stephan. "The Terra Restoration Group understands that. They understand there is a planet here worth recovering, a planet that was wounded, but where humanity and the rest of nature can adapt. You can't be upset with them for trying to save our species. They're the victims here. Block 9X are the criminals."

Stephan cleared his throat. "Might I be straightforward with you, Chief Ishimura?"

"I'd prefer that, Mr. Bauer." Takashi folded his arms.

"As a senior member of the TRG Oversight Board, when I came here the other day, I came here with the express reason of gathering evidence to cut funding to many of the projects. I've visited on occasion and had grown weary of seeing money spent propping up primitive tribes in the ruins of old cities."

Takashi nodded. "I'm assuming big cuts are coming, then?"

"No." Stephan gave a firm shake of his head. "Everything I've seen proves that we only need to increase funding. I won't claim to speak for every member of the board. Others have made it clear they will never be returning to Earth and may leave their position, but what I've seen has changed my perspective."

"Are you kidding me?"

"No. Every time I've come here in the past, I've only come to this area or small TRG projects, the city ruins I mentioned. I flew from place to place in shuttles, not paying attention to the beautiful surroundings and the planet that I intellectually understood needed to be saved but that I hadn't felt it in here." He patted his chest over his heart.

Takashi frowned. "You're telling me that getting kidnapped and dragged across the wasteland convinced you this whole waste of money is a good idea and not an insane boondoggle?"

"It's beautiful out there if you look. That's one of the only good things that came from this crime." Stephan held up his damp sleeve. "There is so much life here, underwater rivers with caves filled with animals, not vicious monsters. Huge, sprawling herds that this planet hasn't seen for centuries."

He lowered his arm. "Of course, I'm not pleased with having been kidnapped and beaten. Many of my associates might never return, but I also understand now, in a deep and visceral way, that Dirtside—no, *Earth*—isn't the wastelands that we focus on. We've been taught an incorrect vision of the birthplace of humanity." He nodded at Dante.

"This place is so much more than lost treasures for Plunderers to take. I was terrified...I'll admit that. I thought I would die out there, but now I know that Station citizens were involved, I'm incensed. I'm furious that someone would conspire to turn the TRG against this planet, that someone would attempt to deny humanity its glory."

He groaned. "Sorry. It's...caught up with me."

Dante caught Stephan as he fell forward. "You've had a rough time. You should let the medics check you out."

Takashi frowned. He gestured for one of his men to come and pointed at another building. "Take him there for treatment."

"Yes, sir," the man replied. He put Stephan's arm over his shoulder and led the man away.

Dante squared his shoulders. "Are we going to stop wasting time whining about whether the TRG can spend their money on Earth, or are we going to focus on what happened?"

"You claim that Block 9X was here?" Takashi asked.

Nasreen frowned. "They were."

Takashi looked around. His frown deepened into a scowl. He stepped closer.

"Block 9X has made a mess on my Station," the chief said, his voice low and menacing. "More than once. You two took on SSS and Slaine. I've heard you're even working with that metal killer that used to be Slaine's executioner."

"What of it?" Dante asked. "Hyde doesn't like Block 9X any more than you do. He also helped us take down SSS."

"I mention him because he wasn't the real threat behind SSS. He was nothing more than Slaine's knife. You working with him means you can understand that Block 9X is nothing more than the knife." Takashi flared his nostrils. "Wasting time and resources on dulling the knife doesn't do much. The man wielding it will go get another."

Nasreen scoffed. "Kidnapping a group of Station citizens isn't something you should overlook because it's inconvenient."

"I'm here because many powerful people have an interest in the TRG. All the men and women I brought with me are here for the same reason. In the end, every Station can band together and make an army, but that doesn't mean anything. We're Station security. Dirtside isn't our jurisdiction. You must have noticed by now, Ms. Joelle, how we don't get involved in your Plunderer spats."

"You don't care that someone powerful is using a mercenary team to attack Station citizens?" challenged Nasreen. "They're not doing it for fun, and they're not doing it to challenge Plunderer teams." She slammed her fist into her palm. "You say Block 9X is the weapon. Does that mean you don't care to find out who is wielding the weapon, or you're too afraid to?"

Takashi gave her a lopsided smile and chuckled. "I don't waste time on investigations that aren't going to lead anywhere."

"It sounds like you've tried to look into Block 9X and came up short."

"I make it a habit to be aware of everyone who might be disrupting the peace and order of my Station." Takashi's gaze flicked to Dante. "The SSS Killers. The two mighty Plunderers who brought down the most powerful man in the Stations. Are you saying you have a new target? Do you know who's holding the knife?"

"We might," Dante replied. "But we're one team. There's only so much we can do by ourselves." He nodded at Nasreen.

She frowned at him. "The question, Chief, is whether you value peace and order enough that you'll take short-term trouble for long-term peace."

"That's what it means to be a security chief." Takashi tilted his head and frowned. "My men need me." He turned away and took a few steps before stopping and looking over his shoulder.

"If you two aren't full of it, we should talk again soon. Just so you know, I'm not convinced about any of this TRG garbage. That doesn't mean I don't want the new Slaine to be throwing around mercenaries whenever he feels like assassinating someone."

He started walking and pointed at their shuttle. "It'd be helpful if you depart sooner than later. There are too many questions I'll have to answer as it is."

"We'll leave soon enough," Dante replied. Once Takashi had disappeared into a nearby building, he said, "This is what we needed. Firewall is a good resource, but their whole cult-vibe means they can't help us in the open."

"If you say so," Nasreen replied quietly.

Suspicion clouded her face. Dante glanced in Takashi's direction.

"Problem?" He was unsure why she'd turned so icy.

"I'm not sure yet." Nasreen headed toward the shuttle. "We can't do anything else here. I'll call everyone back, and we can discuss this new alliance of ours on the way back."

Hyde slapped his knee. "Ha-ha. You're ready to try to recruit the chief of Atlantica Central Station, *Papi?* I didn't see that coming."

Once they'd gathered everyone, Dante explained the situation and told Ambrose to wait a few minutes before takeoff. Nasreen's frown the entire time left Dante unsettled.

"Yeah," Dante replied. "We're not going to win against the Omega Syndrome without more help."

Mugoi leaned against a corner. Its shoulder was dented and chipped from their recent Dirtside adventures. "It would be helpful to have additional allies."

Jolo nodded. "The incident in the club would have unfolded in a much different way if Chief Ishimura was on our side."

"Ain't nothing about the ASF that bothers me much," Braelin chipped in. "I bet those Block 9X bastards wouldn't be so choppy-chop with their blades fighting security."

Dante shook his head. "They didn't see a problem fighting them outside the club. That doesn't change the fact that having another major force to back us up would come in handy."

Hyde scoffed. "You believe that?"

Between the travel and the focus on the hostages, Dante hadn't focused much on the sorry state of Hyde's body. Now, sitting in the back of the well-lit shuttle with nothing else to distract him, the full impact struck. Nanopatches and foam had produced an uneven quilt of colors over his body. The huge chunks missing from his legs and arms exposed wiring, servos, and actuators. It was amazing he could move so well with all that damage.

"Why wouldn't I believe that?" Dante asked.

"I don't give two shits if the Omega Syndrome is another greedy bastard in a suit or a crazy AI," Hyde replied. "But they're good at corrupting and infiltrating systems and people." He jabbed his finger toward Dante. "You think they haven't been smart enough to infiltrate the ASF? You were the one so concerned with them being on somebody's payroll before."

Dante shrugged. "I think there's a big difference between influence and control, and also a big difference between an entire organization and individuals in it. If Ishimura was an Omega Syndrome puppet, he would have his tank blow us away the second we landed. He wouldn't care about Block 9X. That's enough proof he's not their tool."

Nasreen cleared her throat. "It kills me to say this, but I think Hyde is right."

Hyde snickered. "Don't feel too bad, *chica.* I usually am. It's why I've managed to live this long."

Dante scrubbed a hand down his face. "Yeah, that's not something I expected to hear today, especially from the woman who convinced me to trust the group that kidnapped and tortured her when I was ready to put a bullet in their leaders' brains."

Nasreen looked away. "That was different. Whatever Firewall's faults, we know they are fanatically devoted to ensuring they aren't under the Omega Syndrome's control. We can't be certain of that for any other organization, no matter how interested an individual is in helping us."

He'd not expected the pushback. He also couldn't say they were wrong. The dynamic situation had presented an opportunity, and he'd leapt on it without too much time to think through all the implications.

Dante drew a deep breath. He didn't need a repeat of his tantrum with Hyde. The cyborg could be annoying, but trying to protect the team from betrayal wasn't a sin. Nasreen's agreement only complicated the situation more.

Every muscle in his body ached. His lungs hurt. He'd half-convinced himself there'd been something wrong with his oxygen system.

"We're all tired." Dante let his head loll back until it hit the wall. "I didn't agree to anything more than talking to him. I also didn't mention the Omega Syndrome."

He closed his eyes. "We don't have to do that the second we get back. It was a big, long annoying ass job this time. We'll figure it out later. For now, let's all get some rest."

CHAPTER NINE

Nasreen set her tray down on the table next to Dante. When she had stepped into their headquarters' dining room to eat her meal after too few hours of sleep, she'd been surprised to see the entire team gathered except for Hyde. He was in the hangar working on his repairs and resting in his way. Even Mugoi sat at the end of the table, its eyes darting back and forth as it read news projected from a sphere on the edge of the table.

There was something pleasant about the whole situation. It was as if they had gathered for a family dinner. Dante and Hyde had often referred to the apprentices as the children. Nasreen chuckled. Dante was the father. Logically, despite their lack of a relationship, that made her the mother. She'd settle for being the aunt.

They hadn't spent that long on Earth, yet it felt like days, if not weeks. After all her time with Dante, Nasreen was still unsure if she preferred the more subtle and constant tension of maintaining a false identity as a freelance spy compared to the spikes of terrifying violence that came with being a Marauder. Both jobs had proven dangerous in different ways.

She'd never regretted teaming up with Dante. Beyond saving

her life in their first encounter, he'd given her something she'd been lacking for far too long, a goal beyond simple professional survival and a true identity beyond whatever false face she was wearing for her jobs. All her skills, training, and abilities turned to help make the Stations a better place. That was worth doing, even if it cost her life.

The rich smell of her soup tickled Nasreen's nose. Her rumbling stomach tugged her thoughts away from her concerns over the deeper meaning of her life to the more immediate concerns of daily survival through food. Downing rations along the way had only pushed down the hunger. The only time she'd eaten any real meals and done more than swallow them quickly on the surface was during their brief time of relaxing with the first Rider tribe.

Sitting next to Jolo, a drooling Braelin picked up a piece of roasted chicken with his fork. Despite his drooling, a distant and blank expression weighed down his face, not something Nasreen was used to seeing.

"Is everything okay, Braelin?" she asked.

He jerked his head up and blinked. "What? Why wouldn't it be? I haven't heard anything's wrong with the kitchen." He eyed his chicken with suspicion. "Is there?"

Jolo's mouth quirked into a thin smile. She otherwise concentrated on slicing up her steak.

"You looked lost." Nasreen smiled and picked up her spoon. "I recognize the look. It used to be on my face far too often, both before and after my career change."

"I've been wondering myself." Jolo nodded at Braelin. "If there's something you want to say, then say it. There's nothing to be gained by holding things back."

Braelin nibbled on his chicken before setting his fork down. He lifted his glass and swirled the water inside. "I was thinking about Dirtside. That river stunt was crazy. What if Dante and

Mugoi had been wrong? All our close scrapes, and we would have gone out drowning. It's weird."

Dante put down his half-eaten turkey sandwich, his expression turning cold. "Every time we go Dirtside, we can die. In the end, it doesn't matter how you die. You're done whether it comes cheaply or heroically."

He nodded at Nasreen. "She gave a nice speech to the Chief down there about Earth. That doesn't mean he was completely wrong. We get paid because most people can't handle Dirtside yet, and no matter how much funding the TRG gets, that will be true for a long time."

"Except we're not getting paid this time," Braelin grumbled. "It's better when you get paid for almost dying. It doesn't sting so much."

Mugoi dismissed the news article it was reading and grinned. "Consider it an extended training exercise then, Klement."

"This ain't a joke to me." Braelin shook his fork like it was Poseidon's trident and far more threatening. "Don't you understand how lucky we had to be to get out of there without losing someone? We were in unfamiliar terrain and running off after enemies who had a good start. We weren't expecting to run into an entire merc company."

"That doesn't sound much different than most of our Dirtside jobs."

"Nothing of that bothers you?"

"Being a Marauder is a poor career choice for people concerned about danger." Mugoi shrugged.

"I ain't saying I want everything safe all the time." Braelin groaned. "I was expecting a more straight-up fight is all, not running and swimming in caves."

Jolo nibbled on her steak, her expression inscrutable. That was enough for Nasreen to conclude she agreed with Braelin. Both were agreeing with each other more and more as of late.

Dante nodded. "I've told everyone involved on this team the same thing for a long time. You all have the same choice. Every time we gear up, our lives are on the line. Dirtside is unpredictable. No matter how prepared you are, something can always go wrong."

He smacked the end of the table so hard his utensils rattled. "The damned Stations are unpredictable. I've done my best to train everyone to survive. That's all I can guarantee you."

Nasreen looked between Dante and Ambrose. She knew, more than anyone, how much Dante had tortured himself over near calls with his apprentices. This conversation risked pushing him back into his dangerous mindset following the Khallabash Brothers' incident.

"Is it even worth it?" Jolo asked quietly. "That's the question I've been asking myself. You admitted that the Terra Restoration Group might be fighting a losing battle."

"No." Dante shook his head. "That's not what I said. All I said was that it's still dangerous down there, but I have rules about Dirtwalker tribes for a reason. It's not about protecting them because I think they're all going to die soon."

He leaned back in his chair and folded his arms. "My experiences Dirtside have changed me. I agree with what Ambrose and Hyde were saying about the TRG. Long-term the Stations are a dead-end. That much is a fact. The TRG and its work will play a role in getting people back onto Earth.

"As for that location, I owe people down there, including the Crescent-Marked community. Helping them out is personal. Without their help, I would have died a year ago."

Trembling slightly, Ambrose gulped down a dark amber drink and slammed the cup down so hard everyone looked his way. Nasreen doubted he'd chosen that moment to move past his disdain for alcohol.

"You don't think I worry about dying every time we go down there?" Ambrose looked between the apprentices. "I'm a good pilot." He shook his head. "I'm a *great* pilot, but I know one good hit will take down my ship.

"I've come close to dying so many times in my life. Every time after, I ask, 'Is this what I want?' You all need to answer that for yourself."

Dante grabbed his sandwich. "You want to know what happened down there? It doesn't matter because the important thing is we all got out of it alive. Yeah, this time it's because everyone did what they needed to, including listening and not questioning me when they didn't have all the information I had.

"We can't ignore that Block 9X was involved, which means that whole thing was a fight against the Omega Syndrome. That automatically makes it worth it." He took a large bite of his sandwich and spoke again, his voice muffled by his full mouth and chewing. "We lost nobody. They lost mercs, and we screwed up their plan. That's winning."

He swallowed. "That wasn't like with the Khallabash Brothers. This time we hurt our enemy and gave up nothing but ammo and rations. We learned more about Dirtside and gained experience riding Nightmutts. More winning."

"I'm not like all of you," Ambrose interrupted. "You all sought out Dante to become Marauders. I'm not working as a Plunderer anymore. At least I wasn't until Dante and Nasreen came to recruit me back."

He coughed. "I'm only here because they needed my help to save you three. Same with Hyde. We were both happy helping the tribes and the TRG. That didn't make it safer work necessarily. Like Dante said, Dirtside is always unpredictable."

"Just because it turned out that Firewall wasn't an enemy doesn't mean it wasn't a sacrifice for Ambrose and Hyde to help us when we recruited them over the first kidnapping incident," Nasreen added. "They both have been critical to our recent efforts. What happened below would have ended badly without their help. Like Ambrose said, he's a great pilot. I'm only a good pilot."

Braelin looked away. "Yeah, thanks again to both of them for helping out." He turned back and looked at Jolo. "Hyde did a good job protecting Jolo and Urshielle in that ravine. He made good use of his metal body. I ain't ready to take him home to meet my parents, but he does good work when he's not being a big bastard."

"Ambrose's flying should be highlighted as well," Mugoi said. With Ambrose beaming, the cyborg continued. "If he'd been a less competent or confident pilot, the mercenaries would have spotted the shuttle, and we wouldn't have been able to escape."

The cyborg cocked its head and stared at Ambrose. Repairs and cleaning had restored its beautiful features. "That does make me wonder about all of this. What if Firewall had failed?"

Dante gulped, swallowing the last piece of his sandwich. He pounded his chest a couple of times until it passed through. "Huh? You talking about the first kidnapping attempt?"

Mugoi nodded. "Yes. From what you've said before, you only brought back your old contacts because of that effort. What if Firewall had failed then? Like Klement, I appreciate Ambrose and Hyde setting aside their missions to join you in rescuing us and staying on to support our tactical operations. But I wonder if this has forced them onto a path that is not best for them."

"I'm here because I want to be," Ambrose insisted.

"Are you?"

"I gave them both the chance to back out before." Dante shrugged. Annoyance showed in his striking green eyes. "They chose to stay. I'm not threatening anybody to keep 'em here."

"It goes deeper than that," Nasreen replied. "Hyde was a shadow of himself on the planet until I got him his new body. Ambrose wouldn't have survived his ambush.

"They are helping us, but we also helped them, even saved them. Ambrose and Hyde have benefited from being involved in all this. I know it's not what you apprentices thought you would be doing when you signed up, but everyone benefits from all this."

"That's assuming we ain't all killed by the Omega Syndrome before this is over," Braelin mumbled. "Danger's not what bothers me. I just want to see whatever's going to kill me coming, so I can curse it out first."

Mugoi grabbed the sphere it'd been using earlier and slipped it into a pocket. "It all comes back to the Omega Syndrome, no matter how we look at it, doesn't it?"

"Yeah," Dante replied. "I'll make the same offer to everyone here that I have before. I get that you didn't all sign up to be part of my crusade. You signed up with a famous Marauder to learn skills and make money finding crap Dirtside while shooting Nightmutts.

"Despite that, I'm going to tell you that being associated with me means you're now an Omega Syndrome target, but if you all want to hide until it's over, I understand. I won't force anyone who doesn't want to be here to stay."

"Our work has meaning beyond money now. The orphanage helped me realize that." Mugoi smiled. "I can make a true difference aiding you. I can also prove to Hyde and the others who the best among us is."

"Don't get ahead of yourself, Pretty Face." Braelin offered Dante a huge grin. "Being a big hero would be nice." He grabbed his lapels and ruffled them. "They might build statues of us. As long as my statue is taller than Mugoi's, I'll be happy."

"I would have left long ago if I didn't want to be here." Jolo chuckled. "As for the statues, that's all assuming we're not killed in the process."

Mugoi replied, "I'd think if we die in the process of protecting the Stations, that would increase the chance of getting statues. I don't mind if mine is smaller as long as it is more elegant."

Dante burst out laughing. "If you can all talk like that after what we went through, I've got no reason to worry."

Ambrose stared at the back of his hand, his eyes widening. "Nasreen's right."

"Am I?" She looked up.

"I would have been killed without your help." He shook his head. "It goes deeper than that." He inclined his head at Dante. "I would have been killed by Slaine's men long before that. Dante saved me when he had no reason to and every reason to kill me himself. He talks about being so vengeful, but…"

Dante lifted his tray and headed toward the cleaning and processing slot in the wall. "Lucky for you that you're such a good pilot when you're not being a bastard."

"You didn't save me the first time because you needed a pilot," Ambrose replied. He sighed. "I don't believe in fate or destiny, but sometimes life works out in strange ways. Bad things lead to better things. Like on the planet."

Dante pushed his tray through the slot. "You finding the TRG after your adventures with me?"

Ambrose shook his head. "I'm talking about the attack itself. On the surface, you'd think the best scenario would have been a complete failure. People were hurt, including people I knew, so I'm not saying it wouldn't have been better if it had never happened. Still, the more I think about it, the mercenaries grabbing those officials might have been better for the long-term mission and arguably humanity's future."

"That's taking optimism to a new level." Dante walked back to the table and sat.

"You heard Bauer," Ambrose continued. "He was convinced the whole project was a waste of time. You don't understand that the TRG is operating on a tight budget. Any major disruption to that money could kill the TRG. Most people from the Stations aren't ready to accept the obvious about humanity's future. They think the TRG is a group of fools wasting money playing around with Dirtwalkers."

Dante nodded. "You've gone full native? Just need better lungs, then you never have to leave."

"You believe in them, too."

"A little. Yeah, I admitted that." Dante shrugged.

"Those officials needed to see the beauty of the planet like I have." Ambrose smiled wistfully. "They needed to understand how important it was to return to Earth and that it isn't a lost cause."

Braelin leaned forward, his frown a strong contrast to Ambrose's smile. "Block 9X don't take a piss without the Omega Syndrome giving them permission."

Nasreen nodded. "That's what all the available evidence suggests."

"So why does the Omega Syndrome hate the TRG? Grand strategy ain't my forte, but I can't be the only man who thinks this whole thing is a giant clusterfuck for them. They might have gotten unlucky that we showed up, but Chief Ishimura might have sniffed around even without us. Stopping the TRG doesn't make the Omega Syndrome stronger on the Stations. So why?"

Jolo frowned. "That's a good question, Braelin."

"Who knows?" Dante shrugged. "They know that Hyde, Ambrose, Nasreen, and I have a connection to the TRG. It might be like the Khallabash Brothers and nothing more than trying to mess with us."

"Nah." Braelin shook his head. "What if it was a trap? They might have hoped we'd come after them and they'd finish us off. It was close."

"Doesn't that seem too elaborate?" Jolo asked. "They have to know that Dante would bring a team down there, and we'd follow the raiders who were trying to evade capture. Using the locals would only complicate things if it was nothing more than a trap for us."

"No," Mugoi said. "They needed the local Long Riders for the plan to work. I doubt Block 9X developed a detailed plan, including riding Nightmutts that far. They would need the help for navigation."

"It's all speculation until we get more information," Nasreen interjected. "Firewall is doing their part. We should continue to do ours." She pursed her lips. "That brings us back to the question we tabled on the way up about whether it's a good idea to work with the Atlantica Security Force."

Jolo nodded her agreement. "I've been thinking about it since we brought it up on the shuttle. There were persuasive arguments against it."

Dante's back stiffened. The change was so subtle that Nasreen wasn't sure if anyone else had noticed.

"We need more help beyond Firewall," he insisted.

"Firewall also has proven they aren't complete paranoid crazies," Nasreen countered.

"Sure, not *complete* crazies." Dante chuckled.

"I'm not defending everything they did to us, but they did find traces of influence in you and Mugoi when you came for me. That keeps leading me back to Ishimura. If the Omega Syndrome is as pervasive as we believe, doesn't recruiting him increase our risk?"

Dante nodded. "Yeah. But your argument goes both ways. They might use the Omega Syndrome to keep their hands clean, but they have influence all over, including what happened with the Khallabash Brothers. We need more allies to take down an enemy with that level of reach."

Braelin, Mugoi, and Jolo kept quiet. They followed the back and forth of the conversation with their eyes. Ambrose had moved on to slicing into his piece of chocolate cake. His face twisted in a faint grimace of annoyance.

Dante continued. "With the Omega Syndrome messing with us, we won't be able to do jobs without risk of claim jumping again. That means no cash flow and having to be careful with resources. I've earned a pile of money over the years but used a good chunk of it taking on SSS and building this place. We're not going to starve anytime soon, but we're limited on major equipment upgrades until we can start pulling in jobs without risking war with every other Plunderer."

He grinned. "We might be able to squeeze money out of Ishimura in all this, too. Saving humanity is good and all, but getting paid to do it would be a nice perk."

Nasreen let out an exhausted sigh. "Ishimura's not going to allow us the freedom we're used to operating under. We were chafing under Firewall's proposed restrictions. How would this be any different?"

"Because those were insane," Dante replied. "Ishimura isn't going to ask us to give up our identities and join a cult."

"But *Chief* Ishimura is going to insist on control," Nasreen countered with a harsh nod. "Having an army backing us is helpful, but it eliminates any ability to launch surprise attacks. There's no way the ASF can mobilize a large number of troops without the Omega Syndrome getting wind of it."

She wrinkled her nose. "This all presupposes that Ishimura didn't tell us exactly what we want to hear to lure us into a trap. It makes more sense to ambush us on the Stations than Dirtside."

Dante shook his head. "No. It's not that. I'm sure."

"How are you so sure?"

"Because I looked into the man's eyes and saw his soul. He was serious about wanting to help us."

Ambrose gagged, choking on his chocolate cake. He hit his chest several times before coughing up an unappetizing dark lump onto his plate. "You saw his soul?" he rasped.

"Yeah."

"We're all going to die. This is insane."

Dante shot out of his chair and glared at him. He motioned at the door. "There's the door if you want out," he yelled.

Ambrose clutched the table, his fingers turning white from the pressure. His wide-eyed look of terror urged Nasreen into action.

She reached over and placed her hand on Ambrose's arm. She was glad Dante didn't have a gun on him. "Dante, calm down. He's not questioning your overall leadership, but you do have to accept the obvious.

"Even if Ishimura is sincere, there's no guarantee that all the ASF is free of the Omega Syndrome. That means it'll be dangerous to share our anti-Omega Syndrome efforts or Firewall with them. It only takes one Security Intervention Squad to blow us away if we let ourselves get put in a bad position. That can happen no matter how good the chief's soul is."

Dante drew slow, deep breaths before sitting. "We won't share anything with him until we know it'll work for us. I'm not an idiot. Right now, all he knows is that we have insight into who is behind Block 9X, and the Omega Syndrome knows that. We've lost nothing reaching out to him."

Nasreen pulled her hand away from Dante's arm. "I hope you're right."

CHAPTER TEN

Sir...sir...sir.

The quiet yet persistent English voice woke Dante from his deep slumber. Growling, he sat up, rubbing his eyes. While he'd gotten a good stretch of sleep, with everything that happened Dirtside, he could have slept a day or two. A fog hung over his mind to match the lingering soreness in his muscles.

"What?" Dante barked. "This better be important. I told you not to bother me, and no, discussing whatever new upgrades you've convinced yourself will save us the next time we're Dirtside isn't an emergency."

Sir, I'm terribly sorry to wake you, but two messages came in. The first, I thought could wait after consideration of the implications. With the arrival of the second, both have become of increased importance. On balance, I thought they were worth disrupting your current sleep cycle.

The AI should have understood better. He was in Dante's brain. Yet sometimes he acted clueless.

Dante grunted an unintelligible response before drawing a deep breath and switching to something more useful. "Yeah. Whatever. I'm awake now. You might as well tell me."

Chief Ishimura contacted you first. Midas' announcement had an odd prideful quality as if he'd personally negotiated the meeting. *He wants to meet with you as soon as possible. The message indicates that he would prefer it to be immediately, although he understands if you need, in his words, 'Time to rest.'*

"That sounds like it could have waited."

Yes, sir, and if it had only been him, I wouldn't have awoken you.

"Yeah. Yeah. You said that."

Dante nodded slowly, his heart kicking up in anticipation of the follow-up message. He couldn't do jobs because of the chance of interference, so he preferred to take down the Omega Syndrome soon. That required someone else's help, Firewall.

"And the second message?" he asked.

Firewall sent a message not long after Chief Ishimura. They sent it using the encrypted channel with the appropriate protocols consistent with their previous messages. They didn't offer much detail other than noting there had been developments and wished to meet with you and Miss Joelle as soon as possible.

They also stressed time is of the essence. Unlike Chief Ishimura, they made no allowance for you to have more time to rest. I'd characterize it as strident, although you can look at it yourself, if necessary.

"That's okay. I believe you."

This was it. His team had raided the deepest bowels of the Station and fought cannibals Dirtside to get all the toys Firewall claimed they needed to fight the Omega Syndrome. The zealot resistance group had every reason to finish the battle quickly.

Dante tossed his legs off his bed and rubbed his eyes again. "Of course, they don't care about giving me time to rest." He stood. "Wake everybody up. This could be big, and we need to plan."

Standing in their main HQ meeting room, leaning over at the end of the table, Dante laid out the situation with brevity and precision before adding, "I don't want to have another damned argument about whether it's a good idea to team up with the ASF. I'm going to meet with Ishimura. That doesn't mean I'm going to give everything up, but we at least need to feel him out and see what he can do for us. With Firewall calling for us, we don't have the time to sit around figuring this all out and trying to account for everything that might go wrong. Something will, and we'll deal with it once it does."

Nasreen's pinched face said all Dante needed to know about how she felt about the idea of teaming up with the ASF. He understood her perspective. He still had to trust his instincts. They hadn't always worked out for him, but they'd kept him alive even when everyone else had betrayed him.

That had to mean and count for something. At the end of the day, Cormac Slaine and most of his old crew were dead because they didn't trust anyone. Dante was running around the Stations fighting the Omega Syndrome because he trusted himself.

"I agree that if Firewall says they need to talk right away, we shouldn't take that lightly," Nasreen said. "They might need tactical assistance for an operation, or they might need us to recover another item to help with their database."

Jolo put her hand to her mouth and yawned. "Meeting with Chief Ishimura after meeting with Firewall isn't a good idea. If the Omega Syndrome has corrupted the ASF, it gives them time to react to whatever Firewall might be doing. Meeting both at the same time lowers that chance."

Braelin shrugged. "We don't know what Firewall is doing. Will it be that big of a deal?"

"It could," Jolo replied. "One misstep could end with us all suffering. It doesn't hurt to be careful."

Hyde snorted. "Knowing Firewall, they're planning to kidnap someone again. Those *pendejos* are more trouble than they're worth."

"He does have a point," Ambrose said quietly.

Dante gave him a dirty look of warning. "They're our allies, and that damned database we spilled so much blood to get will help them contain the Omega Syndrome. I'd like to punch a couple of them—not going to play like I don't—but they are providing something we can use. With the Omega Syndrome targeting us Dirtside, we now need Firewall as much as they need us. It's only a matter of time before the Syndrome decides to come at us full force."

"Then we'll fight them," Hyde replied. "I don't care how many shit Reapers they throw at us."

Ambrose winced at that. He sighed and shook his head.

"Can we fight the entire Station?" Dante asked. "Because the only reason they've limited themselves to Block 9X is plausible deniability. If they get serious, we might end up in a war with half the Plunderers, Reapers, and security forces. We had a year to get ready, and the battle's begun."

"I wouldn't mind fighting the entire Station." Hyde grinned. "It'd be fun to see how long I could last."

Dante didn't know how much the cyborg was messing with him. Judging by the looks he kept giving Urshielle on the planet, Hyde had something to live for.

"I mind," Mugoi replied. "Unnecessary and unprofitable battles don't help our team or the Stations. We must always remember who the true enemy is."

"Agreed." Nasreen leaned back in her chair. Her brow creased deeply. "Jolo's right. I'm not going to object again to meeting Chief Ishimura, but it's not unreasonable to at least plan around the possibility of corruption. A simultaneous meeting is our best bet for that. The only question remaining is about who goes to what meeting."

"Yeah. I agree, too." Dante drew a deep breath and slowly let it out. "Let's play to our strengths. Ishimura isn't going to like it if you show up and give him the evil eye. You don't want an alliance, so it will come through."

"I used to be a freelance spy. I can fake it."

"Sure." Dante nodded. "I get that. But I've always been a Marauder."

"I don't understand."

"I want the alliance with the ASF, but I can't fake it. We have the alliance with Firewall, but every time I think about what they did to you, it makes me want to beat them down."

"Ha-ha," Hyde replied. "Now we're talking. I like the beatings plan."

Dante didn't like the fact that Hyde was on his side. "If I show up to talk to them, and that Exploit fool shows his face, I might not be able to stop myself. You got your punches in, Nasreen. You can control yourself better. So, it makes it easy. I talk to Ishimura, and you talk to Firewall."

"I see. It's a reasonable strategy, and I can't fault your logic."

Dante nodded. "Firewall is full of assholes, but we've got no reason to suspect they'll do anything to you at this point. They would have taken the chance when we handed over the parts for the database."

Hyde frowned. "What about the rest of us, *Papi?* We're supposed to sit around here doing nothing but staring at our hands?"

"He's got a point," Braelin offered. "It might help to have better numbers before you talk to assholes, ASF *and* Firewall."

"These are meetings, not Plunderer jobs," Dante replied. "Showing up to either meeting with a huge team, including two combat-augmented cyborgs, will send the wrong message. Right now, we're trying the diplomacy route, not the Dante Shale intimidation route."

He patted his chest. "I'll go alone to meet with Ishimura. Nasreen will go to Firewall. Everyone else will remain on standby in case this shit all falls apart, and we need you to pull our asses out of the fire."

"This is going to be great." Hyde slapped the table with a grin.

"They told me you looked into his soul. Did you look into my soul when we first met, Shale?"

"Yeah. I saw a gateway straight to Hell. I should have trusted my instincts. It would have saved me a pile of trouble."

Hyde cocked his head before nodding quickly. "That sounds about right."

"Somebody else might want to take their shot while we're distracted," Dante continued. "Going after our place when Midas has done a good job of locking down the systems isn't as viable. We've got too many defenses and weapons here. It makes more sense to go after us somewhere else."

Jolo frowned. "You make it sound like you're expecting an ambush."

"Then we should go with you," Braelin added.

"I agree," Mugoi seconded. "We don't need to be with you at the meeting. We should be nearby."

"Expecting one?" Dante shook his head. "Nah. I'm not going to pretend it's impossible, though. You being on standby here with access to the vehicles will give you the most mobility. Nothing may happen, or we both might get jumped. With the shuttle and hovercar available, you can split the team as necessary for up to two separate rescue missions."

"It sounds like a good plan to me," Nasreen interjected. "I have one addendum. Neither of us should commit to anything until we've had a chance to talk it over."

"Makes sense. No point in pissing anybody off until we have a good reason."

"I also suggest that you don't tell the Atlantica Security Force anything about Firewall," Nasreen added.

"That might be difficult. Ishimura wants answers."

"Without being a hundred percent certain this bet will pay off, it's not worth the risk."

Dante tried to find a good argument against her conclusion. He couldn't come up with one. There was no such thing as excessive caution when dealing with a conspiracy that spread throughout the Stations and reached to Dirtside.

"I won't tell Firewall about your meeting with the ASF," Nasreen continued. "They don't have to trust one another. They only have to trust us if this is going to work. Once we have a better feel for what's going on, we can exchange notes and figure out where we're going from there."

Dante looked around the table. Other than a bored-looking Hyde, everyone else seemed satisfied. On second inspection, Ambrose couldn't look Dante in the eye. He wasn't sure what that meant. He'd worry about it later.

"Yeah," Dante said. "That also makes sense. If I can trust Ishimura enough to mention the Omega Syndrome, I can talk about that Voices crap that happened when we finished off Slaine, if necessary. It gives me a way of explaining why we know all this without mentioning Firewall."

"If you don't have to give up anything, that'd be for the best," Nasreen suggested. "Firewall at least has proven what they could do for us. I think the ASF should earn our trust."

Dante surveyed the table. Eagerness had returned to the faces of the apprentices. Hyde's smirk was expected enough to be a relief. Ambrose's scowl surprised Dante.

"Everyone arm up and get ready," Dante ordered. "I'm not expecting you to launch at a second's notice, but don't get too far from HQ. Midas, send a message to Chief Ishimura telling him I'm on my way."

Nasreen stood, along with the others. "I'll contact Firewall myself. I want to use specific verbiage in my reply."

"I'll leave that to you."

The apprentices filed out of the room, followed by Hyde, who glanced at the sitting Ambrose. Dante waited in his chair until everyone departed.

"You got something to say?" he asked Ambrose. "You could have asked it during the meeting. No one was shy about sharing their opinion. I don't care at this point about how people think this ASF alliance is a bad idea. They might be right. We still have to try."

"No. It's not about that." Ambrose's voice was quiet but steely. "This is more…personal. There was no reason to get everyone involved in the discussion. That's why I didn't bring it up."

"Then get on with it." Dante made a circle with his hand. "I've got a meeting with a security chief. Lay it out before I go."

Ambrose narrowed his eyes. "What's your plan?"

"Were you asleep during the meeting?" Dante asked. "I told you the plan. I'm meeting Ishimura. Nasreen's meeting Firewall. The rest of you are on standby to pull our asses out of the fire if needed—simple and straightforward."

"That's not what I'm talking about." Ambrose stood and squared his shoulders, puffing out his chest with a defiant glare that made Dante want to chuckle. He looked like a puppy pretending to be a great wolf.

"What's your plan for dealing with the Omega Syndrome? I'm not talking about a vague idea that Firewall contains them, and we blow something up. You intend to take on a power that might very well control the Stations and now is, by your admission, targeting us on Dirtside missions. You should have something more concrete lined up."

He scoffed. "There's no guarantee Firewall will succeed at anything they've claimed. They might be dedicated, but you were able to track them down and fight their people. Zealotry isn't enough to assure victory."

"True. The plan's still coming together. We need more information. You know that. We need them to get their information out of the database. Once we have that figured out, we can proceed with all this."

Ambrose's shoulders slumped as his defiance and attitude drained away. "I…" He shook his head. "When I agreed to keep helping you fight the Omega Syndrome, I thought something would happen sooner."

Dante frowned, trying to tamp down his flaring anger. "What? You're bitching now after I gave you a choice? You said you chose to be here. Now, things are moving forward, and you want to cut and run. Give me a damned break. Can you be a man for five seconds, Igento?"

Ambrose waved in front of him. "It's not like that. This isn't what you think it is. This isn't about cutting and running."

"This isn't what I think it is?"

"Yes. No… I don't know! Just hear me out, please!"

"What do you think you know about how my mind works?" Dante asked.

Ambrose looked away. All his earlier gathered courage had vanished from his slumped form, leaving the familiar broken man Dante had almost killed a year ago. "We have a history that colors all of this and makes it hard for you to be objective. This isn't like before. I admit I was a greedy coward before, not once but twice. Now things are different. This isn't about me being greedy and afraid."

"Oh? That's the line you're going with?" Dante snickered. "How the hell isn't it? You were fine with helping me, then we had a close call on the planet, and you want to quit.

"I'm not going to beg you to stay, but I'm not going to pretend this isn't you doing what you do best, looking out for yourself. You've always been a good pilot, so I looked the other way. I thought you'd found your balls along the way. But same old Ambrose Igento, right? The man who wants to go play piano and pretend he doesn't owe anyone anything."

"That's not fair!" Ambrose shouted, smacking the table. He winced and shook his hand.

"That's not fair?" Dante threw his head back and laughed. "You're going to talk to me about fair? Let's invite Hyde in so he can join the game."

"I don't understand."

"You're the man who stabbed me in the back more than once, and you're bitching to me about being fair. Maybe Hyde's right. Maybe I should have killed you both when I had the chance. I keep telling everybody how good at vengeance I am, but here I am, letting you screw me over yet again and doing nothing about it."

Ambrose waved again in frustrated negation. "Just…just listen to me. You're taking this all the wrong way. You…you don't understand what I'm getting at and why I'm saying this."

"I am listening," Dante spat through gritted teeth. "You're not saying anything worth listening to. It's all excuses and fancy bull-shit to justify being a coward."

"I was doing good work with the TRG!" Ambrose snapped.

Dante's brow lifted. "What's the TRG have to do with this?"

"I was doing work with them that I felt equipped to handle and do. Work, for the first time in my life, that felt…like it meant something. I was doing more than making money as a Plunderer."

Ambrose shook his head. "You should understand that. You might have gone after SSS and Slaine for revenge, but it started because you didn't want to ignore your conscience. This is the same thing. About a cause greater than money."

Dante smashed his fist on the table. "What the hell do you think we're doing now? Fighting the Omega Syndrome isn't about money, asshole. Don't you get that? We're trying to save our species, you spineless prick."

Ambrose groaned and rubbed his temples. "You're not listening to me. You're so busy being self-righteous that you won't allow me to explain myself. I had setbacks below, and I came close to dying, yes, but that last mission reminded me of what I should have been doing.

"If I'd been there during the raid, I could have gotten to the shuttle and saved those people. I could have stopped everything.

I've been thinking about it. Those officials could have seen the beauty of Dirtside, of Earth, in a different way. I could have taken them on a tour."

Dante shook his head. "Block 9X and their Rider buddies would have sniped your ass. You would have been another body in the pile. You think you would have been a big hero down there?"

"I believe I could have made a difference, yes." Ambrose sucked in a breath. "You're still overreacting. It's not that I want to quit. I stayed on because of you and Nasreen. I do get that the Omega Syndrome is a threat.

"All I want to know is how long I'll be indebted for my past actions before I can get back to what I really want to be doing and what I'm better at. Is that too much to ask? I wanted information about a plan, and all you've offered me is the same 'Stand by, Ambrose. We're still figuring it out, Ambrose.'"

Dante clenched his hands. It would have been one thing if Ambrose had turned him down from the beginning, not run off with his tail between his legs because of one close call. The pilot had tricked Dante into believing in him, and that made Dante question his judgment.

"I don't need a man who isn't dedicated to the mission." Dante's voice was ice-cold. "I thought you were one-of-a-kind. I used to tell people you were one of the best pilots in the Stations." He shrugged. "I guess you're replaceable after all."

Ambrose's eyes widened. "Dante, look, I'm sorry. I'm just scared—"

"You're scared." Dante snorted. "Fine. You want out? You can get out. Find a replacement, then you can get the hell off the Stations, and we never have to see one another again. That might be for the best before I remember all the times you screwed me over and decide to act on it."

"I didn't want it to go down like this. I'm trying to…to…"

Dante snorted. "Spit it out, asshole. I have something far more important to do than deal with your self-pitying crap."

"I'm not trying to abandon you guys." Ambrose's eyes grew pleading. "That's not what I want. You have to believe that. That's not why I said all of this."

Dante shook his head. "But you also don't want to be here doing what matters. Can't have it both ways. You want me to pat you on the head and tell you no hard feelings? Screw that. You made your bed of nails. Now you have to lie on it."

Ambrose collapsed into a chair with his face in his hands. "Okay. Okay. I'm sorry. I won't go. No, seriously, I won't. You're right. This is important, and—" He shrank back under Dante's withering gaze. "Please…listen to me."

"I already told you," Dante growled. "I don't want anybody not dedicated to this mission. Fighting the Omega Syndrome isn't about money or fame. Our enemy will kill us if they can. Just find your damned replacement and leave. It was a mistake to bring you on. It was a mistake to believe that someone like you could change. People never change."

"But I—"

"*I* don't want you here anymore. Don't you understand?" Dante stomped over toward the door. "This conversation is over. I have a meeting to get ready for that might help us save the damned Stations. The only thing I want to hear from you is who your replacement will be."

CHAPTER ELEVEN

Dante strode confidently from the grav train onto the platform standing in front of the Atlantica Security Force Headquarters. People stopped and stared at him. That didn't bother him. Having fame had proven helpful, and he doubted the Omega Syndrome would send Block 9X after him in front of the ASF HQ.

He snickered at the thought. That might be entertaining. He wasn't sure if he should be applying human logic to an AI. Midas acted very human at times and was explicitly designed to aid humans. He still displayed unexpected emergent quirks.

Freed of any link to its creators, a rogue AI might become the closest human beings would ever come to encountering an alien intelligence. He planned to defeat the Omega Syndrome, but what would happen in the future? The coming of another Omega Syndrome was all but assured.

The solution lay below the Stations. Humanity had to return to Earth. Defeating the AI would enable that to happen.

Dante jogged down the ramps leading toward the headquarters. The building complex was tall concentric rings connected with covered walkways and transparent sky bridges. Shuttles and hovercars flowed in and out of hangars and garages, but almost no one was walking toward or out of the front door. He imagined it looked more impressive from the air, making it an odd design choice for a Station.

He wasn't much of a history or architecture buff. He had no idea if they'd modeled the headquarters after something on Old Earth.

Until meeting Urshielle and the other Crescent-Marked, he hadn't thought of the Earth as anything more than a way to make a living. History wasn't something to be remembered. It was something to be looted and sold off. Now, everything was different.

A year after those events, he hadn't fully processed them. His last trip Dirtside had only brought that more into relief.

He didn't plan to give up being a Marauder. More selectivity in jobs would have to be part of any post-Omega Syndrome future. His policies that prohibited unnecessary violence against Dirtwalkers were only the start.

Standing at the bottom of the ramp, a well-manicured man in an expensive suit looked away from a heavily gesticulated conversation with his friend, and his brow lifted. "Isn't that Dante Shale?" he whispered.

"The Marauder who took down SSS?" asked the other man. "Why would he be here? He's back to Plunderer work last I heard. They're about nothing more than a paycheck."

"I'm telling you it's him. I guarantee it. This is another vendetta."

"Does that mean the ASF is corrupt?" The second man glanced at the headquarters with a suspicious look. "He couldn't be taking down the entire ASF by himself, could he?"

Dante fought the urge to laugh. While he didn't go out of his way to promote himself anymore like he had when he'd adopted a fake identity, he also didn't pay that much attention to his public reputation. It was good to know the Omega Syndrome hadn't poisoned all the citizens against him.

Planting the occasional negative rumor or ill-source news story would be a subtle way to turn the Stations against him. The use of blunt tactics like sending Block 9X after targets had pushed him into believing the Omega Syndrome was a rogue AI. Overwhelming force seemed more like the strategy an AI would use as it involved less uncertainty and reliance on social manipulation, which was far too dependent on understanding the vagaries of human nature.

He passed from the platform down the ramp to a path lined with the flag of Atlantica Central Station on either side of a forest of statues. The closest figures depicted men in armor and with swords or poleaxes and proceeded to uniformed men and women holding batons and firearms. From what he'd read, they were supposed to represent the historical advances in security and policing throughout the millennia rather than famous individuals.

Despite the dearth of tourists, uniformed and armored ASF officers patrolled the plaza with shock batons on their belts. A show of force at headquarters made a certain sense. Order was as much about attitude as it was ability. None of the ASF officers approached him, but their attention lingered on him longer than necessary.

Dante arrived at the front double doors. Conspicuous cameras stared out at the front. Small indentations marked where sliding turrets could deploy in the event of a frontal assault. Granite topped the doors with an inscription carved in Latin.

Pax sequitur ordinem.

"What's that mean, Midas?" Dante asked.

Peace follows order, the AI translated.

"Whatever." Dante snickered.

The ASF thought that was inspiring. It sounded rather sinister to him. For people claiming the mantle of justice and order, they'd spent too long letting corruption fester in the

Stations. A Marauder shouldn't have had to be the one to take down Cormac Slaine.

Nasreen might have been right. The Omega Syndrome might have hopelessly compromised the ASF.

The doors slid open as Dante approached. A clear partition separated him from the scowling sergeant working the front desk. A bright blue field moved across the front lobby and passed over him. With a *whir*, a drawer popped out of the wall and extended toward Dante.

"Shale, Dante," the sergeant announced. She pointed at the drawer. "Place all weapons there. Any failure to comply will be treated as an implied threat to ASF members. An appropriate response will be employed."

"No reason to be prickly. I'm here to see Chief Ishimura at his invitation."

"I'm aware of that, and the chief didn't provide any orders saying that you get to walk around headquarters armed." The sergeant nodded at the drawer. "Stop wasting my time, and I'll stop wasting yours, Mr. Shale."

Dante reached into his pockets. He fished out his razorfist and dropped it into the drawer. A backup knife followed. He wasn't stupid enough to bring a firearm or grenades into ASF Headquarters.

The sergeant reached beneath the desk to press a button. A seamless door slid open in the partition. She motioned at a young, uniformed rookie standing ramrod straight around the corner. "He'll escort you to Chief Ishimura's office. Do not attempt to leave your escort. Any attempt to do so can be interpreted as an implied threat to ASF members."

"If I sneeze, will that be interpreted as an implied threat?" Dante asked.

The sergeant's grin showed a lot of teeth. "Depends on how and where you do it, Mr. Shale."

Fame didn't buy automatic respect from everyone. He wasn't there to push a low-ranking security officer around.

Dante stepped through the door. It slid closed immediately. He wandered over to the rookie and nodded. "Lead on before she decides my breathing is an implied threat."

"Yes, sir." The rookie was still as stiff as before. He pivoted like a robot and marched away.

The HQ hallways curved off in different directions matching the general architecture he'd seen outside. Door after door marked with different departments and senior officers lined the hallways. Many ASF members who spotted Dante froze and stared at him, watching him as he proceeded through the hallway.

Furtive whispers and murmurs filled the air, accompanied by quick nods and gestures. More than one armed officer lowered their hands to their batons, glaring at the Marauder in their midst as if he'd planned to take the entire ASF down by himself with no weapons.

On most days, he'd take it as a compliment. This trip, he found it annoying.

Dante's silent escort led him to an elevator. The rookie punched in a code on a keypad and motioned him inside. Once Dante entered, the rookie made a point of standing behind him with his arms folded behind his back.

"You been in the ASF long?" Dante asked.

"Four months, Mr. Shale. Two, if I don't count training."

"Do you like it?"

"Yes, sir. May I ask you a question?"

Dante shrugged. "Sure. I won't answer if I don't like it. People have told me I can be an asshole."

"Is it true that you once killed six Nightmutts and a cyborg with a depowered sphere when you ran out of ammo?" the rookie asked.

Dante laughed. "I've killed tons of Nightmutts and cyborgs. I don't remember doing it with a sphere. There was a Dirtwalker years ago who once got the drop on me, who I bashed over the head with a sphere. Broke the damned thing, which was inconvenient because I didn't have a backup. Mostly I like to stick to guns or razorfists down there. Why mess with a makeshift weapon when you can use the real thing?"

The rookie looked disappointed. "People say you've fought huge odds and survived."

Dante wasn't there to be the rookie's fantasy of the ultimate killer. He also wasn't there to downplay his skills.

"That's true. You can't be a good Marauder if you can't win an unfair fight. Dirtside doesn't care about fair. The TRG's doing their best, but it's going to be a long time before it approaches safe for the average person."

"How do you always win, then?" The nervousness vanished from the rookie's face. "I've received riot training for dealing with multiple opponents, but they stressed it's about maintaining formation for force multiplication. They taught us if we get separated from our unit to retreat until we can reform. Strength in numbers."

"I win by making sure the fight was unfair in my favor. It's not about honor, glory, or any of the crap people go on about. It's about surviving. Sometimes that means running and coming back later. Sometimes it means doing something crazy. I'm a Marauder. My main job's to grab things. Fighting is incidental to that."

"Running and coming back later like with Cormac Slaine," the rookie mused, the name coming out like a curse and accompanied by a huge scowl. "One Marauder versus SSS and a criminal o-harvesting ring used by the elites. It shouldn't have been a fair fight. It wasn't a fair fight, but you still won." He raised his chin. "I joined the ASF because of that incident."

"You did?" Dante couldn't hide the surprise in his voice. "A Marauder taking down a corrupt businessman convinced you to join the ASF rather than become a Plunderer? How does that work?"

"You proved that justice isn't gone from the Stations," the rookie replied reverently. "Everyone knew the harvesting was going on, and everyone knew it was against the law. No one did anything about it until you. You proved one man can make a difference even when he's up against the most powerful people out there."

"I had help," Dante reminded him. "One man can make a difference. A group of people can make a much bigger difference."

The lift slid to a smooth stop at the top floor, and the doors opened. A waiting lieutenant jerked back when she spotted Dante. An angry scowl ate away the bland boredom she'd been displaying before.

Dante tried not to smirk and failed, offering a polite nod after following the rookie out of the elevator. The lieutenant rushed down the hallway and turned the corner. Hurried words floated from there, too quiet at a distance to make out. He had to imagine the insults and implied threats.

His headquarters adventure continued with more curving hallways, the plaza and surrounding grav lines visible through the clear walls. The entire experience made it feel like he was walking on the edge of a mountain. He didn't care for it.

After taking a turn, the path curved inward, away from the exterior walls and straightening into a long hallway filled with the offices of impressive-sounding ASF staff. He ignored them all and the whispers and glares of the scattered officers and commanders until he and the rookie arrived at the end of the hallway and a massive door marked with CHIEF TAKASHI ISHIMURA.

Sitting behind a desk with two spheres and numerous feeds, a receptionist—a stern-looking dark-skinned man—leveled his cool gaze on Dante before dismissing the rookie with a nod. The younger man returned it, resumed his robotic pivoting, and marched away.

The receptionist pressed on one of the spheres. "Chief, Dante Shale is here."

Ishimura's door opened itself, and his stern voice came out next. "Get in here, Shale. We've got too much to talk about and not enough time."

Dante nodded at the receptionist and headed into the office. Ishimura sat behind a desk flanked by holographic statuettes and images. All were security force personnel from the different Stations, and not a single celebrity or politician that Dante could see. Not that he was an expert or paid much attention to who was popular.

They were less impressive than the huge curved sword hanging on the wall directly behind him. The shiny blade looked as if it was forged yesterday.

Ishimura nodded at the weapon. "I see you've noticed my *tachi*. It belonged to an ancestor who fought in the Battle of Dannoura. Although my understanding is he only used his bow during that battle."

"I'm not that great when it comes to ancient history," Dante admitted. "I know they say history repeats. It's hard to believe that when most of humanity lives in space now."

"It was the last battle of the Genpei War fought in 1185," Ishimura explained. "A great civil war in ancient Japanese history that marked the changeover in central, bureaucratic control of officials to the military control that marked my ancestors' home-land for centuries.

"It started because of the greed and ambition of two different clans. Blood spilled all over, noble and peasant, until the power changed hands. The story's much the same in most of the ancient world."

"Wasn't one of those greedy and ambitious guys your ancestor?"

"He was a man of minor distinction, following what he felt was right, or so the stories go." Ishimura looked away.

"Those who rule begin the battles. Those below suffer. We can only hope if we're the men fighting at their behest that in the end, something better comes. What's best is to avoid the struggle entirely, to keep order before the greedy and ambitious let it get out of hand."

"Like Cormac Slaine?"

Ishimura narrowed his eyes. "It would have been far better had someone kept his greed and ambition in check before he rose to his heights of power."

"Yeah, I agree with that. Don't worry. I solved the problem."

"So you did." Ishimura leaned back and steepled his fingers. "That's where we're at, Mr. Shale, and why I wanted to speak to you. Based on your reputation, you and I appear to want the same thing, to stop greed and ambition from hurting innocent people.

"The nobles who ruled those ancient clans used their forces and allies to fight in the battles. At least they had the honor to participate and suffer alongside their followers. Now, someone is sending mercenaries around the Stations and Dirtside, killing and maiming out of greed and ambition. Yet at the same time, they use their connections to push back enough to keep their tools from being tossed into the garbage."

Dante eyed the comfortable-looking chair in front of Ishimura's desk before taking a seat. He adjusted his butt for a moment and made a mental note to buy a similar chair when he had a chance. "That's all fancy of you to say, Chief. Block 9X keeps getting in my way. I'd like to see them taken down. This is less about honor and nobility and more about taking down an annoyance."

"I don't believe that. I think you don't want me to believe you're a good man, only a pragmatic man, and I also believe we want the same thing. But the best way to accomplish our shared goals is to take down the people who control them. Why don't you start from the top with information about that?"

"Yeah, well, Block 9X are just the dogs," Dante replied. "Somebody else has the leash. I'm glad you understand that."

"Who are they? What do they want? Leftovers from SSS and Slaine?"

"I don't think we should go into that yet."

Ishimura frowned. "Why wouldn't we? I thought it was obvious that's why I wanted to talk to you."

"I have my reasons." Dante shrugged. Nasreen would have been better at deflecting. He still didn't regret sending her to Firewall. He'd need to punch Exploit in the face before this was all over. A good kick to the guy's crotch would be satisfying too.

Ishimura sighed. "You have reasons?"

"Yeah. Reasons."

"I can't help you, Mr. Shale, if you don't give me something to work with. I'm reaching out my hand here."

Dante rubbed the back of his neck, trying to think of his next answer without offending Ishimura. Things were so much easier in the past. A year ago, he strode confidently into Cormac Slaine's office convinced he could handle a bad man. Now he sat across from a man his instincts told him was a good man who wanted the same things he did and had no idea how to handle the situation.

Ambrose had complicated matters. Dante was off because of the argument. That wouldn't justify messing things up.

"You'll have to trust me, Chief. You know me, and you know my rep. You know what I've done and who I've done it against. I'm a stone-cold bastard, but only to people who have it coming. The problem is the people who've pissed me off this last year aren't sublevel scum that I can go finish off without making waves. Ambition and greedy people have pull in society."

"You're implying that the people behind Block 9X are well-connected," Ishimura said. "High-ranking businesspeople, politicians? Can you give me names?"

Dante shook his head. "No, I can't."

"Because you don't have them, or you won't? You think I'm going to hand your name over to a corrupt politician."

"I can't. That's all I can say. This isn't a game for me."

Ishimura turned his chair around and stared at the *tachi*. "Showing up and telling me powerful people are pulling the strings isn't telling me anything I don't know, Mr. Shale. There's a reason Block 9X still operates, and it's not because I want to look the other way."

"Yeah, I get that. I also have my own constraints. I don't mind risking my life, but I don't want to get taken out because I was too trusting. No offense, but I've had trouble with that."

"You don't trust me?" Ishimura turned back around. "Have I given you any reason not to?"

"We both know it's not that simple," Dante replied. "I've got a small team. I can vouch for every person on it. Can you do that for every last member of the ASF?" He nodded at the door. "For all I know that guy out there is calling Block 9X right now and telling them to send a kill squad to ambush me when I get off the train."

"Rupert is the most loyal man I know." Ishimura scowled. "Are you questioning him?"

"I'm using an example. Everyone has their price. That's human nature."

"Everyone has their price except you?" Ishimura asked with a trace of mockery.

Dante allowed himself a grin. "I took on Cormac Slaine and SSS because some things were worth more than money. I think I've proven myself."

"Then you're wrong about human nature. Don't you think the ASF has proven themselves?"

Dante shrugged. "I think large organizations have factions,

which answer to different people. Not all those people care about anyone but themselves."

Ishimura stood. He walked over to the sword and ran his finger along the blade. "Do you know the moral status of a weapon?"

"Huh?" Dante shrugged. "Weapons are for killing people. They don't have a moral status. People are the ones doing the killing."

"You're right. A weapon isn't evil or good. It just is. It's nothing more than a tool. A righteous man wields his weapon to protect the weak and fight injustice. The wicked man uses his to terrorize, murder, and take what he wants without concern for others. Organizations can be like that, too, if not guided properly."

He turned back toward Dante. "You're right, Mr. Shale. You and Miss Joelle have proven yourselves in a way few people can these days. At the same time, you have to give me something to work with. It's obvious you know more than you're letting on."

"I'm not a hundred percent sure on all this myself. But there's a way you can help without worrying about everything else."

"How is that?"

"Putting direct pressure on Block 9X," Dante explained. "You start that up and sustain it, especially with us helping out on the side, and certain lines of evidence will start popping up you can follow. Then we both get what we want."

"That'd be a bold move." Ishimura sat back down. "I'd be putting my career on the line and angering many well-connected people."

"They attacked and kidnapped Station citizens," Dante replied. "Isn't that an excuse enough?"

"They did it Dirtside."

"It's still an attack." Dante shrugged.

"There are options that have been brought to my attention," Ishimura admitted. "This would be far easier if you'd start trusting me. It'd help me understand whom I could reach out to and whom I need to be careful of."

Dante didn't answer for a moment. Memories from all the close calls of last year swirled through his mind. Gambling on the ASF could end with his entire team dead if he was wrong.

"The one time I really needed to trust people, and these were people whom I thought would have my back no matter what, those people betrayed me. That's when I learned everyone has a price. Following that, I also learned that people can redeem themselves and prove themselves trustworthy."

"You want me to prove I'm trustworthy?" Ishimura looked insulted.

"All I'm saying is you have plenty of reason to go after Block 9X between the TRG attack and the club incident. You shouldn't need anything from me to do so."

Ishimura frowned. "We haven't released anything publicly about the club incident. I take it you were the other party there? I know that Eduardo Curtidor was present, although we can't find anything on the cameras that proves you were there. We're assuming you wore a disguise, which raises other questions about what you were doing there and why you felt the need to wear a disguise."

"I hear things." Dante was unwilling to give too much information away. "I heard they were at that club. Right now, my people have trouble moving because Block 9X keeps breathing down our necks. You put pressure on those mercs, and that might free us up to poke other people higher up the food chain. Then evidence will show up where you least expect it."

Ishimura stared into Dante's eyes. "My grandfather always said you can see a man's soul through his eyes."

Dante chuckled. Now that he heard someone else say it, he had to admit it sounded ridiculous.

"What do you see in my soul?"

"A man who might not care as much about law and order as I

do but wants to do the right thing." Ishimura offered a curt nod. "Very well, Mr. Shale. Block 9X has run rampant. I've spent years cultivating favors in the Station governments. I think it's time to cash that in and put pressure on those killers who call themselves mercenaries."

"Good. I'll do what I can on my end."

"I hope so." Ishimura motioned at the sword. "This time I want to be on the winning side. You should get ready, Mr. Shale."

"Excuse me?"

"Strike first and fast," Ishimura declared. "Disrupt the enemy operation, and don't give them time to prepare. By now, they know you've come here. I'm gambling here and trusting that what I see in your eyes and what I've seen from Block 9X will lead me somewhere. It's time to gather help. We happen to have good intelligence on Block 9X's main base."

"You mean the one in Nuevo Rio?"

Ishimura's brow lifted. "You are well-informed. Yes, that one. While it's not like I can take all my people over there, it's time to push their chief to offer support. We can raid their base and see what that knocks loose."

"You're prepared to go that far?"

"Yes." The chief nodded. "I have been for a while. I just needed a reason to convince myself."

"Then I'll be ready."

CHAPTER TWELVE

Led by a sullen-faced Firewall operative, Nasreen stepped into a small dusty room. Based on the counter and the long tables, she suspected it used to be a small cafeteria. Like many of Firewall's other bases, this room was in a hidden base along an abandoned grav line station.

When Nasreen contacted the organization, they'd instructed her to go to an address across town where she'd met an operative with a code phrase. Her fleeting nervousness had left her when a group of stab-happy operatives looking to kidnap her didn't jump her.

She didn't recognize the operative, and he didn't seem interested in communicating with her other than offering the bare minimum of orders and direction.

A circuitous walk led by the operative took her to a sublevel, an officially decommissioned grav line, and a waiting train. She'd not bothered with small talk. There wasn't any point until she dealt with someone farther up the ladder. She knew that much about working with Firewall.

That was fine with Nasreen. She respected Tether and Lock. That didn't mean she needed to befriend everyone in Firewall.

They'd passed through a guarded door without the fierce array of inspections she'd expected. That surprised her given they knew she carried several implants.

The operative motioned at a chair. "Sit. Tether will be here soon." Without waiting for a response, he stepped out of the room. At least he hadn't stabbed her or tried to kidnap her.

Nasreen took a seat, grateful she was meeting with Tether and not Exploit. A shudder passed through her as she recalled her treatment at his hands during her imprisonment.

Dante was right to be angry at the insane zealot. She clung to her anger, only having set it aside for the good of the alliance. Dealing with only Exploit would have taken all her self-control. Trusting him made her nauseous.

Lock had done what he had out of a sincere desire to ensure the safety of the organization and his belief that Firewall would save humanity. Exploit claimed righteousness and a higher calling.

She'd seen through to the truth. He was a petty, evil man who enjoyed hurting others, found a place to do it, and claimed a moral justification. Once they'd taken care of the Omega Syndrome, she'd ensure he couldn't get away with hurting anyone else.

Nasreen didn't have to wait long before Tether entered. Her gaze drifted to the operative's arm. Block 9X blades had taken it in the club, setting in motion the chain of events that led to Nasreen getting kidnapped and tortured by Exploit in the guise of interrogation. All the while, her team had desperately tried to keep Tether alive.

Instead of an autoclamp or bandage, Tether sported a new biomechanical arm and hand, obvious by its dull gray color. The articulation of the fingers was stiff. She'd not even tried to match it to her skin tone or the skin tone of anything remotely human other than a corpse.

Nasreen's brow lifted. "Of all the things I'd never expect from a Firewall operative, a major cybernetic augmentation is at the top of the list. Your organization is changing in a big way."

Tether sat across from Nasreen and rested her arm on the table. "You think I'm a hypocrite? That all that talk about implants was just that, talk?"

"I don't know what to think," Nasreen admitted. "I go back and forth about the truth about the Omega Syndrome, but you've convinced me of how dangerous implants can be. I'm also surprised you didn't check me out before letting me in here."

"We were planning to get rid of this base." Tether flexed her fingers. "This area is shielded, and we're monitoring for any suspicious transmissions. Our enemy may have infected you since our last meeting, but building a trusting relationship goes both ways. Lock has stressed that we should compensate you for your treatment last time by showing you more respect and deference than we'd normally extend to anyone outside the organization."

"It'd be nice," Nasreen said. "We could have avoided that entire situation with more openness on both sides."

"I am aware and am grateful that your team saved my life despite my actions that night." Tether raised the arm. "I'm not a hypocrite."

"I'm not here to judge you for your implants. Your friends will do that, such as Exploit."

She indulged her petty side by spewing out his name like a foul curse.

"You don't understand." Tether lowered her arm. "The Omega Syndrome has limits. It needs a true software interface to invade.

"This prosthetic is mostly a glorified mechanical machine that responds to my muscle movements to mimic the function of an arm and hand. No wireless capability, no neural interface, and almost no real computing involved. It's clumsy and far less effective than a modern advanced augmentation, but its fundamental design ensures its protection from Omega Syndrome infection." She rotated her shoulder. "A working replacement with no risk."

"That's useful."

"It is." Tether flexed her fingers again. "You're right. There's no way my comrades would let me stay in the organization with a true cybernetic augmentation. They'd be right not to. There's too great a risk even when you're being careful."

"I'm not here to debate your security again unless it involves strapping me down in a small room."

"That won't happen again." Tether stood and motioned for Nasreen to follow her. "We don't have much time. There's somewhere I need to take you. Consider this conversation my way of verifying you aren't infected."

"You don't want to talk here?" Nasreen looked around. "Is there something wrong with this room?"

"No, it was just a useful place to meet you." Tether headed toward the door. "This station is next to a convenient line to get us to where we need to go next."

Nasreen stood and hurried after Tether. "What's this all about?"

"You'll find out soon enough."

"I thought you trusted me."

"That doesn't mean I need to tell you everything right away." Tether smiled. "Mystery can be fun."

"It can get you killed."

"That too."

They transferred between two old lines before jogging down a long, winding sublevel path past suspicious scavs and other undesirables with nowhere else to go. The mazes of metal hallways and tiny rooms left Nasreen uneasy, but at least the area looked stable and lacked the obvious signs of collapse that

Dante had described during his last journey into an old sublevel.

The Stations mirrored all the glories and failures of past human civilizations. The men and women who couldn't fit neatly into the order of things were shoved aside or convinced to stay out of sight. People claimed to care, but most lacked the resources or will to do anything other than complain about it.

For a species on the verge of extinction, humans might be better served taking care of the existing population. It was as if everyone was stuck in the patterns of the past and on a fundamental level, they hadn't adjusted to the new reality that accompanied leaving Earth.

A dirty little girl with a cybernetic arm and solid chrome-colored eyes clung to a doll. Nasreen didn't look away, but she didn't speak to her. The Omega Syndrome had to come first, which meant playing by Firewall's rules.

Nasreen had expected to run into fewer people given who was escorting her, but the longer and farther they walked, the more people they passed heading to and from their general direction. Desperate scavs and addicts grew less common, with a mixture of fashionable young people with obvious money and more distinguished-looking older people feeding the growing crowd.

A building roar slowly ate away at the earlier quiet and scattered chatting of the sublevel. Cheering and yelling echoed through the narrow, dusty metal hallways. A familiar high-pitched whine mixed with the noise, although Nasreen couldn't place it until Tether pushed past a group of red-faced men drinking alcohol in dark cups and blocking a doorway.

"Hey," a man greeted, slurring his words.

Tether spun and glared at him. He grimaced and backed away, holding up his hands.

Three brightly colored thrustbikes screamed through a narrow tunnel in front of Nasreen. Side-by-side, their hard turns had them scraping the ground, leaving sparks and offering no sign of standard gravitational safety shields being active. They disappeared into another winding tunnel as another group of bikes flew by, none marked by anything less than an obvious and unnatural color.

Nasreen had assumed that Tether was leading her to another Firewall base. They stood in a thick crowd of people who weren't operatives. She doubted Firewall operatives could smile and cheer so much. That only left her confused and frustrated. She hadn't come for a social call.

Nasreen narrowed her eyes. "Is this what I think it is?"

"This is underground thrustbike racing." Tether gestured at a blur of green zooming through the tunnel. "These are daredevil drivers who are directly neurally wired to their thrustbikes. They fly them through the twisting tunnels and passages of the underbelly of Atlantica Central Station in these races. People love to bet on them. It's big business."

"It's an illegal business."

"Many things are. That never stops them. The authorities crack down. They move for a while. Then they come back."

A red bike scraped the ground, leaving a spray of parts flying behind. The rider chasing the red bike rotated his bike and surged over his red competitor before turning back over and waving at the roaring crowd. He disappeared around the corner.

"Are they purposefully not using their safety features?" Nasreen asked. "It's like they're trying to get hurt."

Tether shook her head. "No rider wants to get hurt, but people want a show. The crowds claim they want to see men and women go fast, but make no mistake. This is a coliseum, and they're hoping to see people die from a mistake. That excitement feeds their betting.

"You'd be surprised. There are far fewer deaths than you'd expect. Being directly linked to the bike gives impressive reaction times. The bikes are missing the features, but their suits have built-in airbags and are a special nanopolymer blend."

The mystery and frustration only deepened. Nasreen doubted Firewall had invited her there to place bets. She couldn't discern the hidden link between illegal racing and the resistance organization.

Nasreen frowned. "Don't you think the more fundamentalist-minded members of your organization disapprove of this place? Men and women using implants for racing? Isn't that tempting your enemy to come?"

Tether shook her head. "To keep the races hidden from the ASF, we use advanced and powerful electronic countermeasures. The enemy would have a hard time penetrating that. The data environment is so toxic to signal integrity that the effective EM storm surrounding the place would shred any infected data packages. The organization has learned from experience how to harden this place from that sort of influence."

"I suppose I hadn't noticed this place was special. My implants have been giving me errors since I first boarded the grav train. I assumed it was one of your special devices."

Two more bikes flew past, eliciting huge cheers from the crowd. Nasreen didn't see what was special about the purple and yellow thrustbikes compared to any others. She assumed they must be the reigning champions or larger-than-life personalities.

Tether added, "Besides, this place has its usefulness. It serves our needs in many ways, and beggars can't be choosers. Our people had previous connections here that have made it worthwhile to help maintain this place despite the risks involved."

"What's so useful…" Nasreen scoffed. "You're skimming from the bets? Is that how you fund your operations?"

"It's one method, yes. You can't win a war against an enemy as powerful as the Omega Syndrome without resources, and we're not in a position to ask for donations." She gestured for Nasreen to follow her. "I didn't bring you here to watch the races. Come on."

Nasreen scanned the crowd. No one was watching her. Everyone was focused on the racing. That was another way such a place could be useful. Even the paranoids of Firewall could have a meeting in plain sight without arousing suspicion.

Tether led Nasreen and navigated through the throng of cheering fans. Farther down, Nasreen spotted holographic signs reporting the state of the race. The names were all unfamiliar to her, but her earlier theory was confirmed when she spotted the numbers for the purple and yellow bikes currently occupying the top two race positions.

The roar of the crowd and scream of the bikes grew less overwhelming as she and Tether moved away from the densest part of the crowd. They turned a corner and headed down an empty side tunnel to an unmarked dusty door with a newer-looking keypad. Tether punched in a code, and it *clicked* open. She ushered Nasreen into the room.

The tiny room looked as if no one had used it in decades. Dust coated the walls and floor. A small table and two chairs lay inside. Calling it a closet was an insult to closets.

"I'm getting tired of being taken from place to place. I understand your security needs, but that doesn't mean you should feel free to waste my time." Nasreen frowned. "Why are we here exactly?"

"You'll see soon enough." Tether folded her arms and stood near the door. She nodded at a chair. "Nothing we do is without reason."

"I hope so." Nasreen sat. "You're the ones who contacted us. Did you have something you wanted to report? I doubt you called me all the way here to brag about how you're funding your group."

"We'll get to that in due time. First, why don't you tell us what happened on the planet? Rumors are flying all over the place. It's obvious that the powers that be, among others, don't want the full story coming out right away. When they don't, that often means the Omega Syndrome doesn't, which makes us believe they were involved."

"You're right." Nasreen drew a deep breath. "That's straight-forward enough to explain. It's important that you understand how the Omega Syndrome is changing tactics."

<hr>

"Now we're hoping you could give us something to work with," Nasreen finished. She'd laid out the team's troubles back to the Khallabash Brothers' incident and the implications. She left out key details such as Dante's strained behavior and their contact with Ishimura beyond noting the arrival of the joint Station security detachment.

"We have theories on why Block 9X was there, but nothing solid. We wanted to minimize unnecessary contact with you, but you contacted us anyway, so here we are. We're not sure if it was a coincidence or Block 9X is attempting to harass our team in an indirect way based on our previous relationships."

Tether never spoke during the explanation, but she did nod to prove she was paying attention. When Nasreen finished, Tether lowered her arms with a slight frown. "Thank you for being so honest. I know someone who could help explain why the 9Xers were there, among other things." She rapped her knuckles on the door. "Which is why we're here. We just needed to make sure you'd be willing to give us something before we wasted our time. Trust goes both ways."

"Right." Nasreen watched the door.

The door opened, and Lock entered. Nasreen let out a sigh of relief. She'd worried Exploit would show up, or someone even worse, if there was such a person in the organization. From what she'd learned, Firewall appeared far more horizontal a group than she'd first assumed.

Lock nodded at Tether. She disappeared through the door and closed it.

"It's good to see you again, Nasreen." Lock took a seat.

"Were you listening in on that entire conversation?" Nasreen asked. "You could have come in here."

"I was spying the old-fashioned way." He smiled. "I apologize for the subterfuge. We had our reasons, and I thought you might be more comfortable somewhere that we didn't completely control after everything that…" He sighed. "I want you to know I have regrets over everything that happened. I shouldn't have let things go so far. If I'd stood up to Exploit sooner, you wouldn't have had to suffer like that."

"We all have regrets about how our team and your organization have interacted. The important thing now is to move forward. We can take those tragedies and use them to stop our mutual enemy and far worse tragedies in the future."

"I know that. It's just that what I was responsible for in helping subject you to…" Lock shook his head. "A woman like you shouldn't have had to deal with that. You and Mr. Shale have done more than your share to help push back the Omega Syndrome without knowing about them. But we treated you and your people like you were no better than Block 9X."

Nasreen couldn't help but reach out and pat his hand. She hated the pain she saw in his eyes. She hadn't been happy in captivity, but now she understood how much the aggression of men like Exploit drove that. Given the scale of the threat, she could empathize with their point of view, even if she didn't agree with their actions.

Lock was different from Exploit. She wasn't comfortable calling him misguided anymore since she'd come more and more to believe in his theories, including that the Omega Syndrome was a rogue AI and not only a tool used by humans.

His gaze lowered to her hand. His brow lifted. Nasreen blinked and pulled it back slowly. She needed to keep it professional.

Nasreen cleared her throat. "Tether mentioned you might have something to share with me. Us. The team. I assume it's not a problem that Dante's not here?"

"Anyone from your team would have been fine, but I'm happy it's you." Lock let that statement linger for a moment before continuing. "Thanks to the parts your team gathered, we've been able to access the database fully. It's proving far more useful than anticipated, including the information we needed on the state of the systems and networks before the Omega Syndrome and the original code we can use for comparative analyses."

"That all sounds great." Nasreen nodded. "I'm glad you have no complaints."

"It's better than you know. What we found aided another operation that allowed us to access what we believe is partial Omega Syndrome source code. Combined, this allows us to start crafting measures to disrupt the Omega Syndrome's tentacles throughout the Stations."

He clenched his hand into a fist. "Once that's ready, we'll need your team's help to deliver that tool in a way that'll finish off the Omega Syndrome."

Nasreen's breath caught. "Then it's almost over."

"Very close, closer than we've ever been, thanks to your team's recovery of that database and the parts from Earth. If you had asked me about this a few months ago, I would have never believed we could come so far so quickly." Lock offered a warm smile.

"For the first time in a long time, we can imagine what victory against our enemy looks like. I have my regrets about how we conducted ourselves, but not about getting involved with your team. You're proving to be the key to our final battle. Your names will go down in history. You didn't have to erase yourselves like us."

"I don't care about going down in history as long as we win," Nasreen replied. "Do you think the Omega Syndrome knows what we recovered? Is that why it's now behaving in a more directed and aggressive manner toward us?"

The Omega Syndrome had warned Nasreen and Dante a year ago that it would be watching. They had proven themselves too hard to manipulate. That in itself might have doomed them.

Lock's smile waned. "We can't be sure. It likely knows something. We've noticed the Omega Syndrome is spending much more time, energy, and resources toward isolating and disrupting the efforts of the Terra Restoration Group, both Station-side and Dirtside."

"Sending mercenaries to join up with local raiders is an elaborate and risky strategy. I don't see the payoff against my team. It's all too indirect."

Lock shook his head. "To be clear, we don't believe the efforts against the TRG are specifically because of your group. Your involvement this time was incidental but obviously helpful to stopping the Omega Syndrome."

Nasreen nodded. Built-up tension flowed from her shoulders and neck. She'd believed the TRG project raid was to strike at Dante, Ambrose, and herself. Innocent people had been hurt and killed, and she didn't like the idea of being responsible for any of that.

"Why exactly then?" she asked.

"Its efforts against the TRG go far back," Lock continued. "Our people found evidence of a major uptick more than a year ago before Mr. Shale and yourselves were tangled up with SSS. Around that time, the TRG had decided on a major increase in projects on Earth, operating on a much wider scale. Before then, they'd concentrated mostly on Dirtwalker relief.

"This was the beginning of them planning for something

beyond that. We didn't know any of this until recently. It's almost as if the Omega Syndrome is becoming desperate and getting sloppier with our recent successes."

"It's scared," Nasreen suggested. "It knows it can lose."

"We can only hope, but scared beings lash out." Lock frowned. "It's not only the TRG it has targeted. Our working theory is the Omega Syndrome is making these moves because more people going Dirtside means more people out of its reach and less dependent on the technological vectors of control it wields. The Earth itself is the ultimate weapon against the Omega Syndrome."

Nasreen nodded. "The tribes are completely free of its influence. A whole part of humanity that it can't control."

"Yes, and if Station-born people begin living there long-term, Dirtside could develop independently enough to not need the Stations at all," Lock replied. "The planet's hostile, but it can be handled with preparation and without the constant need for networked Station systems. Humanity spent most of its existence that way. It's not crazy to think it could happen again."

"Exactly, but it goes beyond that." Excitement filtered into Nasreen's voice. "There's evidence that human biology is adapting down there and here. You've noticed it yourself, and the o-harvesting scandal highlighted it. The longer we choose to live on the Stations, the more and more dependent we'll become on cybernetic augmentations and tech."

Lock bobbed his head. "Which, in turn, makes us more vulnerable to the Omega Syndrome. It has every reason in the world to promote that. It's a vicious loop guaranteed to end with AI control over humanity."

Nasreen continued. "If humanity can stabilize our gene pool on Earth, the Omega Syndrome is done. It might think it can handle the Dirtwalkers with Reapers if the rest of us stay on the Stations, but Station-born people helping uplift the Dirtwalkers while adapting to more natural childbearing will doom the

Omega Syndrome completely. Even if it takes decades or centuries, the more cities and villages reestablished on Earth, the more pressure there will be for people to leave space and return to the surface. It's more natural."

Lock stared at her, his eyes questioning. "You've been down there many times. Is this all nothing but a dream? I want to believe it's not because our enemy is trying to stop it."

"It's not a dream." Nasreen shook her head. "The Earth will need to be tamed again, but it's not the dying planet we have been taught to believe. It's adjusting itself, and the Dirtwalkers prove humans can change to survive those adjustments. Our species has a future in our original home, as long as we're patient and don't destroy ourselves in the meantime."

Lock nodded. Relief flooded his features. "This is all of it then. For whatever reasons, the Omega Syndrome has decided this is the critical juncture in human history, where we decide if we will all be slaves to an AI or free." He squeezed his eyes shut. "We can win this. We're so close."

Nasreen smiled. "Yes, we are." A muffled roar from the crowd made her look at the door. When she turned back to Lock, she found him staring with a vacant expression at the door. "Is something wrong?"

"Sorry." Lock chuckled. "I let the race distract me."

"I'm surprised a man like you enjoys heathen neural-linked racing." Nasreen winked, hoping he took the joke for what it was.

Lock sighed. He put his arm on the table palm up. "I'm sorry."

"No, no. I'm sorry. I didn't mean anything by it. I was surprised Tether brought me here. It felt all overly elaborate if it was about meeting you, not that I'm not happy to be talking with you, I…"

"You're misunderstanding." Lock rolled up his sleeve to reveal deep scarred-over grooves in his flesh. "Do you know what these are?"

"I…no." Nasreen stared at the grooves. "I believe they are scars from excised implants?"

"Yes." Lock inclined his head toward the door. "They were where my neural racing interfaces were installed when I was a racer."

"Oh." Nasreen grimaced. "I see."

"I used to be involved in this type of racing," Lock explained. "I was good. Damned good. I made money, and I enjoyed the thrill and the danger. Then the Omega Syndrome tried to use me as a carrier to infect the other racers." He sneered.

"Even before Firewall secured it completely, this place has been locked down for a while to protect it from the authorities. That meant the Omega Syndrome couldn't use me the way it wanted. Instead, it became bolder and more blatant."

Nasreen shivered. "Meaning what?"

"You and Mr. Shale still don't understand what it's capable of, not really." Lock tapped his forehead. "The brain is the seat of the soul in the body. To hijack a man's brain is to hijack his soul.

"The Omega Syndrome was frustrated by the data-toxic environment and kept pushing me to do more dangerous things on and off the track, almost as if it was trying to punish me for my resistance." He stared at the grooves. "I hurt people I didn't want to hurt. No one cared. That was part of the race. But I cared. If it weren't for Firewall freeing me, it was only a matter of time before I murdered someone and died myself at the hands of a soulless AI."

Nasreen reached over and squeezed his hand. "It wasn't your fault."

"I know." Lock sighed. "That doesn't mean I don't remember the faces of all those riders I hurt."

"I'm more understanding now of why you have the beliefs you have." Nasreen gave his hand another gentle squeeze. "And why you are so grateful to Firewall. I believed it before. Now I know for sure. You're a good man. You didn't deserve what happened to you. Remember, you're as much a victim of the Omega Syndrome as those other racers."

"Thank you. That means something coming from you." Lock looked into her eyes. "You're a good woman. You didn't deserve any of what happened to you."

The door flew open. Lock jerked his hand back and jumped to his feet, reaching into his pocket and pulling out a knife. Nasreen had her hand on a hidden blade. She didn't pull it out when she spotted an unarmed, heavy-breathing, red-faced Tether.

"Lock, ASF raid!" the woman shouted.

Nasreen grimaced and prayed Dante hadn't pushed the ASF into doing something stupid. She released the knife and reached into a pocket to pull out her wrist dart launcher. "Great timing."

CHAPTER THIRTEEN

Dante strolled into his team headquarters' lobby, looking back and forth for Nasreen or any sign of trouble. He'd taken the grav train back with no ambushes, suspicious mercenary attacks, and nothing worse than a boy asking him if he'd ever killed a man with a fork. He'd made a mental note to investigate where these rumors about his choice of non-standard weapons had come from. The last thing he needed was a Reaper showing up to take him on thinking their pulsecore could beat his fork or depowered sphere.

He was only grateful that hadn't happened much before. The closest was Hyde's initial attitude toward him when Slaine had hired them both.

"Midas, is Nasreen back yet?" Dante asked.

He'd received a basic curt response to his earlier messages to Hyde and the others about Nasreen. No one had called him to complain about any ambush or kidnapping attempts, always a consideration when Firewall was involved. They also hadn't seen Nasreen yet.

Dante might have been worrying over nothing. Calling her when she was meeting with Firewall was a security risk. He didn't want to do anything that might point the Omega Syndrome to her current location when she was dealing with Firewall. While he assumed the paranoid members of Firewall would shield her once she arrived, giving out data along the way could point the enemy toward its greatest foe and doom their alliance.

"No, sir, Miss Joelle is currently not accounted for," Midas replied through a nearby terminal. "She's yet to return or interface on a network to send a message to the base. I can't account for her once she left the camera range of headquarters."

"Knowing Firewall, they're probably taking her on an EM shielded grav train blindfolded, spinning her around three times, then making her cross the tracks before they can begin to talk." Dante grunted. "I get why they do what they do. It's still annoying. I hate all this spy crap."

"I'll leave the planning of organizational liaison strategies to you, sir. Although I should note there are certain upgrades that might prove useful for future such dealings."

Dante snickered. "Of course there are. Make a list. We'll talk about it when I'm not readying for war."

Hyde stepped into the lobby, twirling a huge knife between his metal fingers. All evidence of the bullet storm he'd weathered on the planet was gone, with almost no dents or exposed circuitry or internal mechanisms remaining. "I could have told you all that, *Papi*."

"You were listening?" Dante asked.

"Yeah. Everyone's ready whenever you are." Hyde nodded toward the armory. "It's less fun taking down someone Station-side. There are too many rules. I bet you before this is over, even Ishimura says to hell with the rules. We're not going to beat the Omega Syndrome with shock batons and strongly worded threats."

"Damn. I wanted Nasreen here. I also can't wait around for her. Ishimura has the Nuevo Rio Security Force ready to move on the Block 9X base. I want to be present in case the Omega Syndrome pulls something. I've managed not to tell Ishimura the complete truth, but I don't want him taken off-guard."

"You sure about this?" Hyde asked. "We've gone from looking into Ishimura's soul to depending on him keeping other *pendejos* on different Stations in line. Block 9X pulls more strings with heavier weight on their home Station, I'd bet. He might not be able to save you if things get rough."

"That's all the more reason to move fast on this," Dante replied. "They wait around trying to be careful, and those mercs will be long gone, along with any trail leading to the Omega Syndrome. This will be a joint raid, not a purely Nuevo Rio operation. Ishimura's staking his reputation on this. He's not doing that if he doesn't think he can get results."

"And what about the rest of us?" Hyde *clanged* his metal fists together. "It'd be fun to neuter more of their Irondogs. Nasreen doesn't need help. Firewall isn't going to mess with her again. They know we'll rip out their intestines if they do anything."

"The rest of you will remain on standby in case Nasreen needs help," Dante replied. "I'm not worried about Firewall. I'm worried about the Omega Syndrome hitting Firewall while she's around."

"You get to help mess up Block 9X, and we have to sit on our asses doing nothing." Hyde growled. "That's annoying."

"Those are my orders." Dante moved toward the armory. "I'm going to gear up and head out to join the strike team. Worse-case scenario, if this goes bad, it'll be easier for me to extract myself with all that security force power around me. You all don't need to worry about it until the joint strike force handles Block 9X."

Hyde tossed the knife into the air and snatched it by the handle. "Sitting around's boring. I'm all repaired and ready to kick ass. Yeah. I get it. You worry. Leave the *hijos* here and take me. They don't use cyborgs in the security force. They might be in trouble facing off against the Irondogs."

"You'll get your chance soon enough," Dante replied. "Don't worry. This is the advantage of having allies. We don't have to do everything ourselves."

"You're assuming those assholes aren't all working together. This whole thing could be a big trap."

"That'd take more trouble than gunning me down when I was alone in his office. He could have planted a weapon." Dante stopped at the door. "Anyway, it's better to find out now rather than later."

"You're willing to bet your life on this ASF alliance working out?"

Dante nodded. "Yeah, I suppose I am."

With helmet under his arm, Dante stepped back into the lobby on his way toward the hangar. His heavy armored boots thudded against the floor. He'd armed up with shock batons, a razorfist, and a knife. He didn't trust Ishimura enough to show up with firearms. He hoped he wouldn't regret that decision later.

Hyde was still standing there with an annoyed look. "Hey, before you go, *Papi*, I want to know something."

"No, you can't come with me no matter how many times you ask me." Dante chuckled. "I'm not trying to keep you out of the fight, Hyde. I want to keep my best resources available if this all goes to crap and we run out of allies. This fight is bigger than me or any one member of this team."

"That's not what this is about." Hyde narrowed his eyes. "What did you say to Ambrose?"

Dante's smile dimmed. "Why? Did he say something to you?"

Hyde shook his head. "I spent a year with him Dirtside. It's not like we lived together, but I got to know him."

"You think knowing proves something?"

"He was okay before the meeting, then he talked to you, and

now he's shook up. He won't tell me what happened." Hyde inclined his head toward the hallway. "The guy looks defeated. That's not a good thing if we have to go into a fight. And you're the one responsible."

A spark of regret lit in Dante. Any other time he might have admitted that things had gotten out of hand. The stress of taking on the Omega Syndrome had been getting to him. He wasn't sure Ambrose should be sticking around if he didn't want to, but he could have handled it better.

Dante sighed. "I don't have time for this right now. I've got a raid to join. I'll talk to him later and figure things out."

Hyde snickered. "Running away won't make the problem go away."

"I'm not running away." Dante headed toward the hallway leading to the hangar. "I can fix it when I have more time."

"So you admit you messed something up?"

"That's not it." Dante shook his head, not bothering to turn his head when he called back. "I've done nothing wrong. I screwed up my delivery of the truth. I should have taken into account I was dealing with Ambrose. He's always been overly sensitive. The guy shouldn't have ended up flying for Plunderers. He might have had a happier life."

"Funny how that works out," Hyde replied. "Ha-ha. The great Dante Shale. He's never wrong about anything, only about how he talks. Is that what you're going with?"

"I told you I don't have time for this. I need to join Ishimura for the raid."

"Fine." Hyde shrugged. "I'll bother you later. Don't let an Irondog kill you. I'd be insulted if you died to another cyborg instead of me."

"I won't. Make sure the team is ready to move. That's all you need to worry about for right now."

Dante headed into the hallway toward the hangar, shaking his head. Managing a team shouldn't be so much like dealing with a family. He slowed and thought that over. He might have the wrong idea about that.

For the moment, it didn't matter. He could think it all over after Block 9X was finished.

The trip back to the ASF HQ in the hovercar helped Dante bypass the whispers and looks of citizens. Using a call-ahead-netted code provided by Ishimura, he flew straight into an HQ hangar filled with ASF troop carriers. Armored ASF officers stood clustered in their squads, all doing last-minute gear checks. The sea of men, women, and weapons would soon wash over Block 9X. It might have been the largest ASF show of force in years.

Dante landed in a thin open strip at the edge of the hangar. He stepped out of his car, grabbed his helmet, and looked around for Ishimura. The rookie from earlier jogged his way.

"Welcome back, Mr. Shale. If you'll follow me, I'll take you to the chief."

"Lead on."

The rookie pivoted hard on his heel and marched through the gathered army. As Dante and the rookie passed through the hangar, nearby ASF officers stopped talking to look their way with mixtures of curiosity and amusement. No one glared or scowled at him like on his earlier trip. He spotted the lieutenant who'd hurried away earlier. She looked up from a riot shield she was inspecting and offered him a polite nod.

Dante chuckled. The rookie looked his way.

"You didn't notice, did you?" Dante asked.

"Notice what, Mr. Shale?"

"It's nothing. It goes back to something Chief Ishimura told me. A weapon is neither good nor evil. It's how you use it."

The rookie frowned. "That makes sense."

"Sometimes people can be weapons, too."

"That makes less sense."

"Don't worry about it, kid."

They wove through the crowd with a squad parting to allow Dante and the rookie to the back of the hangar where Chief Ishimura stood poking away at a holographic map of the Nuevo Rio neighborhood holding the Block 9X base. The chief turned toward Dante.

"Good timing, Shale." Ishimura gestured toward the ASF troops around him. "These are the main tactical team leaders. We were getting ready to fly out and rendezvous with the Nuevo Rio teams. Any last-minute intel you care to share with us? We don't want to run into any surprises in there."

Dante's gaze flicked around the room. While everyone wore armor and carried batons or stun poles, half the gathered forces carried holstered pistols or rifles strapped over their shoulders. Most squads contained at least a single officer with a pulsecore carbine. Plenty of EMP grenades and more than a few plasma grenades were on display.

"You're using firearms and explosives?" Dante asked. "Isn't that...a huge-ass deal?"

"I've called in favors to get special dispensation because we're dealing with a heavily armed terrorist group that is only surface-level operating as a mercenary company," Ishimura explained. "We have a reasonable expectation they will engage us with heavy weapons. Nobody's happy about this, but they have to be practical about this as well. Criminals would have long taken over the Stations if we could never fight back."

Dante shrugged. "I'm not judging. Block 9X is vicious. I'm glad you're taking them seriously."

"Standing orders from the top insist we don't engage with firearms unless we have no choice. Recon of the facility suggests we can engage, if necessary, with minimal risk of collateral or dome damage. Block 9X made this more convenient that way."

The chief nodded at the rookie and motioned to a weapons rack holding assault rifles. "Feel free to grab a rifle and ammo. You don't fire anything until I give permission, Shale. If you do, you're going to prison. Half of my contacts are happy you're coming along. The other half think it's a terrible mistake."

Dante gestured at the rack. "You're going to need those guns. These people have used everything from pulsecores to explosives on Station in casual encounters. They have combat-augmented cyborgs they call Irondogs and armed gunships. They've demonstrated zero concern about collateral damage when using those weapons. Their bloodbath at the club was restrained compared to what they're capable of."

"Duly noted." Ishimura rubbed his chin, but a slight scowl darkened his face. "We knew most of that information from recent incidents. Your confirmation makes me believe I won't have to resign for overreacting once this is all over."

"I don't think that'll happen unless there's no one there."

Ishimura shook his head. "We have eyes on the base. We've spotted mercs entering. None leaving."

"They get wind of the raid?"

"Block 9X doesn't appear to be in a panic. We believe it's the standard flow of personnel. They run now, and we can track them." Ishimura pointed at a large ASF gunship parked in the center of the hangar. "Shale with me. Everyone else to your teams. We have mercenaries to arrest."

The ASF troops threw their fists into the air and uttered a resounding cry of, "*Pax sequitur ordinem.*"

Dante held onto his reservations about how the ASF often supported the power structures of the Stations more than the common citizen. He couldn't fault the brave men and women gathered in the room who wanted nothing more than to take down a dangerous group of brutal mercenaries who'd been operating unchecked. He was glad he'd trusted his instincts and approached the chief for an alliance.

Ishimura strode away from the group, heading toward a larger command gunship parked in the center of the hangar. Twin turrets threatened from the bottom. Extra antennae and sensor dishes lay on the top. This was a complete electronic warfare package in one modestly sized aircraft.

Dante followed Ishimura across the hangar and up the folded stair-ladder leading into the cockpit of the command gunship. Troops jogged across the hangar, gathering weapons and ammo before loading into the backs of shuttles. Techs ran around performing last-minute inspections of the vehicles.

The earlier distaste of the encounter with Hyde had faded. He had his team problems, but the full might of the ASF was flexing at his direction. They would work together to take down one of the Omega Syndrome's deadliest forces.

Dante slipped on his helmet to make his grin harder to spot. Fame brought its privileges. Ishimura wouldn't have listened to any random Plunderer. Being the best damned Marauder ever had earned Dante an instant army to throw against Block 9X.

Ishimura sat next to the pilot and gestured for Dante to sit behind him. "I'm staking my entire reputation on you being right, Shale. As I noted, we've confirmed Block 9X is still present at the base, but if there's nothing more than a skeleton force, we might not have a chance to pull off another operation like this. The inflow points away from that, including at least four men with obvious combat augmentations, your Irondogs, but they've done a good job of shielding the exterior. We've got nothing on the total force disposition inside."

"You don't have to worry about them running." Dante shook his head. "Those assholes thought they could come Dirtside and kidnap who they want. They don't think anything about using explosives on Station. They're not afraid. I think even if they knew you were coming, they might not care." He shrugged. "After all, they have every reason to believe they're above the law."

Ishimura snorted. "Today we prove that no one is above the

law on the Stations." He reached over to the gunship's control panel and a switch. "This is Chief Ishimura to the task force. We'll now be rendezvousing with the second group of Nuevo Rio forces. Their first group will establish the initial cordon around the Block 9X base shortly before our arrival.

"Remember your briefings. We expect extreme resistance. Standing orders still apply. Firearms and explosives will not be used without the explicit permission of either myself or your tac team leader. Good luck and Godspeed. We will bring order back to the Stations."

Dante frowned as they approached the perimeter of the hidden Block 9X base. Nuevo Rio security forces stood scattered about in a haphazard manner. There were no local support gunships and only a handful of vehicles. Their favored shields and stun poles were more appropriate to breaking a riot than raiding a heavily armed merc base. He didn't spot a single rifle among the Nuevo Rio SF teams.

"All gunships, follow your standard patrol and containment paths after deploying your squads," Ishimura ordered while glancing between the console readouts and out the windshield. "Nuevo Rio command, please confirm your status." He nodded. Dante wasn't privy to the comms response. "Roger that. Be prepared to initiate operation based on the next transmission. Our tactical adviser, Mr. Dante Shale, will announce it."

Dante's brow lifted. He'd not heard he would be on active comms with the teams. "I'm ready. Are your people?"

Ishimura frowned. "We can't access cameras throughout most of the block. No Block 9X gunships. No cyborgs are coming out to probe our cordon. It's almost too easy. We have to assume they'll make a big push once we head inside."

"It might be more arrogance," Dante suggested. "They're not

afraid because they don't think they can lose in their territory. They think they have total control of this situation. Once you take down their front ranks, that might break their morale. Be aware their ops leader and company commander are ruthless sons of bitches."

"As expected, but we've brought a huge force. Call me arrogant if you want, but I'm confident we can win." Ishimura nodded at the windshield. "Whenever you're ready."

Dante cracked his knuckles. This was it, the end of Block 9X.

"All teams, go, go, *go!*"

CHAPTER FOURTEEN

Nasreen threw an elbow into the chest of a snarling ASF officer. The man grunted and stumbled back. Two red-faced drunks tackled him. The officer knocked a man off with his shock baton before jabbing at the other man.

"Screw you!" the drunk screamed. "I just wanted to watch the race."

Taking advantage of the officer's distraction, Nasreen ran away, trying to maneuver through the chaotic brawl between the ASF and the half of the crowd who weren't going down quietly. Although unarmed, their sheer numbers made it difficult for the ASF to gain control.

The officers had miscalculated, not taking into account the cramped, uneven shape of the main race viewing area. That made it difficult for them to reinforce their riot-control squads.

The ASF forces operated with overlocking shields and stun poles, as they had at the club incident. Unlike at the club, their formation had too many gaps, a product of the tight quarters and abundance of exits. A squad would advance and jab out their stun poles, sending a group to the ground only for people to rush their flanks and force them to lock their shields into a defensive circle as the angry crowd rained feeble blows against them.

Nasreen kept close to a wall, trying her best to retrace the general path Tether had followed when she brought them to the races. An exit was nearby, but so was the ASF. An officer ran her way, armed with a shock baton. His helmet was scratched up and crooked.

"On the ground!" he bellowed.

She didn't understand why he'd thought that would work. She must not have looked as drunk or crazed as the angry fans.

Nasreen ducked his swing and punched him, knocking his helmet off. He stumbled backward as it rolled along the ground. Tether rushed up behind him and smashed him over the head with a shock baton, sending him to the ground in a heap as she whipped out a knife from her pocket with her free hand.

"No!" Nasreen shouted, waving her hands. "No killing!"

"This is the enemy's doing," Tether insisted, gritting her teeth. "The timing is too perfect. They sent them here because they knew we would be here. This man is a pawn."

The anger in her voice and eyes was palpable. It cut through the din around them. That didn't make it reasonable.

"A pawn we can free," Nasreen countered. Firewall's penchant for stabbing people in confusing situations was getting annoying. "That's assuming you're right."

"Are you saying you don't believe the enemy sent them?"

"Even if they did send them, the ASF isn't Block 9X," Nasreen replied. "Don't get so wrapped up in your war that you assume everyone's the enemy. Don't make the same mistakes you did when first dealing with Dante and me."

Tether glanced between the fallen officer and Nasreen before sucking in a breath and dropping the knife back into her pocket. The short exchange had given reinforcements time to arrive.

Lock shouted and smashed an officer into the wall with his shoulder. Three quick throat punches sent the ASF enforcer to the ground, leaving his stun pole free for Lock. Nasreen hadn't realized he was that close.

"Are you sure?" he asked Nasreen, jabbing at an officer with the stun pole.

The officer twitched before collapsing to the ground. Killing ASF would end any alliance Dante might have been in the process of establishing. Nasreen would need to be careful. She believed everything she'd said. The ends didn't always justify the means.

"They're not trying to kill us, so we have no reason to try to kill them," she replied. "It's as simple as that."

Lock nodded. This time he swung the pole wide, smacking an officer across the neck and downing him. "We'll follow your lead."

Another officer jogged behind Tether with a shock baton. Nasreen snapped up her arm and launched a dart. Her dart hit the small part of his exposed neck. He stumbled, dropped his weapon, and fell to his knees.

"We have to stop meeting like this!" Tether shouted with a grin.

Nasreen didn't find this whole affair nearly as delightful. She hadn't planned to run from security forces and talk people out of murder that day.

"At this point, I'm starting to think you're bad luck." Nasreen ran over and grabbed the shock baton. She was running low on darts. "Every time you're involved, someone tries to capture me."

She blocked an ASF shock baton before sidestepping and cracking hers against the officer's shoulder. He groaned and fell to one knee. Their armor could only do so much against the weapon's charge. Her next strike across the face sent him to the ground unconscious and twitching.

The scream of the bikes had receded into the distance. The riders had fled deeper into the tunnels.

Chaos reigned all around her. Shouts and cries of pain filled the air. The passion of the race fans and numerical advantage kept them from being quickly overwhelmed. Still, the ASF discipline paid dividends, with the officers stunning and disabling fans so quickly that a carpet of moaning and twitching men and women soon covered the floor.

Nasreen burst through a doorway into a side tunnel. One more turn should take them back to a main tunnel. Sullen-looking men and women knelt on the ground with their arms behind their backs and bound.

"Drop your weapons!" an ASF officer shouted from behind a riot shield. His squad marched down the tunnel, blocking most of it.

A group of young men wearing brightly colored jackets charged from a side tunnel with knives and batons in hand. Nasreen wasn't sure if they were a gang or frustrated fans. The lines blurred in a place like this. Their leader wore a bright purple jacket, which looked ridiculous. His carbon-fiber blade was less so.

The jacket brigade slashed and stabbed at the shields. Stun pole tips jammed into them, dropping them one by one.

Tether and Lock took advantage of the confusion to flee into a different side tunnel. Nasreen followed them, now lost since they'd deviated far from their original course. Their next turn took them right into a pair of officers with shock batons.

Lock lunged with his stolen stun pole like he'd been born to the weapon. He jabbed at a charging officer, hitting him in the chest. The officer stumbled back, his armor insulating him from the worst of the pole's effects but still leaving him staggered.

"We need to keep moving," Lock shouted, motioning Nasreen and Tether forward and waving his pole around to disperse the scowling thugs.

The three ran forward, passing into a wider chamber. Pockets of weeping, bound people filled the corners of the room. Police stun pole squads had circled up here, thrusting and jabbing at the crazed men and women throwing themselves against their shields and screaming obscenities. The brawl continued with no sign of slowing down.

Nasreen wasn't above taking advantage of the rage of drunk and drug-addled race fans unwilling to accept arrest over their pastime. Firewall might have planned for this scenario, too. She didn't believe the Omega Syndrome had sent the police. Still, she could easily imagine the ruthless Firewall depending on the use of the crowd as a shield when escaping the authorities.

They made it through a door to an area fed from several smaller tunnels. Fleeing fans choked the area. Dark armor and uniforms pushed into the crowd, herding them together. Nasreen had never thought much about the size of the Atlantica Security Force. They surrounded the group, pushing in with relentless determination.

Taking advantage of the ASF's focus on the larger group, Lock grabbed a riot shield and sprinted toward an open side door. Nasreen and Tether hurried after him.

A pack of scavs with knives screeched and rushed out of the corner swinging at anyone nearby, interested only in spilling blood and not caring whose. Three quick shots from Nasreen put them all down before she reloaded her launcher. Two ASF officers turned a corner, revealing the reason for the scavs' flight into the room.

Lock charged toward the officers with the shield and pole in front of him. He smashed through the formation in the hallway, shoving officers to the side. Nasreen and Tether surged forward, swinging away with their batons to stun the officers. They only needed a few seconds to pass them.

"A group's getting away that way," came a shout from behind.

Nasreen didn't look back. She pumped her legs, doing her best to keep up with Lock's and Tether's impressive flat-out sprinting speed.

The trio continued down a narrow hallway that led to

another intersection. Loud yelling ahead proved they'd not escaped the authorities. She depended on Lock's knowledge of the tunnels and passages to get them out. Despite their constant changes, there was no desperation or fear on his face, only determination.

Shouting ASF officers chased them, shaking their batons. One woman reached down for a grenade. Nasreen couldn't tell what type it was at a distance, most likely aerosol.

Nasreen glanced to the side as she passed through a doorway. They were deep enough into the sublevels that she spotted an old-fashioned emergency fire suppression door release box. She smashed the glass around it and flipped the switch, praying it would work.

The ASF officer hurled her grenade. With a groan, a thick but corroded secondary door slid down to block the doorway. The grenade *thudded* against the door. Nasreen made out a muffled *hiss*. She'd been right, aerosol.

"Shit!" came the muffled shout. "*Gas, gas, gas!*"

Lock glanced over his shoulder. "Good move and fast thinking." He tossed the riot shield to the ground. "We're almost free." He wiped the sweat from his forehead. "It feels like half of the ASF is here."

After drawing a deep breath, he burst away, sprinting through the new hallway. Tether and Nasreen pumped their legs, breathing hard while sweat poured down their faces. The shouts had grown far more distant and muffled. Their escape crystallized into reality with each passing moment.

Lock ran around the corner through another doorway, disappearing for a brief moment. "Don't come!"

His warning arrived too late. Tether and Nasreen skidded to a halt around the corner. They'd stepped into what appeared to have once been a garage. A large contingent of baton-armed ASF officers waited for them. Two officers on the flanks held snap guns and kept them pointed at the new arrivals.

"Drop your weapons and put your hands above your head!" bellowed an officer. "You're under arrest."

Nasreen spotted a touch of red out of the corner of her eye. "On the count of three, go through the door," she whispered, holding three fingers behind her back.

"I won't repeat myself," shouted the officer. "Any further resistance will be treated as obstruction of justice and felonious assault upon Station security. You may also be charged with terrorism and general offenses to public safety and order."

Nasreen folded back one finger. "There's been a misunderstanding. We're not criminals."

"Then drop your weapons! Threatening Station security is illegal."

She turned toward Lock and winked. "Get ready for another good move."

He frowned and edged toward the door. Tether matched his movement.

"I'm going to count to five," the officer explained. "One, two, three…"

Nasreen pulled back her last finger. Lock and Tether darted through the door. She didn't go through, instead spinning and smashing open an emergency door release. The door collapsed with a loud groan in time to deflect two snap gun rounds and absorb their crackling buzz.

The remaining authorities all turned toward Nasreen. She tossed the shock baton to the ground and yanked off her dart gun.

Lock banged on the door. "You can't do this."

Nasreen dropped to her knees and put her hands behind her head.

"There's no easy way to get those back up on this side. Get out of here. I'll get this figured out. You can't get caught. You don't exist. They'll figure that out right awa—"

"Nasreen!" Lock shouted.

The ASF swarmed her. They shoved her face against the cold metal floor and kicked away the baton and dart launcher. A man put a knee in her back as he pulled out restraints.

"You're not figuring out anything, bitch. You're under arrest."

Nasreen's cheek throbbed. Her shoulder and back didn't feel much better. She still offered her best charming smile, the product of countless hours of practice when she was a freelance spy. Every part of her body could be on fire, and she could produce that smile on command.

Everyone liked a smile, even hateful people. The expression disarmed others, put them at ease, and made them more suggestible. It was then a simple matter of pushing them the right way to get what she needed.

She'd been taken from a long line of prisoners unloaded and marched into the back of a local station for processing. They'd taken a DNA sample and retinal scan to confirm her identity before shoving her into a seat in front of a bored-looking middle-aged sergeant scanning through the projected display and glancing between the file holograph of her and the real woman.

His brow lifted and he frowned. "Wait, a second. Nasreen Joelle. I know that name. It couldn't be. You aren't here. I mean you have that name, but I'm saying you're not *the* Nasreen Joelle. You couldn't possibly be."

She fluttered her eyelashes. "I'm the one who was working with Dante Shale. I'm the one and only. I helped him in his campaign against SSS, and if I'm being honest, I was the one responsible for framing the PR campaign."

"You're the woman who helped take down Cormac Slaine and gut o- and t-harvesting." The sergeant looked her up and down and scoffed. "And now you're hanging out with trash at illegal races? Talk about how the mighty have fallen. You fell so far you hit Dirtside."

"I was there as part of a job." Nasreen was amused that she was speaking the truth. "I wasn't there to bet on illegal races. It's all been a big misunderstanding. I tried to explain it to your associates, but they were rather aggressive at the time." She shrugged. "I don't blame them, given the situation, but it did make things more complicated than they needed to be."

"Being a Plunderer doesn't mean you get to ignore Station law just because you feel like it." The sergeant frowned at her. "Just because you did something good in the past doesn't mean you can do whatever you want in the future. I think you better get that through your pretty little head right now."

"I know that, and that's not what I'm saying." She winked. "I'm glad you find me pretty."

"If this is the part where you ask me to let you go, that's not going to happen." The sergeant gestured at his sphere on his desk. "You've been processed, which means without someone way more important than me saying so, you're not going anywhere until you make your way through the system.

"I appreciate you doing what you did against SSS, but I'm not losing my job because you're a gambling addict. Those races are dangerous. People get killed. No responsible person should support them."

"I understand." Nasreen nodded. "I would never ask that. But there's nothing in the rules against passing information along, is there?"

"You watch too many movies," the sergeant replied. "You don't have a right to guaranteed contact with anyone but your lawyer, and we can hold you for a while before we have to let you speak with one."

Justice had always been a secondary concern in the Stations. Living in space meant the cost of disorder could spiral out of control. Order, first and foremost, trumped most rights and liberty. That fed into why the corrupt elite could get away with so much. Their crimes ate away at the soul of society without producing as much obvious immediate disorder.

Nasreen leaned forward and tilted her head, injecting a tad more coquettishness into her smile. The pain in her cheek made it hard. "I don't want to contact a lawyer. It's just I happen to know that Dante Shale is meeting Chief Ishimura today.

"Again, to be clear, I'm not asking you to let me go." She stuck her bottom lip out. "You can tell I've gotten in trouble in a big way that I didn't expect. All I'm asking is if you can pass a message to Ishimura's office that I'm in holding. Then he can choose whether he wants to pass that along to Dante. The chief isn't the type of man I suspect who'll ignore legitimate crime he feels undermines the public order."

The sergeant glanced between his display and Nasreen. He sighed. "I suppose that won't hurt. You might be waiting a while. You're right. The chief's out in the middle of something big. Taking down illegal racing isn't the only thing we do."

"I can wait." Nasreen smiled. "Thank you."

CHAPTER FIFTEEN

"Roger that." Ishimura hopped out of the side of the command gunship. "Understood. Shale, you're with me."

Dante jumped out and kept a tight grip on the baton, surveying the gathered security forces. Officers followed Ishimura's advance with looks of concern and even pity. Two men exchanged whispers. One shook his head.

Something was wrong. He'd expected Block 9X not to make a big show of resistance until they breached the compound. ASF and NRSF officers had swarmed the building without a single shot or a man jumping at someone with a razorfist.

There was no way Block 9X would give up that easily. They'd been willing to take on the ASF outside the club. It made no sense they'd surrender at their base without putting up at least token resistance.

The men and women around him didn't display the energetic cocky triumph that should have accompanied a major victory against a dangerous mercenary outfit involved in illegal activities. They all looked defeated.

A sergeant held a young officer, who was bent over vomiting

into a helmet. Others were pale and noticeably not looking away from the base.

Other than the ASF and NRSF officers' expressions and weird behavior, nothing looked wrong. They all had untouched armor and weapons. A single Irondog should have forced a major battle with even a well-equipped tactical squad.

For now, all Dante could do was listen to Ishimura's side of the radio conversations. The majority over the last several minutes had ended with rote confirmation of receipt or request for confirmation. Each new message left him looking more and more confused. Dante's curiosity got the better of him as they proceeded down a hallway leading into the front of the Block 9X base.

"What's going on? They give up?"

"That's unclear," Ishimura replied. "We've had zero active resistance. I'll put it that way." Something heavy strained his tone.

"They ran. Your people spun themselves up for a big fight, and now the adrenaline is wearing off, and they're disappointed." Dante grunted.

"Damn it. Block 9X saw this coming after all. Don't feel too bad, Chief. It's hard to mobilize this many troops without somebody finding out. It was a good plan. There's no way that many mercs disappeared. We just have to find them."

Ishimura gave him a cold look. "That's not necessary because they didn't run. Not in the way you're talking about, although they might have caught wind of this raid and that set in motion… certain results."

He stepped around a corner and flared his nostrils. "They definitely didn't run. This is…" He shook his head. "Strange. You'll see soon enough. We both will."

Dante turned the corner. Grim-faced ASF and NRSF officers lined the hallway with their weapons stowed. One man clasped his hands together and prayed quietly.

"What the hell happened here?" Dante's eyes widened. He now understood the prayers.

The mangled bodies of Block 9Xers littered the hallway. Blood coated the walls and floor, leaving few spots untouched.

The mercenaries hadn't suffered clean deaths. Throats were ripped open. Men had limbs torn off and heads and backs bent in unnatural ways. Abject terror showed in their frozen expressions.

Other injuries were different but no less obvious. A man had a hole punched clean through his chest with his heart missing. Another man had been decapitated with a blood-stained carbon blade now sticking through his body.

Dante couldn't even tell how many men had died. There were too many bodies in too many pieces.

"What the hell did your people do, Ishimura?" He shook with anger. "This is sick. This is over the line."

As the words left his mouth, Dante grasped the security forces hadn't massacred the mercenaries. Too many of the injuries would have required excessive strength to pull off. That pointed to one likely class of culprits, one not represented among the ASF or NRSF.

Ishimura shook his head. "My people couldn't do this even if they wanted to." He shuddered and looked away from a tangle of bodies. "You're right. This is evil and sadistic. This is Dirtwalker garbage. I'm only subjecting myself to it because my men have been forced to see it. They deserve a leader who will suffer along with them."

"I could have done without the suffering," Dante admitted.

"I knew describing wouldn't be enough."

"No, it's not. Even for someone who's seen as much death as I have."

They continued through the hallways. More mangled bodies lay all over the floors of both the main hallways and side rooms. The deeper the pair moved, the more they found.

There was evidence of a less one-sided struggle, including chipped blades and razorfists. Discarded rifles lay next to those broken in half. Bullet holes marred the walls. Blood painted small piles of shell casings. A blackened hole through a partially collapsed wall was from a pulsecore carbine, but the weapon itself wasn't nearby.

"No, Ishimura." Dante surveyed the carnage. He connected his baton to his belt. The weapon was useless now. Everyone was dead. "You've got this all wrong."

"How so?" Ishimura asked. "This is one of the cruelest murder sites I've ever seen in my entire time in the ASF."

Dante shook his head. "You're right about this being evil, wrong how you described it as Dirtwalker garbage." He looked the chief in the eyes. "I've fought cannibal Dirtwalkers, and this isn't something even they would do. This is like walking into a rabid Nightmutt feeding pit."

"Agreed. Whatever did this isn't human in any sense of the word."

The horror show continued as Dante and Ishimura proceeded deeper into the facility. Destroyed bodies lay everywhere, bent and broken in every conceivable way. Dante had half-convinced himself someone had smuggled a pack of vicious Nightmutts into the Station except for the fact that whatever had killed all these men hadn't torn away any flesh with fangs or teeth. The victims were butchered as a threat, not for food.

Two pale ASF officers stood on either side of a door to the hangar. They nodded at the approaching chief.

"Sir," one officer greeted. His hands shook. "We've not touched anything."

"Open it up," Ishimura ordered. "You don't have to follow us inside."

"Thank you very much, sir."

The officer turned and opened the door. Dante followed Ishimura in. Bile rose in the back of his throat, and his stomach churned. A life of violence didn't always prepare a man for everything he might see.

No matter how much death and destruction a Marauder might have witnessed, there were always new frontiers in cruelty and mayhem. Bullets and pulsecores tore the body apart in brutal ways. They were a mercy compared to what he saw in front of him.

Untouched except for blood splatters, the shuttles and gunships sat in neat rows with no evidence anyone had tried to fly them out. That was normal enough, although the banal contrast with the *de facto* morgue around them heightened the impact of all the bodies present. Even the fields of dead mercenaries didn't shock Dante anymore.

The carnage of those men and women, including the victims on the way in, hadn't prepared him for what remained of the Irondogs, his main suspect for the killings. Cyborg strength was the only way to explain what they'd seen, but they hadn't survived either. Blood and dark fluids mixed beneath the heap of torn remnants of what had once been powerful bodies.

The cyborgs had been torn to pieces, sliced or crushed, depending on equipment nearby. Many were strewn in so many separate pieces that it would take a puzzle master to put their bodies back together. An Irondog had dozens of sharp punctures in its body. Its nearby head was a crushed and unrecognizable mess.

Dante knelt next to a body missing a leg and an arm. A trail of drying blood and blue fluid lay behind it, suggesting it had crawled to its current position.

That didn't bother him. What bothered him was it had pushed its metal fingers through the brain of another Irondog before dying. The man's last living action was to murder his ally.

Ishimura stared at a cyborg beneath him, his dark eyes smoldering with barely concealed fury. This Irondog's hand lay atop his chest with his artificial heart power unit resting in his palm.

"He tore himself apart," he whispered. "He reached into his chest and tore out his own heart." He gagged and looked away. "Ancient samurai who dishonored themselves committed seppuku by slicing open their stomachs, but the bravery was the point, not the suffering. Assistants were ready to decapitate them after they'd proven themselves with the first cuts. But this…"

He motioned around the room. "Turning on their allies to tear them apart then killing themselves. You're right. These are like rabid animals who have lost control."

Dante stood and drew a couple of deep breaths. "Yeah. Based on the bodies we've seen, the Irondogs turned on the normal troops first, the ones at the perimeter. They looked like they barely had time to react. Some must have warned the others, who managed to scrape together their guns and blades."

He flared his nostrils. "It wasn't enough. After killing the rest of the mercs, the Irondogs turned on each other. Whoever was leftover finished themselves off. Like that guy." He gestured at the Irondog near Ishimura and another who'd torn off his arm to stab it through his head.

"They all went berserk together. Otherwise, I think we'd see missing shuttles or gunships." He pointed at bullet dents and holes among the dead cyborgs. "If anyone had seen it coming from the beginning, they might have had a better chance. Or at least they would have had a better chance to run."

He gestured at a half-burned cyborg lying near the wall. "Someone got him with a plasma grenade or a pulsecore."

Ishimura glared at Dante. "To be honest, you don't seem surprised. It's almost as if you expected to find something like this."

That wasn't right. Dante was disgusted and surprised. What he couldn't hide from his eyes was how this entire incident was a shocking confirmation of every warning they'd received from Firewall about the Omega Syndrome's capabilities.

He'd thought Block 9X was arrogant. Instead, he'd been the

arrogant one not believing the enemy would ever go so far as to treat living human beings like nothing more than disposable tools to be discarded when they were no longer useful.

"I didn't expect this," Dante replied. "I'm the one who warned you about all this. You think I'd want to come with you to see all this crap? I already need a drink."

Ishimura stepped over a mangled set of metal legs. "In my entire time working for the ASF, I've never, ever seen anything like this, and I was the man who helped bring down the Grav Line Slasher. He was genteel compared to what happened here."

Dante acknowledged the statement with a shallow nod. The Omega Syndrome didn't care who or what it killed, even its servants. He turned his head and grimaced when he spotted two corpses near a gunship. There was enough left of DeFrieze and Sheer that he could at least recognize their bodies.

"I can't tell you what you want to know," Dante offered. "It's dangerous." He motioned around the room. "This is the proof of how dangerous it is."

"I'm through playing games, Shale," Ishimura shouted. He flung his arm in a wide arc. "This was a damned massacre aboard a Station, not Dirtside. They might have been mercenary scum, but they didn't deserve to die like this, and I can look at you and know that you have the answers. And…one second."

He put his finger to his ear. "Yes. What? Are you sure? Thanks. Separate her from the other prisoners."

He glared at Dante. "Now your associate Nasreen Joelle was picked up at an illegal underground bike race. You care to explain yourself? For a man concerned about mercenaries and criminal conspiracies, I would think you'd keep your people under closer control. The timing is suspicious."

Everyone believed in good luck, but few people believed in bad luck. Dante scrubbed a hand down his face. Everything was spiraling out of control. He couldn't make any moves without first coordinating with Nasreen. Her being arrested only made that more complicated.

"I can explain, but only if I have a chance to speak with Nasreen," he said. "That's the only way I can guarantee you can get the full picture while keeping everything safe for you."

"You're trying to bargain with me?" Ishimura snorted. "I can arrest you right now for obstruction of justice, Shale. You're not Dirtside now. You can't claim I don't have jurisdiction. This is a joint operation between the ASF and the NRSF. They'll be more than happy to let me drag your body back to Atlantica Central Station. I doubt they want to deal with the hassle of sticking Dante Shale in jail."

Dante held his hands in front of him and tried to keep a calm tone. "I'm not trying to mess with you, Chief. The situation's complicated. Way more complicated than you realize."

"An entire mercenary company slaughtered themselves," Ishimura replied. "That goes beyond complicated. It's evil."

"Yeah." Dante nodded. "I'd agree it's evil."

"Here's what's going to happen, Shale. You and your entire team are coming to ASF HQ. You're going to contact them right now and inform them that I'm sending people for them. If they resist, we will use whatever force is necessary to take them down."

He shuddered at a bent Irondog at his feet. "Especially the cyborgs. I'm not letting any other berserk cyborgs butcher people today."

"It's fine. I'll contact my team and tell them to stand down."

"Good. You can come along to make sure they play nicely." Ishimura waved for his men to enter. "Because I'm going to get answers, or you're all going to be locked up for a long time until you decide to give me those answers."

Shall I take emergency measures, sir? Midas asked.

"No," Dante whispered. "We're going to contact the team and

tell them exactly what Ishimura said. The last thing we need is more trouble with the security forces."

Dante began to doubt the usefulness of powerful allies.

CHAPTER SIXTEEN

The apprentices, Hyde, and Ambrose all waited in the open hangar, out of their armor and not armed with weapons as the ASF gunship carrying Dante and Ishimura set down. Dante was relieved. He'd worried Hyde might mount a defiant resistance rather than surrender to the authorities.

He wasn't sure if he'd screwed up by not telling Ishimura everything he wanted to know. Talking about the Omega Syndrome in public in the middle of a charnel house created by the enemy's corruption was too risky. He couldn't be sure if the officers with implants might have turned their weapons on him. Now that had left him on the wrong side of the ASF and the team in a worse position than before he'd talked to Chief Ishimura.

Tactical teams holding stun poles surrounded the hangar. An officer holding a grenade launcher caught Dante's eye. The man had a row of EMP grenades on his belt. Firewall might have developed their methods for dealing with technology, but it wasn't as if there weren't existing cruder tools available. After what they'd found in Nuevo Rio, they were ready for any powerful, out-of-control cyborg.

No weapon, no matter how powerful, lacked a counter.

Hyde's original body had been based around technology less sensitive to anti-cyborg weapons partially out of that concern. His current body was far more sensitive to EMP and anti-electronic weapons.

Dante jogged toward his team. The first step to controlling the situation was to keep everyone calm on both sides. Nasreen had told him that. Once he had a chance to get Ishimura to calm down, he could reason with the chief and get their alliance back on track.

"Is everyone all right?" Dante asked.

"Ha-ha." Hyde threw his head back and cackled. "We're about to be arrested. You see, *Papi*? Joelle was right, and I was right. This blew up in your face faster than I thought it would. This is why you should never trust security forces. Think about all those years Slaine pulled crap, and Station security looked the other way."

"This is a precaution," Dante replied. "And we don't need anyone saying 'I told you so' right now. You have to understand what happened. The Block 9Xers were dead. All of them. From what I saw, it looked like the Irondogs had been forced to kill them, then forced to rip themselves apart."

Hyde's brow lifted. "Huh. Didn't see that coming."

Braelin wrinkled his nose. "Are you serious?"

"Do I look like I'm joking?" Dante asked. "Trust me. I've never seen anyone who has punched through his own head before."

"That's not fair." Hyde growled. "Those *pendejos* should have let me do it if they were going to do that anyway. Instead, I had to sit here and do nothing except wait for the security forces to come and arrest me. That's bullshit."

"That's also not the point." Dante frowned. "Pay attention to what I'm saying. The entire damned mercenary company was slaughtered down to the last man and woman. Nobody survived."

"No witnesses, no evidence," Jolo concluded.

Dante nodded. "Exactly."

Mugoi glanced at Hyde. "That's disconcerting, Captain."

Ishimura cleared his throat loudly behind him. "We're not here to discuss the raid, and you can leave the rest of the investigation to the ASF." He motioned his men forward. "Everyone's going to be restrained. If you resist, we will take appropriate measures to ensure your compliance. After the day I've had, I'm not taking anything for granted."

Hyde grinned. "You afraid of me? Good. You should be. I'm the scariest fucking cyborg anywhere."

Ishimura narrowed his eyes. "I'm cautious by nature, Mr. Curtidor, and your reputation precedes you. Today, I've seen enough cybernetic carnage to last me the rest of my life."

"I don't care. I'm just messing with you. Beating your guys up wouldn't be that much fun." Hyde put his hands behind his back. "Use whatever you want to keep me in check."

He nodded at Dante. "He said to cooperate, so I'm cooperating. That means he still believes in you. Once that stops, this will be a very different conversation. You better have way bigger guns then."

"I need a Class Two Restrainer for the big cyborg," Ishimura called while eying Hyde. "Make sure we have a dedicated squad on him until we get back to HQ."

Another ASF officer jogged over to the area, holding what appeared to be dark black cuffs. A team advanced on Hyde all holding up their stun poles while their comrade edged behind the hulking cyborg with a nervous look. The ASF officer drew a deep breath and closed the restraints around the snickering Hyde's wrists.

"I can still headbutt you," Hyde announced, still snickering. "It'd be easy to cave your skull in. Bones are weaker than my metal."

The ASF officer jumped backward and scrambled for the shock baton on his waist. The others jabbed forward, keeping the tips of the stun poles inches from Hyde.

"Hyde," Dante yelled. "Don't make this worse with your bullshit."

He couldn't bring himself to make one of his more colorful threats. Even thinking of them reminded him of the Block 9X base.

Hyde shrugged. "I didn't say I would cave his skull in, only that I could. Everyone shouldn't be so jumpy."

After a moment of hesitation, ASF officers swarmed the apprentices and a weary-looking Ambrose to slap on less impressive restraints. Dante noticed they'd used standard restraints on Mugoi. That was a mistake, but he didn't feel any reason to point it out. People always underestimated Mugoi because its metal body lacked Hyde's bulk, but the smaller cyborg was no less dangerous.

Ishimura grabbed a pair of restraints from a passing officer and headed toward Dante. "Put your hands behind your back, Shale. You're under arrest, too."

Dante grunted. "Is this necessary? If I was going to pull something, wouldn't I have done it on the way over? Or when I was alone with you in your office?"

"Yes, it is necessary until I know what's going on." Ishimura shook the restraints. "You were as shocked by what we saw as I was, but you're also hiding something."

"Sure." Dante shrugged. "I'm not the one screwing with the other guy."

Dante put his arms behind his back and his wrists together. He snorted when Ishimura secured the restraints and pushed him toward the back of an ASF prisoner transport shuttle docked right outside the hangar.

"You're making a mistake, Ishimura. You need my help."

The chief glared at him. "You refuse to tell me the truth. How am I supposed to trust a man who is holding out on me? Vague warnings aren't enough."

Sir, Midas chimed in. He restricted his communication to

Dante. *I understand this is a difficult time, but Firewall has transmitted a sample of the code they plan to use to disrupt the Omega Syndrome. Oddly enough, the message seems to indicate they anticipate you using me to help facilitate the transmission of this to a target node in the final attack on the Omega Syndrome.*

Firewall reports they are still adjusting settings and refining it but appear confident they will soon have something lethal to the Omega Syndrome. It might bolster our situational defenses should we be forced to confront the Omega Syndrome corruption before we can implement Firewall's final plan. I believe it can be a useful temporary weapon and enhance my existing anti-Syndrome abilities. I will start the process of compiling the code with your permission.

"Go ahead," Dante replied.

Ishimura frowned at him. "Go ahead?"

Dante hadn't realized he'd spoken aloud. He preferred to do that when dealing with Midas. It made things easier to process overall. As much as he'd gotten used to another intelligent being living in his head, he'd never liked the idea of mental communication.

"Go ahead and arrest us," Dante continued. "But it's a big mistake."

He didn't dare mention the code or Firewall, not when they were that close. While he didn't believe Ishimura was a tool of the Omega Syndrome, any hint that their ultimate weapon was close to being completed could doom the entire operation and allow the enemy to develop countermeasures prematurely. Dante was happy to sit in a cell for a few days if it meant defeating the Omega Syndrome.

"You've got to be kidding me."

Dante groaned loudly when the shock baton-wielding ASF guards marched the team into the large room devoid of anything but chairs secured to the floor. The stark gray and thick layer of dust pointed to its use as something else before being repurposed as an interrogation room. He didn't understand why the ASF would maintain a room large enough to fit a good-sized shuttle or two and put nothing in it. He doubted they needed to interrogate entire teams together all that often.

That's not what was bothering him.

The ASF had prepared chairs for each of them, including a huge, reinforced seat for Hyde. Nasreen was present, sitting in a chair, light bruising on the side of her face and a tear on the side of her shirt as if it were her perpetual lot to be battered.

Dante's cavalry would be less convincing after being arrested too. He'd need a new plan, or he'd have to rely on the most dangerous one, telling Ishimura the unvarnished truth.

Ishimura stepped into the room last, surveying the chairs with a cold frown. "I want the cyborgs shackled to the chairs." He patted his shock baton. "The others I can handle if they get out of line."

"Yes, sir," a guard answered.

Braelin looked at Dante for direction. He nodded at the apprentice. This wasn't the time to fight back. This wouldn't be like Firewall. The ASF wouldn't torture them and claim near divine justification.

A snickering Hyde stomped over to his chair like he was looking forward to being locked down. The whole encounter was nothing but a game to him, another way to exert and challenge others for dominance without fighting. Ambrose stared at the floor, sighing deeply.

With no one resisting, securing the entire team to the chairs with nanofilament-reinforced chains took only seconds. Even Hyde and Mugoi would struggle to free themselves in those conditions. Whatever plan Dante had clung to in the back of his mind at the hangar had fallen apart.

Ishimura motioned at the door. "Everyone else out."

A guard frowned. "Are you sure, sir?"

"What are they going to do? Break out of those restraints in the middle of HQ, kill me, and get away? If they could pull that off, they deserve their freedom." Ishimura frowned. "Besides, I have a feeling Shale might talk if he feels more comfortable. I can see it in his eyes."

There was nothing inherently wrong with that conclusion, but Dante was far from comfortable.

The Block 9X massacre portended more blood. They needed to move on the Omega Syndrome. At least Firewall had made progress, but their lack of operatives would make any major operations difficult.

The guard glared at Dante while patting his baton. With an incline of his head, he led the other guards out of the room and closed the door, locking it with a loud *click*. No one was getting in or out easily now.

Ishimura stood in front of the door. His dark gaze bored into Dante. "You're going to give me answers, real answers, not bull-shit half-answers. I'm tired of these games. I said it at the base, and I'll say it again. It's like you expected to find those bodies."

"You think I'm responsible for that?" Dante asked. "If I had that power, why would I let you take me in?"

"I don't think you did it, but I think you know who and how." Ishimura narrowed his eyes. "All my years of investigating crimes tell me that."

"We're not the enemy, Ishimura," Dante replied. "You've seen what the enemy is capable of. We're fighting that, and it's also why we've had to be careful, why I still have to be careful."

"So you were expecting the death." Ishimura stomped over to the seated Dante, leaning over him with one arm on his shoulder but keeping his head far enough away to avoid an easy headbutt.

"What we saw there?" Dante shook his head. "No, I wasn't expecting that exactly, but seeing the entire Block 9X butchered by their Irondogs and those same Irondogs having torn themselves apart is on par with what we know of the enemy capabilities."

Nasreen's eyes widened. "What? Is that what happened?"

Ishimura's gaze slid her way, and he backed away from Dante. "At least one of you has the decency to be shocked. Is it that you don't know all his secrets, Miss Joelle?"

He walked up and down the line of seats, stopping in front of the smirking Hyde. "Mr. Curtidor looks like he thinks this is a big joke, but what about the rest of you? Mr. Igento? Mr. Klement? Miss Neburu?

"Everything your boss said was true. Block 9X had been destroyed, murdered by their cybernetic operatives. Awful carnage. This is your chance to help me help you."

Braelin spat at Ishimura's feet. "I ain't saying nothing to you, asshole."

Ishimura smiled. "Oh?"

"That's not helping, Klement." Dante frowned at him. "We need him on our side."

"Oh. Sorry." Braelin offered a sheepish grin. "Sorry, Chief."

Ishimura walked over to Jolo. "There's no reason to go down for loyalty."

Jolo stared at Ishimura with a steely intensity that would have made Dante uneasy had it been directed at him. "I have nothing to say."

Ambrose sighed when Ishimura stood in front of him. This sigh lasted far longer than any of his recent others. "I'm just the pilot."

Hyde jumped in. "Hey, Ishimura, if whatever you saw made you piss yourself, then you should worry less about us and more about what did that." He nodded at Dante. "I told him before that asking you people for help was stupid. What did it get us?"

He rattled his restraints. "It got us here. You're wasting your time and getting more people killed, this time somebody other than merc and Reaper scum."

Ishimura frowned at him. "Forgive me for not trusting the character-evaluating abilities of a known murderer." His gaze flicked to Nasreen. "You made a point of having my people get hold of me. That must mean you have a better idea of how to handle this conversation."

"I trust and believe in Dante if that's what you're asking," Nasreen insisted. "And he insisted, Chief, that involving you with our operations was necessary and good for the Stations. This might have turned out this way, and I find his evidence not persuasive for that being a good idea. But he is a man I've learned to trust my life to, so I'll do it now. His instincts serve him well."

"I agree with her," Mugoi added. "I won't give you any information that he doesn't want you to have."

"I'm just the pilot," repeated Ambrose morosely.

"Too many damned lives," Hyde added. "He might not go by Hellcat in public anymore, but he kept the extra lives. You think you can win against that, Ishimura?"

The chief moved away from the chairs and back over to the door. "You keep saying I'm not your enemy, Shale. Friends and allies share information. Right now, the only thing you've done is urge me to go after Block 9X. Conveniently, the day I do that, Block 9X is all dead. You have to understand what this looks like from my perspective."

Dante sucked in a breath. Spending too much time dancing around the truth would end with them spending weeks locked up in the system. That made them easy targets for the Omega Syndrome.

He couldn't leave everything to Firewall. They might understand the technical requirements, but their tactical operations left something to be desired. He needed to make a hard choice.

Ishimura wasn't under Omega Syndrome control. That much was obvious. He wouldn't be acting the way he was if he'd been working for the enemy. Killing Dante at the Block 9X facility or while they were in close quarters on the gunship or transports would have been trivial. He could have covered it easily, or the Omega Syndrome could have killed the chief and tried to frame Dante.

There was only one way forward, trusting his instincts and hoping his extra lives applied to everyone.

"Do you have any augmentations or implants, Chief?" Dante asked.

Before getting Midas, Dante wouldn't have thought much about the question. He tended to assume the average person was like him. Midas' installation and his dealings with Nasreen and the orphanage changed that impression. He understood he'd been unusual in being an adult without implants before getting Midas. Implants and augmentations would define the future of humanity in space.

Ishimura frowned. "What business is that of yours?"

"Because it's about everything that's going on here." Dante's tone was serious. "And everything that happened at the Block 9X base."

Nasreen looked Dante's way. "Are you sure about this? Once you tell him, there's no going back."

Ishimura looked between the two with a frown. "I need to know the truth to protect this Station."

Hyde laughed. "Oh, this is going to go great. We'll be executed by the time this is over. I can't say I'm surprised. This was high on the list of ways I thought I might go out."

Braelin and Jolo exchanged confused looks. Mugoi rolled its shoulders, pulling against the restraints keeping it pinned to the chair. He narrowed his eyes on the chief.

Ishimura threw up his hand. "Shut up. Only one person needs to talk at a time. I'll ask questions, and you'll answer."

"Yes or no, Chief," Dante continued. "Do you have any implants? You have to answer my questions if you want me to answer yours."

"No. I don't have any implants." Ishimura shook his head. "I've always been healthy, and I've never liked the idea of anything that permanent, especially the brain interfaces." He glanced between Mugoi and Hyde. "The idea creeps me out. Are you saying that the Block 9X cyborgs all malfunctioned at the same time because of the implants?"

"It's close to something like that. I'm about to tell you a story. It's going to be hard to believe, but I swear to you that every word is the truth." He turned toward Nasreen. "We're out of time. I'm going to lay it all out for him."

Nasreen nodded. "I trust you. Do what you feel is appropriate."

Despite saying that, Dante wasn't going to mention Midas' work on the Firewall anti-Omega Syndrome code. He only needed to keep them from being locked up and win Ishimura back to his side.

"I'll decide what I believe." Ishimura folded his arms. "Go ahead. I've been with the ASF for a long time. Whatever you're about to say, I guarantee it won't be the craziest thing I've heard over my career."

Drawing on his preferred brevity, Dante laid out their first encounters with the Omega Syndrome as the Voices Dirtside when they finished off Slaine and their encounters with Firewall at the communications relay. To avoid complicating the situation, he left out the various kidnappings, only referencing stumbling across the resistance group and joining forces. Continuing, he finished with the most controversial reveal.

"We're not sure if the Omega Syndrome is a rogue AI or a program an asshole is using," Dante explained. "The more I've seen of it, the more I'm convinced it is an AI. The sheer callous brutality we've witnessed goes well beyond ruthless asshole rich guys trying to control things. Even if it's not a rogue AI, it's out there infecting systems, and almost no one's trying to stop it because almost no one understands it's out there."

Ishimura stared at Dante. "I stand corrected."

"About?"

"That is the craziest thing I've heard over my career." Ishimura scoffed. "You expect me to believe there's a corrupting virus out there, infiltrating people's implants? What's worse, you're saying it might be an old rogue AI that somehow did all this without being noticed for years."

"Yeah, I am." Dante shrugged. "Because it's the truth."

"Let me get this straight. You expect me to believe your ghost program is out there secretly pulling the strings of human society but also that you and a small resistance group are the only ones opposing it? Doesn't that sound rather convenient? You're the brave hero at the center of humanity's valiant last stand, fighting a war in the shadows. The rest of the authorities are all the tools of the evil AI."

Dante scoffed. "Convenient? The Omega Syndrome's trying to get me killed. It's messing with my work and friends Dirtside. None of this crap is convenient. I'd much rather security forces kept assholes like Slaine and threats like the Omega Syndrome in check so I didn't have to worry about them."

"There might be other people opposing it," Nasreen offered. "But anyone aware of it has to be careful, as we have, which limits cooperation. Half of the Stations could be standing up to the Omega Syndrome yet believe they are fighting alone. That's the difficulty that comes with its fundamental nature. Too many of us have made it too easy for it."

Ishimura walked away from Dante and stopped in front of Braelin. "What about you? Do you believe this crap, or do you think your boss is crazy?"

Braelin shrugged and chuckled. "The first part, yeah, not the crazy part, at least not most of the time."

After a moment of consideration, the ASF chief stopped

before Ambrose. "What about you, Mr. Igento? You've been the quietest of all of them. If you have something to share, now is the time to do it."

Ambrose lifted his head. His face was a mask of defeat. "I only wanted to do the right thing. That's new for me, but it's true."

Ishimura frowned. "Do you believe in this Omega Syndrome nonsense or not?"

"It doesn't matter." Ambrose dropped his head. "Nothing matters now. I fucked up."

Ishimura eyed Ambrose for a moment longer before rolling his eyes. "You have an interesting and loyal crew, Shale."

"Is this all that much of a stretch from what you asked me?" Dante asked. "You saw what I saw with your own two eyes. The Block 9X cyborgs butchered their own men. It's easy enough to write that off as them being paid off, but how else do you explain them tearing themselves apart?

"One guy, sure, he might have lost it. But all of them at the same time? The Omega Syndrome is real. You've seen what it can do when it wants to cover its tracks. The more machines we have in us, the easier we are to make into puppets."

Ishimura's eyes widened. He stumbled backward as a shudder ran through his body. "You don't work Station security as long as I have without seeing awful things, and what I saw in Nuevo Rio is about the worst and most inexplicable thing I've ever seen."

He scrubbed a hand down his face. "Part of me is screaming to call you a liar or nut job, lock you up, and tell them you need a psych adjustment. That'd be easier because I wouldn't have to believe anything you're saying. I wouldn't have to *act* on what you're saying."

Nasreen leaned forward. "What do your instincts trained by your years of service tell you? If we were to come up with a lie, wouldn't we pick something far less outlandish? I understand what you're going through because we all did the first time we heard the truth."

"I've run into too many strange loose ends these last few years, and this Omega Syndrome could explain them all. I've always felt like there was a common thread we were missing, something about the basic corruption at the top." Ishimura backed toward the door, his breathing ragged. "Accepting it as the truth is almost worse. How do we even begin to face something like that?"

"We're working on things with Firewall," Dante explained. "It's too dangerous to give you details at the moment. We can't risk the Omega Syndrome learning about it. The enemy is obviously on the move. Nuevo Rio proves it."

"I suppose that makes sense," Ishimura replied. "Then you're close to being able to beat this thing?"

"Yeah." Dante nodded.

Hyde growled and pulled at his hand and leg restraints. His chair shook with the effort.

Ishimura's hand dropped to his baton. "Mr. Curtidor, I'd advise you to stop."

"What the hell are you doing, Hyde?" barked Dante. "He's finally listening to us. This isn't time for your bullshit games."

Hyde grunted, threw his head back, and howled. He shook his head. "Damn it, *Papi*. We screwed up. It's in my head. It's trying to turn me into a damned puppet. Fuck that. I only kill who I want to kill."

"Midas," Dante shouted so loudly his chair shook. "Use the code, damn it. If the Omega Syndrome kills the chief, we're finished."

I'm not sure if it's rea—Midas began.

"Just do it! Anything!"

Ishimura jerked his head toward Dante. "Who's Midas?"

Hyde's eyes glowed red. He roared a bestial and bone-shaking sound. Nasreen shrank in her seat, pale and trembling.

Hyde's specialized restraints buzzed, and his body arched, his eyes rolling up in the back of his head. His roar grew louder. He continued pulling, and with a wrenching and cracking noise, the leg and arm restraints ripped apart and skidded across the floor.

"That's impossible." Ishimura backpedaled and slapped the door control. It wouldn't open. He yanked out his baton.

Hyde lurched toward him with uneven movements. He threw a metal fist at the chief. Ishimura lifted his baton to parry the blow. The cyborg's punch bent the baton and ripped it from the chief's hand. The damaged weapon twirled through the air and bounced off the wall.

Another wide swing missed Ishimura only because of the older man's surprising agility. He stumbled backward, wide-eyed.

"Hyde!" Dante shouted, tugging against the restraints and the chair. "Fight it, damn you! You're nothing but the Omega Syndrome's bitch right now."

Ishimura glanced at the door. Dante was also confused. Somebody had to be watching the interrogation from outside, yet they were letting a murderous cyborg attack their chief. They needed reinforcements with anti-cyborg gear.

"Release our restraints, Ishimura," Dante shouted. "We can stop him."

Ishimura ducked Hyde's next sluggish punch. The ugly form proved Hyde was fighting the enemy who'd hijacked him.

Running across the room, Ishimura reached into his pocket. A moment later the restraints unlatched from the rest of the team and clattered to the floor.

"Fight, damn you!" Dante launched from his seat and charged Hyde. He dropkicked the back of the cyborg. "You're stronger than that AI."

Hyde jerked forward and snapped his head toward Dante, growling.

"Any day now, Midas!" Dante shouted.

Working on it, sir.

Mugoi tackled Hyde, wrapping its arms around the larger cyborg's legs and knocking him off-center. Braelin, Jolo, and

Dante leapt on Hyde, grabbing a separate arm or leg to take the huge cyborg down to the floor with a loud crash that echoed in the barren room. It was like wrestling a metal bear.

Hyde smashed an elbow into Mugoi's chest and knocked the smaller cyborg away. He flung Braelin away like an unwanted toy. He bowled into a surprised Jolo, taking them both down. Jolo flew through the air and bounced against a wall, wincing. Dante managed to hang on a few seconds longer before Hyde tossed him across the room. Fire shot through his side as he hit the hard floor.

Shaking, Nasreen grabbed a pair of fallen restraints and pitched them at Hyde's head. They bounced off with a dull *thud*. He caught one in the air and threw it back. The heavy restraint struck Nasreen in the forehead. She fell to the floor with blood running down her face.

Gritting his teeth, Ishimura tried to pull open the door. Hyde sat up. His glowing red eyes fixed on the ASF chief. He stood and stomped forward, his mighty stride ominous yet slow before he strumbled and pitched face-first to the floor, his eyes no longer glowing.

Dante managed to push himself to his feet. "Good job, Midas." He blew out a breath. "That was too close."

Mugoi bounced to its feet. Hyde's attack had left a huge dent in its chest. Dante was about to ask the apprentice if it was okay when he noticed the glowing red eyes.

"Damn it," Dante muttered. "Not our day."

Mugoi advanced, slowly, halting step by step toward Ishimura, raising its hand and pressing its metal fingers together.

"You don't want to be outdone by Hyde, do you, Mugoi?" Dante shouted. "Show that big bastard who's got better self-control. I can tell you're fighting it. Just give Midas more time to help you."

He stumbled toward Mugoi, his movements still unsteady and pain accompanying each step. Bleeding and bruised, Nasreen,

Braelin, and Jolo lay on the ground, breathing and half-conscious.

"Midas, Hyde, I need your help," Dante begged.

I'm working on it, Midas insisted. *It's taking all my processing power.*

Ishimura stood tall, swallowing. He squared his shoulders, his eyes admitting his defeat and his desire not to spend his last moments alive cowering before a cyborg.

A plaintive cry followed an angry bellow. "Fuck the Omega Syndrome! You cowardly AI piece of shit!"

Dante was so focused on the other combatants he'd forgotten about Ambrose. The pilot charged from the corner of the room and collided with Mugoi, taking the cyborg down in an impressive bearhug.

Mugoi yanked an arm free of Ambrose. It chopped Ambrose's shoulder. The sickening *crunch* and Ambrose's piercing scream turned Dante's stomach.

Dante tried to shake off his injuries and rush toward Mugoi. The cyborg snapped a kick into his chest, knocking the wind out of Dante and leaving him gasping on the floor, desperate for air.

Mugoi tried to stand. Its red gaze locked onto Ishimura. With tears streaming down his face, Ambrose tightened his bearhug around Mugoi. The cyborg crawled toward the chief while raining thudding blow after blow onto Ambrose's soft body.

The pilot finally fell free, bloodied, and with his arms and legs wiggling in unnatural ways with his impact on the floor. Mugoi cocked its head, reached down, and lifted Ambrose by the neck. The other arm now free, Mugoi smashed a palm twice into Ambrose's chest before tossing the wheezing man to the floor.

Ambrose's eyes rolled up in the back of his head. He wheezed deeply and coughed up blood.

Mugoi snapped its head toward Ishimura.

The chief's gaze hardened. He raised his fists. "No. I'm going to make you work for this kill, you bastard."

Mugoi's eyes stopped glowing. It dropped to the floor with a thud, limbs splayed.

Ignoring his pain, Dante scrambled over to Ambrose, whose breathing grew more ragged and irregular. "Damn it. You didn't have to do that. You're supposed to stay in your lane. You're the damned pilot."

"I'm…not…just…the…pilot. I'm…sorry. I…got…scared."

"Don't talk." Dante glared at the door. "Where are your damned people, Ishimura?"

Ishimura pounded on the door. "How do I know this wasn't all a trick?"

"You think I'd kill one of my people to trick you, asshole?" Dante snarled. "He needs medical attention immediately. He saved your fucking life. Why didn't your people come in here to save you?"

Ishimura's eyes widened. He backed away from the door, staring at Ambrose's broken body on the floor.

"Stay with us, Ambrose." Dante cradled the man's head. "I was a dick before. You're part of the team, part of the family. That's why I kept going back to you even after everything. I was mad when I said all that crap. We wouldn't have made it this far without you, and I still need you to help me take down the Omega Syndrome. I was going to apologize. I just needed to find the time."

"Thank…you," Ambrose wheezed. "And…I'm…sorry…for…everything."

His eyes glazed over, and he stopped breathing. Dante started chest compressions.

"No, you don't die until I give you permission, asshole," he shouted. "And you don't have permission to die."

Ambrose's body shook with the compressions. He didn't react or start breathing. Everyone watched in horror as Dante continued the compressions. After a minute, he stopped and sat back, staring down at his dead pilot. He stood, his hands coated in Ambrose's blood.

Nasreen, Jolo, and Braelin managed to grab the chairs to pull themselves to their feet. Despite all being bruised and battered, no one else had any serious injuries. Hyde and Mugoi weren't moving. Their eyes weren't glowing red.

"Damn it." Dante turned and kicked the wall. "Damn it!"

Ishimura shook his head. "I'm sorry, Mr. Shale. You're going to need to spend time in custody until I get this figured out."

Dante snapped his head toward Ishimura, his voice a predatory growl. "Haven't you been paying attention? We don't have time to get caught up in bullshit when the Omega Syndrome is using this type of attack."

"I just…I'm not sure."

Dante resisted the urge to punch Ishimura in the face. Ambrose had given his life for the man. He deserved better.

The door slid open. Three ASF personnel advanced into the room. Their stylized unit patches marked them as members of a Security Intervention Squad.

The delay now made more sense. Fearful guards must have locked the room down to request specially trained unit reinforcements.

Dante scoffed. The bastards might have saved Ambrose if they'd gotten through the door earlier. He was about to tell them as much when they all lifted their hands, revealing they held pistols. A telltale red glow shone from their eyes.

"Not for nothing!" Dante tackled Ishimura to the floor as the first SIS member fired at the chief. The bullet whizzed overhead and ricocheted off the wall, narrowly missing Braelin.

Another SIS member fired at the apprentices and Nasreen. They ducked low, the metal chairs taking the rounds.

The remaining SIS member walked toward the downed Ishimura and Dante. Something moved out of the corner of

Dante's eyes. He was too busy scrambling to his feet to worry about it before the controlled SIS opened fire.

Mugoi flew in front of Ishimura. The rounds bounced off the cyborg's chest and legs.

Thunderous steps marked the return of Hyde to action. He smashed his shoulder into the first man, sending the would-be assassin into the wall. He spun toward the others who concentrated their fire on his chest. All they did was add more sparks to the air and metal shavings to the floor.

"Don't kill them," Dante ordered. "Disable them until Midas can transmit the code or we can restrain them."

Hyde snorted. "You're never fun, *Papi*." He snatched the weapon from the closest man and shattered his kneecap with a powerful kick. "He'll survive that."

Despite the dangling limb and collapse, the red-eyed SIS member never cried out. His active partner stopped firing at Hyde and sidestepped to empty his magazine at Ishimura.

Mugoi wrapped its body around the squirming Ishimura. The bullets struck up and down its body, only a single bullet grazing the chief's arm. Quick trigger pulls didn't save the SIS member from Hyde grabbing and crushing his hand before smacking the man backward.

Hyde turned to the grimacing Dante. "It'll heal. We did worse to Klement when he broke his arm."

Ishimura wriggled out of Mugoi's grasp. He eyed the door, but Hyde stood between him and his escape.

"You really want to go out there and have other people trying to kill you?" Hyde asked.

"They saved you." Dante gestured at Mugoi and Hyde. "Your men will be saved in a moment once they get the counter-code. It's a temporary solution, but at least it's something."

"You're telling me the Omega Syndrome took them over?" Ishimura asked.

He looked at the fallen SIS men. They were breathing, but

Hyde's blunt assault had knocked them unconscious.

"Wait." Ishimura walked over to the nearest man and crouched. "These aren't just SIS. These are SIS snipers."

"Is that supposed to mean something to me?" Dante asked. "Because one of my men just died saving your ass from the Omega Syndrome, and you're still acting like you don't believe me. That's pissing me off in ways you don't want."

"SIS snipers have neural weapon uplinks to enhance firing performance." Ishimura stood. "That's not standard gear in the ASF. It's something you see in certain units. You asked me earlier if I had implants. Most ASF personnel have either none or very few implants. The ASF is concerned about the expense of maintaining them and how it can affect force readiness. Good implants cost money anyway. We're not rich enough to invest in serious implants like you Marauders."

Hyde walked over to Ambrose's body. His mouth twitched. "I'm tired of playing around, *Papi*. That toy in your head freed me. That means we can take the fight to them, right?"

"Midas isn't sure about its long-term effectiveness," Dante replied. "We're waiting on Firewall for the real AI murder code."

Nasreen walked over to Ambrose. She knelt and took his hand in hers, sighing. "We can't survive if it's going to keep on like this. Another close call will cost more of our people."

Dante turned toward Ishimura. "No more games. No more delays. If you're not ready to help us, get the hell out of our way and let us go. We have an AI to kill."

"I believe you," Ishimura replied. "And I'm going to put together a team with minimal to no implants. That's all we need? It can't take over people with no implants."

"Get them ready soon because I have a feeling we're about to go into the final battle." Dante nodded at Ambrose. "Please make sure they don't do anything to his body. We'll be ready to honor him when this is all over. By saving your life, Ambrose might have just saved humanity."

CHAPTER SEVENTEEN

No one said more than a handful of words until the police shuttle dropped the team back at their headquarters. Nasreen kept stealing glances at Dante, seeing the pain hidden behind the mask of anger. She was still processing Ambrose's death too, a dull aching pain that wouldn't leave.

The theoretical loss of a friend and comrade against the Omega Syndrome had always hung over them. Now they had to face the harsh reality without proper time to grieve.

Dante had been right. The Omega Syndrome was determined to crush them.

They needed to move fast to ensure Ambrose hadn't sacrificed his life for nothing before the Omega Syndrome finished them all off. The bold play in the heart of the ASF HQ proved the enemy understood they were a unique threat. Firewall's apocalyptic warnings now seemed less insane.

Nasreen wondered if they'd waited too long. They'd tried to follow up on the Voices but hadn't gotten anywhere. Still, she kept thinking they'd missed something that would have led them to Firewall earlier and a scenario where Ambrose hadn't been killed because of an Omega Syndrome possession.

"Everyone arm up with every implement of damned death you can find," Dante barked. "The clock's ticking. With the code revealed, we can't be sure how long it is until the Omega Syndrome comes up with countermeasures."

He stomped toward a door leading into the main building. "I'm going to contact Firewall to let them know what's going on, so we can get a move on. If you're tired, rest in your gear in the hangar."

He glanced at Nasreen. "In all this bullshit, I never did get a chance to ask you why you were in custody. Did Firewall screw up again? If they did, I'm shooting Exploit in the head the next time I see him, and damn the consequences."

"I stalled to help Firewall escape a police raid," Nasreen replied. "As best I can tell, it wasn't their fault, nothing more than unfortunate timing." She shrugged. "Now they owe me and should trust me more."

"Good. We might need that." Dante stopped at the door. "Firewall's going to come here. I don't want to waste time riding around old grav lines because of their paranoia, and I'm tired of doing everything based on everyone else's terms. They can play by my rules, or they can stay the hell out of my way like I told Ishimura. We don't have time for bullshit."

Nasreen nodded at Hyde and the apprentices before jogging after Dante. Once she'd followed him into the hallway, she asked, "Are you okay? You can talk to me."

"Am I okay?" Dante let out a low, harsh laugh. "Hell no, I'm not okay. Ambrose is dead. But that's going to have to wait.

"We need to make everything that's happened count. We need to take down that AI bastard." He clenched a fist. "I'm going to ensure that happens if I have to drag Firewall kicking and screaming into this."

"It's not your fault," she said. "Remember that. It's the Omega Syndrome's fault. Everything that's happened, even back to SSS, is the Omega Syndrome's fault."

"I'm the team leader. It's my fault. But guilt has to wait, too, and you know what I always say. I do vengeance well."

He ground his teeth. "Midas, get ready to send a message over the encrypted channel. Message is as follows: 'T, L, and E to come to my HQ immediately. Countermeasures successfully deployed in field. Block 9X destroyed. Mass suicide due to infection.

"'The war has begun. If you don't come, you will all die. We need an immediate plan, and I've lost people. I don't have time to deal with your issues, and I've lined up non-augmented support. We need to move ASAP. If you're not here in two hours, we'll proceed without you.'"

"Sir, are you sure you want to send that message?" Midas asked.

"Yeah. Send that exact message. No changes. They need to understand the stakes."

Nasreen shook her head. "They have a better understanding of the code we need to do more than roll back and block individual Omega Syndrome infections. We shouldn't pressure them unnecessarily. We can't win the war without them, only battles."

Dante gave Nasreen a look of warning. "Now is not the time to tell me to calm down. There's nothing unnecessary about me telling those self-righteous and sanctimonious assholes to hurry up. I've never liked working with them. I only have because you convinced me it was a good idea."

"I'm not telling you to calm down." Nasreen emphasized it with a firm nod. "It's as you said. We have to make Ambrose's sacrifice meaningful. That includes making sure Firewall's on our side. We don't have to like them, but we need them."

"Let's get ready for our meeting."

"You're sure they'll come so quickly? If they did the same thing to us, we might refuse. That's all I'm trying to say."

Dante stopped and frowned. "I'm not sure of anything anymore other than I want to beat the hell out of something big. I'll settle for a sinister AI secretly controlling the Stations."

Nasreen had expected a counteroffer of a different meeting place and later time, or at least a response message. Instead, Tether, Lock, and Exploit showed up at the front door by themselves after twenty minutes. Either they had supreme trust in Dante or understood there was no turning back, and the best way to defeat the enemy was to work together and strike while they still could. Looking apologetic, she led them to the meeting room where Dante sat at the front of the table, glaring at the wall.

"How dare you treat us like this," Exploit spat as he sat. "I think you forget yourself, Mr. Shale. We're the ones who have led the charge against the Omega Syndrome. Don't think that you call the shots because you collected a handful of trinkets. You're a tool of Firewall, nothing more."

"Shut your mouth, or I'll shut it for you with my fist and boot." Dante brandished his fist. "I don't have time for your crap or arrogance, asshole. I lost a man today and came close to losing two others. I've seen Omega Syndrome horrors you can't begin to imagine."

Exploit narrowed his eyes. "You're not the only one to ever lose people and far from the only man to see evil from the Omega Syndrome."

Nasreen looked among the Firewall members. Before, they'd not shared the same opinions about the nature of the Omega Syndrome. She'd not noticed until now that they all seemed to agree the enemy was a rogue AI. There must have been information on the database or the other information they discovered that confirmed its true nature. She didn't care as long as their code worked.

"Block 9X Irondogs massacred their own men before ripping themselves to shreds earlier today," Dante continued. "ASF SIS snipers with targeting neural implants almost killed the chief when I told him the truth. The only good thing that came out of that is my AI's manipulation of the code proved effective, but he's assured me he believes his efforts are only temporary. We need your plan. We need to kill the Omega Syndrome."

"What?" Exploit narrowed his eyes. "You told the head of the ASF about the Omega Syndrome. Are you insane? You may have doomed us all, you idiot!"

"Idiot? Yeah. I am. Crazy. That too." Dante shrugged. "That's why I'm fighting a sadistic AI. Get over it. Get over yourself. Ishimura knows, and he understands he can't trust anyone with too many implants."

"You used an AI to process the code?" Exploit glared at Tether. "This is your doing, isn't it? We'd discussed this. Asking that thing to help is the same as capitulating to the Omega Syndrome."

"Fight the enemy on their terms," Tether replied. "We always knew we'd need that level of processing power to end this. There is poetic justice to using an AI to fight an AI."

Exploit sneered and nodded at her arm. "You're thinking like a machine now. The Omega Syndrome will corrupt the AI as it corrupts all implants and augmentations it touches. It's unfortunate Block 9X didn't kill you at that club."

Tether narrowed her eyes. "And it's too bad Nasreen didn't snap your neck at our base."

Dante smirked. He liked Tether's idea.

Lock cleared his throat. "That's not appropriate. Everyone calm down."

"These fools have brought the Omega Syndrome to us before we're ready." Exploit pounded the table. "Our plan was years in the making, and it'll now be for nothing."

"No, now we will carry out the plan," Nasreen interrupted. "Emotions are running high. I understand. Much like Dante, I can't and won't care until we take down the Omega Syndrome. We have a brief window of opportunity to press our advantage.

"Like Dante said, Chief Ishimura of the ASF is gathering a

non-augmented strike force as we speak. He's seen the horrors of the Omega Syndrome firsthand. If we wait, it will assassinate him soon, and we'll lose that strike force and access to more resources in the following chaos."

She blew out a breath. "We need to figure out how to best leverage that force and stop the Omega Syndrome because if we sit around here for weeks arguing about who's an idiot, we'll all be dead or enslaved by the AI. Humanity will follow. Got it?"

Exploit flared his nostrils. "No. You have doomed us all."

"Assuming we haven't done that, we still need to come up with a plan. I say we try to take down our enemy. At this point, we have nothing left to lose."

"We have a plan," Tether replied. "The hard part was coming up with enough people. You've solved that issue by recruiting the ASF. We wouldn't have thought it possible, although I am sorry it cost you one of your men."

"Don't tell them anything more," Exploit spat. "These Marauder fools will get us all killed. They don't have the right to finish off the enemy."

Lock glared at him. "This is a fight for humanity's freedom. It's not a holy crusade for only Firewall members. Without Dante's and Nasreen's help, we wouldn't have found the database or the parts we needed to access it."

"If you tell them and we fail, we'll never get another chance at this. You're betting our species' future on this thuggish fool and this corrupted spy woman."

Nasreen gave him a thoughtful look. "That's an interesting description. I don't find it all that insulting."

Dante narrowed his eyes on Exploit. "Yeah. I'm a Marauder. I'm good at getting in and out of places while fighting dangerous shit. That's why we won't fail. Now shut up. Your objection is noted, asshole." He let his harsh-tinged words hang in the air for a moment before turning to Tether. "What's the plan?"

She gestured at both walls. "Atlantica Central Station is situated at the center of the Station networks, especially computing and communications. We can hit and take over the comms relays all over the Station with the help of the ASF troops. Once they're secured, we can start uploading the code. That'll limit the Omega Syndrome's escape routes."

Exploit shook his head. "I've never liked this plan. What's to stop the Omega Syndrome from isolating those areas to limit the damage and buy it the time it needs to come up with counter-measures?"

Lock replied, "If we strike all of the relays simultaneously, it won't have time. The code will spread throughout all the Stations, cutting off its tendrils. Then we can strike the—"

"No!" Exploit shrieked. "You can't tell them about that. It's our only chance of surviving." He shot up. "We should have never come to this meeting."

Dante stood and walked over to Exploit. He shoved the man back into his chair. "This isn't your base. This is my home. I have every reason in the world to hate you for what you did to my partner, but there are more important problems. You're not walking out until we have a plan. You try to leave and I'll knock your ass out. Understood?"

Red-faced, Exploit ground his teeth. He harrumphed and folded his arms.

"Our analysis has revealed the heart of the Omega Syndrome," Tether explained. "The central most important part that we've long theorized existed. The AI isn't fully distributed through all systems."

Exploit shrank into his chair. "This whole alliance will kill us all. We should have gone after his people to begin with."

"Thank you, Tether." Dante nodded at the woman before heading back to his chair. "You're saying that if we cut the Omega Syndrome off everywhere else, all we have to do is take out his heart, and we win? The digital equivalent of bleeding it out and shooting it in the brain?"

"Interesting imagery and not all that inaccurate," Tether replied. "The heart is a critical central hub of processing that the database helped us locate. Heart, brain, whatever you want to call it." She gave Dante a pitying look. "You'll never guess where it is."

"Somewhere annoying, like hidden deep in a jungle in South America and surrounded by packs of wild Nightmutts and murderous cannibals equipped with pulsecore weapons?"

Tether shook her head. "It's in the old SSS Central Tower, in the basement. It's been in front of our faces all this time, almost like it's trying to mock us."

"That explains why no one else took over that building." Dante nodded with a knowing look. "No wonder the Omega Syndrome threatened me when we finished off Slaine. I was sniffing around too close to its heart."

Nasreen frowned. "If this heart is the most important part, I don't understand why we don't go straight for it. A complicated plan with different teams has more that can go wrong. Overwhelming force applied to that tower will assure our victory."

"This is the problem with these people." Exploit snorted. "They're ignorant. They learn one fact and think they know everything about our enemy. Being able to shoot mutants doesn't make them worthy allies."

"Being able to string words together doesn't make you a worthy human being," Nasreen answered cheerfully before turning back to Tether.

"You're lacking knowledge of certain technical details," Tether said. "I can see why that plan would make sense to you because of that." She patted her heart. "The Omega Syndrome's primary neural network is centralized, but the second we subject the heart to attack, it would be able to begin transferring its core data via one of the relays. It'll escape, and we'll have to track it down again."

"I don't get it," Dante said. "Why isn't it constantly doing that now? Even Midas has backups. Why is it sitting around waiting to get attacked?"

"Because the Omega Syndrome is a unique entity integrated with the Station systems in a particular way," Tether answered. "Our information suggests that doing so would fragment its control and coordination ability."

"Then it'll kill itself? That works." Dante shrugged. "All the more reason for a front-door attack."

Lock shook his head. "It's not that simple. It would only be a temporary setback until it reconstitutes itself in a new location and with better knowledge of our operations and capabilities.

"Our only choice is to coordinate the raids with the relays first, then the heart. We salt the ground with the killer code to make sure the heart is trapped and vulnerable. Then we finish it off." He emphasized it with a firm nod.

"This has always been the plan. It's why we were investigating comms relays in the past. The two biggest problems we faced were developing a transmittable method to contain the Omega Syndrome and how to hit that many targets at once simultaneously.

"You finding the database and the parts to help open it solved the first issue. Bringing the ASF aboard solves the second. It's no longer theoretical. It's a viable plan."

Dante nodded as a hungry smile grew. "Then we win. We make the bastard pay. We burn out the relays, and we cut out the heart. We show the AI that humans will run human affairs, not a rogue-ass piece of software with delusions of grandeur."

He half-expected Midas to chime in, but the AI remained silent, perhaps understanding the intensity of the emotions running rampant in the meeting.

"Nothing's assured." Tether sighed. "Every second counts, and there's also the more fundamental threat of what a desperate Omega Syndrome might do."

"So?" Dante shrugged. "It'll be cut off."

Exploit rolled his eyes with all the attitude of a man who thought he was dealing with a child. "It'll be cut from the relays. There will still be thousands of people within the heart's reach. Our Firewall people have removed or disabled their implants. But what about everyone else? There will be vulnerabilities."

"ASF will have limited implants, but I can't guarantee they'll have none." Dante shrugged. "Most of my team has at least some. It doesn't matter. Midas can help fight the attacks."

"Oh?" Exploit raised an eyebrow. "You're that confident?"

"Every second counts, like Tether said. If we don't make this happen right away, we've lost, and everybody who might oppose the Omega Syndrome will get picked off. Your little club might continue, but without help from the outside, you won't have a chance. By then, the Omega Syndrome will have relocated."

Dante leaned over his table with his hands palm-down. "Firewall should get your people together. If the worst shit happens, you have the fewest implants to worry about. You should be a major presence at the heart."

"We still haven't agreed to go along with this." Exploit folded his arms. "You haven't accounted for every possibility. And Firewall operatives will be carrying the final kill code. That's non-negotiable."

"Yeah, I haven't accounted for everything, but it's like fighting Dirtside. Sometimes the only thing you can do is push forward and hope the Nightmutt bleeds out before you do."

Lock stood with a look of determination. "We'll need eight hours."

"Shouldn't we move before that?" Dante frowned. "We just got done saying seconds count."

"We need the time to gather our people and finish tuning the code."

Dante grunted in frustration. "I hope we don't all die in the meanwhile because you people can't work fast enough."

Exploit snorted and stood. "If this plan fails, it'll be your fault,

Plunderer, not ours. You're the one who struck such an obvious blow and revealed our weapon."

"If I hadn't, we'd be screwed."

Tether nodded at Dante. "Make sure your ASF allies understand the timeline and mission. We won't transmit any information about the heart until we're within thirty minutes of being ready to strike."

"Makes sense." Dante gestured at the door. "You know the way out. The sooner you leave, the sooner you can finish preparing your part of this."

Exploit offered a final sneer for Dante before making his way out. Tether and Lock nodded with worry lining their faces before departing.

Dante sat back in his seat and turned to Nasreen. "Get the team in here. We need to brief them."

"Simple as that," Dante explained. "In eight hours, we take down the Omega Syndrome or die trying. We'll have all of Firewall's people and several ASF teams backing us up all over the Atlantica Central Station."

Hyde frowned. "Are me and Pretty Face going to be able to do anything? I owe the Omega Syndrome."

"As do I," Mugoi added quietly.

"The code I can broadcast should be sufficient," Midas answered. "Until the Omega Syndrome has time to come up with a countermeasure, you should theoretically not be re-inoculated in my direct presence."

"Theoretically?" Dante asked.

"Nothing can be assured when dealing with such an unusual AI."

"I'll take the odds."

Braelin ran his hands through his hair. "Damn. No rest for the wicked. I'm still catching my breath from Dirtside, not to mention…" He looked away. "Sorry. It's not the time."

Dante shook his head. "We've got no reason to ignore what happened. Ambrose is dead. He sacrificed himself to save Ishimura. That's why we have to finish this, for the Stations and him."

Mugoi looked down. "It's because I couldn't control myself." It lifted its hands. "I killed him."

"It's not your fault. You didn't kill him. It's the Omega Syndrome. We knew about the threat. We didn't take it seriously enough. If it's anyone's fault, Ambrose is dead because of me."

Dante scoffed. "He felt like he had to be a big hero because I told him he was a coward who should get the hell out. I should have fought harder. Then he could have stayed put."

"Is that so, *Papi?*" Hyde's voice was a near growl. "That's why he was so messed up?"

"He'd complained about a plan and a timeline." Dante shook his head. "I got angry. I yelled at him. It was a mistake. I knew it not that long after. I figured I could apologize to him when all this crap was over. Too late now."

He rubbed his temples. "I might be the greatest Marauder ever, but I'm shit as a leader. If any of you don't want me to take point on this, I understand. My gun needs to be involved, but I don't want anyone worried about the mission. There's too much at stake."

Nasreen shook her head. "We all make mistakes, Dante. Ambrose didn't die because you yelled at him. Ambrose died because he had enough courage to sacrifice himself for a greater cause. It's not because you called him a coward. It's because he was heroic in his way."

Dante let out a low, dark chuckle. "That's what he wanted to go back to, a greater cause. I couldn't see anything but cowardice. I couldn't see the real man because I was too blinded by my bullshit."

"Every man lives on borrowed time," Hyde rumbled. "It doesn't matter if he's made of metal or not. You didn't kill him when he deserved it, just like you didn't finish me off. I don't know if I like you that much, Dante Shale, but for a little *pendejo* without useful combat augmentations you can do damage when you want to."

He chuckled. "Nobody else could have taken down SSS. Shit, I had to run to you when Slaine figured I was no longer useful. So did Ambrose. You cut and run now, then you might as well be pissing on his grave. You're the only man who can lead us against the Omega Syndrome."

"I agree, Captain," Mugoi concurred. "I don't want to take orders from anyone else. I don't trust anyone else. You've led us this far. You need to lead us over the finish line."

Jolo offered a shallow nod. "To honor Ambrose, we need to defeat the Omega Syndrome. Our best chance to do that is with you leading us. It's as simple as that."

Braelin grinned. "You know how to lead a man, Dante. Sure, you might be leading us to death, but there ain't no perfect way to go out. If I have to die fighting beside my friends and with my mentor leading me against an evil AI…" He slapped the table and whistled. "Damn, I hope I get my statue out of this. Bronze? Stone? Gold?"

Hyde snickered. "We need to win first, Klement."

"We've had our ups and downs." Dante stood and looked around the table. "We've fought on the Stations, all over Dirtside. We've faced Nightmutts, Reapers, Plunderers, and Dirtwalker cannibals who wanted to have our spleens for dinner. Every time, we've shown them why they picked the wrong crew to fuck with. We came back, and they ended up in the ground."

"Hell yeah!" Braelin shouted and pumped his fist. The others nodded their eager agreement.

Dante continued. "We won't only do this as a team. We'll do this as a family. I've never believed in fate or providence or anything like that, and I'm not sure I believe in it now, but it's hard not to see this as what we were meant to do together. So that's what we are going to do.

"We might be plunging into the lion's den, but we are doing it together, and well... That's got to be something, right?"

CHAPTER EIGHTEEN

Sitting in the back of the shuttle, Dante couldn't stop flexing his fingers. He looked up on occasion at a holographic image of Ambrose projected into the center of the bay. With Nasreen flying the shuttle, he wanted a small memento of the man who'd helped protect Ishimura.

Dante still blamed himself. There was nothing he could do to change the past. The best he could do was ensure that Ambrose's dreams carried on by stopping the AI that wanted to interfere with the TRG's work.

The team had geared up in armor and full weapons. Ishimura was allowing firearms for the assault. Dante had worried the man would shy away from it given the public nature of the op. Humanity couldn't fight for its freedom and continued existence with only shock batons and razorfists.

Dante didn't bother to ask permission for the gel explosive packs he'd slipped into his tactical vest pockets. He'd not needed it for years Dirtside and never anticipated using it on a Station.

This was war. Firewall had understood that from the beginning. It had taken Dante a while to figure it out. The ASF and

Ishimura accepted that, and now they had an army to take on their enemy.

Tether, Lock, and Exploit sat together in the back of the shuttle. They wore tactical webbing but no armor. Dante had handed over rifles and shock batons for each before they set out.

He would have preferred that Exploit not accompany the team on the mission. Defeating the Omega Syndrome would provide the added benefit of never having to deal with the asshole again.

A report came over the comms. "Tac Team 42 in position, awaiting go orders."

"Tac Team 24 in position, awaiting go orders."

"Tac Team 12, thirty seconds until position. No go."

Other team reports streamed out from all over the Station. Ishimura had linked Dante and the crew into ASF comms. Nasreen circled the SSS tower in the shuttle with a wide flight path to make it less obvious. Two ASF gunships manned by non-augmented personnel flew what appeared to be practice runs in the nearby area but secretly acted as an escort for Dante's team and carried additional ASF tactical teams.

The Omega Syndrome was a terrifying enemy, but it had demonstrated that for all its power, it wasn't omniscient.

A countdown flashed below the hologram of Ambrose as additional ASF tactical teams gave their status. The final battle for the future of humanity lay only minutes away, yet most people on the Stations had no idea what was about to unfold. Even if they learned, they'd find it hard to believe.

Dante took a moment to reflect on everything that had happened since Slaine's betrayal. He'd not been much better than the average Station citizen. He didn't put much thought into who might be running things. All he cared about was his reputation as a Marauder and his next paycheck. He would not have imagined a powerful corrupt man's betrayal would lead him to where he was today.

He looked over the team. Braelin tapped his boot against the shuttle floor. Jolo rubbed her hands together. Mugoi stared straight ahead with a haunted look in its eyes. Defeating the Omega Syndrome was the first step for Mugoi to learn to forgive itself for what had happened.

"Remember the plan," Dante declared, breaking the tense silence hanging over the team. "Don't get yourself spun up too much. After setting down near the loading dock, we'll use the ASF overrides for the service tunnel to get us to the stairs that lead to the basement. We can't make our move until the joint ASF-Firewall teams hit all the relays. It should be a straight shot."

"And if they fuck up?" Hyde asked from the corner of the shuttle. "What if they don't secure every relay?"

"We still proceed toward the heart," Dante answered. "We have no other choice. If we can't kill the Omega Syndrome, then wound it badly. I don't intend to lose, though. I intend to kill that AI son of a bitch even if it means tearing down the entire tower with my bare hands."

Hyde grinned. "That's right. Burn it all down, Hellcat."

Exploit stared at him. "I'm glad that despite all your other foolishness, you've accepted the true nature of the threat. This creature, this rogue AI, is worse than the ancient evils mentioned in religions. People could claim those, at least, were beyond their control. This was birthed from humanity's hubris, a cruel, twisted angel that wants to spread its corruption through our souls until only evil remains."

Even when the man was right, he sounded like a nut in need of a good ass-kicking.

"I don't care what I'm facing," Dante replied. "The only important thing is that we win and it loses, AI, human, or Nightmutt. When this is over, you can hide somewhere and meditate all day on your non-AI soul. You probably should before I decide to follow up on what Nasreen did before."

"You're nothing more than a thug." Exploit snorted. "Doing this doesn't change that."

"Yeah, and I'm damned good at being a thug."

Jolo stared at Ambrose's hologram. "We will win today. For Ambrose."

"For Ambrose," Braelin chanted.

"For Ambrose," Mugoi added.

"For Ambrose," Hyde agreed.

Dante nodded. "For Ambrose!"

"All relay teams," Ishimura transmitted. "This is Command Team One. Begin assault. I repeat, *begin assault. Go! Go! Go!*"

The final battle had officially begun.

Different units rattled off their receipt of the message. Out in his command gunship, Ishimura was no doubt paying attention to screens of status reports. Dante didn't need to worry about that. All he was waiting for was a direct go order from the chief to the heart teams.

Waiting on others didn't suit Dante. That didn't matter. Being the best Marauder on the Stations didn't make him a god. He couldn't have come this far without his teams and friends. Now he owed it to the fallen to finish what they'd all started.

Much like with SSS, he might have had a noble goal in the background, but in the end, it was personal. He needed to deliver Hellcat vengeance to the Omega Syndrome.

Dante drew a deep breath. "It won't be long now for us. Make sure you do last checks. If we screw up here, there might not be a second chance."

Mugoi flexed its fingers. "You're sure Midas has hardened us enough?"

Dante cast a warning glare at the scowling Exploit. "If I wasn't confident, you wouldn't be coming along. We need your and Hyde's strength."

"I owe this to Ambrose," Mugoi replied. "I'll do whatever it takes, even if I—"

"Shut up," Dante interrupted. "We don't need to lose anybody else. Today is about killing the Omega Syndrome. That's how we'll all make it up to Ambrose—by taking out the enemy and assuring everyone else survives."

Dante's radio crackled to life. "Command Team One to Shale."

"This is Shale," Dante answered. "We ready for go?"

"All teams are encountering heavy resistance at relays," Ishimura reported. "Heavily equipped mercenaries, including a higher-than-expected number of augmented troops. You're not cleared to go."

"Damn it." Dante's hands clenched together. "You saw what happened in the interrogation room and Block 9X. If we lose here, that's going to happen everywhere. Don't trust in a Plan B because there might not be a tomorrow."

"Calm down, Shale. We're not losing. They might have been well-guarded, but they seemed surprised we showed up. Our teams are confident we can secure the relays."

"I'll take whatever little luck we can find."

"I'll be in contact soon. Command Team One out."

Dante looked at Lock. "Have the relays always been that well-defended?"

He avoided Dante's gaze. "Not always. We did notice an uptick in defense after recent Firewall operations. It might be that the Omega Syndrome understood a portion of our plan."

Hyde snickered. "All that crap about how great you guys are at security, and you tipped them off. All the while, your friend was screaming about how it was our fault."

"Because it was," Exploit mumbled.

"Operational failures are inevitable," Lock replied. "Your team understands that."

Nasreen frowned. "The real question is whether the Omega Syndrome will run. It might be too late."

Tether shook her head. "Dispensing with human tools costs

nothing. It won't run unless there's no other choice. The cost is too high, and we don't believe it's convinced it can reestablish itself if weakened and actively hunted."

"How can you be so sure?" Nasreen asked. "It's not as if we have a history of such missions to draw on."

Tether drew a deep breath. "We found evidence on the database that someone attacked the heart before."

"What?" Dante shot up. "You didn't think that'd be nice to mention before we launched a major one-way operation to take it out?"

"We believed if you heard that it'd been attempted and failed, you might pull back from the efforts." Tether lifted her chin and stared back at him defiantly. "We're committed now. It's not as if we're gambling with others' lives. Three important Firewall leaders are on the frontline with you."

"That doesn't make me feel as comfortable as you think." Dante sat. "Why did it fail last time? Because they didn't have code? They didn't secure the relays?"

"Yes, because they hadn't secured every relay. From what we can tell, the Omega Syndrome was able to relocate, although weakened for a period. We did notice that it chose to stay on Atlantica Central Station, but its heart wasn't in the same location. The building hadn't been constructed yet."

"Staying on Atlantica Central Station assures easier access to the entire Station network," Dante concluded. He glanced down at the EMP grenades clipped to his tac belt. "How did Firewall not know about this earlier attack?"

"Because the other organization was wiped out, and all but the faintest scraps of evidence concerning their existence deleted from Station records. They might as well never have existed. The Omega Syndrome wanted to ensure that no one learned from their mistakes.

"It covered up the incident using false terrorist reports and used its influence among the security forces to maintain the lie. It's not clear if anyone alive knows the truth other than us. That same data proves the origin of the Omega Syndrome as a rogue AI."

Dante grinned at Braelin. "Statue after a heroic death or getting erased from history. Not liking our options."

Braelin laughed. "Nah. We return triumphant, and we get statues. You just see."

"Yeah. Let's hope for the best."

There was nothing left to do but sit there for tense minutes. Everyone sat as if collected in quiet meditation, the rumble of the shuttle engines soothing in a strange way. Dante focused on Ambrose, gathering his guilt and anger to fuel his coming battle.

Everything about the mission was strange, a strike deep in the heart of a building constructed by the company he'd helped destroy. About the only thing he could guarantee would be no Nightmutts. It would be nice to run a mission that didn't involve anything twisted and corrupt.

Time blurred. Dante's mind drifted to blank until a message from Ishimura snapped him back into the here and now.

"Shale, this is Command Team One."

Dante sat up and rolled his shoulders. "Give me good news, Chief."

"All relays secured," Ishimura reported. "Firewall teams report successful uploads. The Omega Syndrome has nowhere to run. Rip out this thing's heart and finish this. You're cleared for go status."

"Take us down, Nasreen!" Dante ordered. "We've got an AI to shred."

Everyone perked up in the back, but only Hyde looked enthusiastic. Heavy resignation settled over Exploit's face. Tether and Lock offered a master example of studied calmness. Braelin bounced his knee as nervous energy got the best of him. He only stopped when Jolo put her hand on his shoulder and offered him a slight smile.

The shuttle banked hard and dove directly toward the abandoned SSS Central Tower. ASF commands had kept commercial traffic away from the building, a maneuver that risked alerting the Omega Syndrome but minimized innocent casualties. All they needed to do was land and force their way inside.

Dante grinned. The relay teams had taken the Omega Syndrome by surprise. The heart might be easier to penetrate.

"Trouble! Come up here," Nasreen shouted.

Dante clambered out of his seat in the back, braced against the wall as he made his way to the cockpit, and dropped into the copilot's seat. "Shit."

Or taking the heart might prove far more difficult. Hard-cased troops streamed from the building's rear, spreading over the loading dock and lifting rifles and more shockingly, missile launchers. The sheer number impressed almost as much as the ruthless choice of weapons.

"There are so many," Nasreen observed. "You think they're all mercenaries?"

"There will always be men and women willing to take on the ASF for enough money. If I had to bet, I'd say it's a mix of love of money and hijacking. In the end, I guarantee all these people worked freely for the Omega Syndrome at some point. We don't have time to feel pity for assholes who'd murder anyone for a paycheck."

Nasreen frowned. "Block 9X were all too eager to work for their mysterious employer."

"Exactly, now stay low and open up with the cannon."

"That'll make it easier to hit us. I'm good, but I'm not Ambrose. We'll crash if I try to be too clever with my maneuvers."

"We can't allow stray missiles to travel too far. The sheer volume of explosives might risk dome damage. I'm sure when this is over, the Marauders would be the easy ones to blame if something bad happened. I'd rather be able to walk around the street without people beating me to death."

"Understood." Nasreen pushed forward on the yoke.

His stomach lurched as the shuttle dropped toward the ground. Nasreen opened up with the pulsecore cannon. Green blasts flashed across the dock, flinging the armored troops through the air. Masses of rifle muzzles flashed. Bullets filled the air.

Nasreen's abrupt dive threw off the mercenaries' aim. Dante was glad he'd skipped a big meal.

Ignoring the impact warning alarm, Nasreen continued the brutal drop, pulling up so suddenly at the end that Dante braced himself for impact and hoped to survive the crash. The shuttle skimmed the ground, cruising across the hard surface of the loading dock. She blasted through a nearby mercenary, the pulsecore round leaving little behind.

"That's a nice start," Dante declared.

A missile screamed past the side of the shuttle and exploded against the ground. The shuttle shuddered from the blast wave and dropped, shaking as the bottom scraped the ground. Nasreen hissed and pulled into another turn.

Bullets ripped into the shuttle. Shrill alarms cried out, red warnings flashing all over the control panel. More missiles exploded around them, forcing Nasreen to cut through dark clouds and showers of shrapnel that thudded against the shuttle.

Nasreen swept the area with the pulsecore cannon, not being stingy with the ammo. Her attacks left a line of craters and broken shells of men, giving the team a brief moment of respite from the overwhelming volleys they'd survived.

Dante nodded, satisfied at the lack of movement among the smoking ruins of the loading zone. Nasreen might have dug halfway to the first sublevel, but she'd also left few of the mercenaries alive. The Omega Syndrome had been so focused on repelling ground-based assaults it had made their job easier.

That's what Dante wanted to believe, but the Omega Syndrome wouldn't be so easily defeated. Reinforcements continued pouring from the building. In a twisted irony, they emerged from the exact access tunnel the team had planned to use.

Once clear of the tunnel, they immediately sprayed into the air, forcing Nasreen higher again. The shuttle had grown heavy and clumsy, the turns not as sharp, the rattling constant as if the vehicle threatened to shake apart.

"At least we won't have to waste time trying to open the tunnel," Dante noted.

"It's nice to be able to look on the bright side in the middle of a battle for our lives," Nasreen offered, her voice tight.

The ASF gunships arrived. They dove, and their weapons came to life. In a sight few on the Stations had seen, heavy auto-cannons delivered withering punishment. The massive storm was more impressive than the sporadic pulsecore explosions Nasreen had delivered. Once the first missile came their way, the ASF pilots realized their mistake and dropped altitude for their strafing runs.

Despite the early success at clearing out the mercenaries, the enemies were now spreading out more and breaking up their formations. Dante's team needed to cut down their numbers if they were going to land before the shuttle got shot down.

"Hyde and Mugoi," Dante yelled. "Go outside and rain pulsecores down on our merc friends."

Nasreen looked at Dante like he was crazy. He grinned and flipped the bay switch. The shuttle trembled with the airflow change. Nasreen concentrated on keeping it steady while Dante watched the cameras.

Two cyborgs scampered out, their augmented grips letting them hang on with one hand as they aimed their pulsecore carbines at the ground to deliver more plasma explosive payback to the mercenaries flooding the smoking and pitted loading zone below.

The ASF gunships swept through the air again. Unlike Nasreen, the pilots concentrated on maximum speed strafing runs that lasted only seconds but made it harder for the mercenaries to target them. Their rounds carved paths through the loading zone, gouging material out of the ground and launching it into the air to join the burgeoning clouds.

Hard-cased armor could be impressive. It didn't allow a man to survive a direct hit from a vehicle-based autocannon. The cannons tore mercenaries apart. Dante was unsure if determination fueled their bravery or the poison touch of an AI in their brains.

With cyborgs on both sides and the forward cannon, the shuttle now had an almost 360-degree firing arc. Nasreen spun the shuttle on its side and zoomed over the enemy formation, letting her cyborg teammates drop more explosive death from above.

The latest disruption of the mercenary volleys allowed the ASF gunships to slow for more thorough passes. They elected for more straightforward strafing runs, walking armor-piercing rounds through the advancing mercenaries, adding new bodies to the growing pile.

After a few more passes from all three aircraft, mercenary reinforcements stopped coming from the tunnel. Dante's team thinned the back ranks of the mercenaries, their overlapping triple punishment overwhelming the enemy. This cleared a path for an ASF gunship to come in from behind the enemies and split the largest surviving formation in half.

At the beginning, the mercenaries had been an impressive army guarding a loading zone with dangerous weapons. Dante's team and the ASF tac teams wouldn't have survived a frontal assault.

The brutal aerial assault had wrecked the army, leaving the

area below a bloodied, smoking mess. Dead and dying mercs lay spread all over, many having rolled into the newly dug craters.

"Prepare to take us down." Dante pointed his thumb down. "We don't want to wait too long and find they're rolling out a missile battery."

"I—" Nasreen gasped and jerked the yoke, spinning the shuttle so hard, Dante worried about tossing Hyde and Mugoi to the ground.

He didn't have much time to register what was going on. The constant bleating of alarms had become easy to ignore, nothing more than background noise. He didn't understand what was happening until the ASF gunship swept over them, autocannon flashing and narrowly missing the shuttle.

"Ishimura!" Dante transmitted. "Do any of your gunship pilots have implants? We're being attacked by one!"

"The team with you doesn't have implants," Ishimura replied. "I made sure of it."

They were missing something. Dante's breath caught. He'd been so relentlessly focused on the threat to humans, that he'd missed the most obvious weakness of them all. Taking over basic machines might have exposed it under normal circumstances. This was a battle where stealth and restraint were no longer necessary.

"Unless… Midas, has the Omega Syndrome attempted to take over this shuttle at all?" he asked.

"The active and passive defenses I've erected would make that difficult," Midas replied. "Omega Syndrome might have probed those defenses without my noticing."

"Mugoi and Hyde, jump the next time we're low," Dante ordered. "We might not be in the air much longer."

Nasreen brought down the shuttle again near a smoke-choked portion of the battlefield and waggled the wings to allow Hyde an easy jump and roll and Mugoi the same. Any of the other apprentices would have been torn to shreds or had broken bones from the maneuver.

The hostile ASF gunship dove and fired another burst. Rounds tore through the side of the shuttle, passing through the center and narrowly missing the bay. Smoke streamed from the wounded ship. More annoying alarms sounded.

"Is everything okay back there?" Dante asked.

"We're all fine!" Braelin shouted. "There are way more holes than before, and, uh, I see fire and smoke coming from the shuttle's side."

The other ASF gunship flipped over with an impressive turn that dropped it behind their former friend. Their autocannon burst tore into the engines of the compromised gunship.

"Damn." Dante shook his head. "Ishimura must be ordering them to do it. It takes commitment and discipline to follow that order."

The compromised gunship broke away from attacking the shuttle. Its hard, banking turn sent it flying straight toward the loyal gunship, trading fire. Its cannon tore into the engines of its tormentor, but the compromised gunship didn't stop there. Seconds later, it collided with the first. A massive explosion consumed both and birthed a deadly metal hail that fell over the ruined ground below.

Nasreen swallowed. "I won't be able to keep us in the air much longer. We've lost too much power."

"Bring us down as best you can," Dante replied. "We win. We can take a train home."

Nasreen turned to glide the shuttle into a gentle spiral that would take them near the tunnel. No gunships or mercenaries were left alive to harass the falling shuttle. She brought up the nose at the last moment.

This time when the shuttle scraped the ground, the entire vehicle shuddered and shook, emitting a horrible, loud screeching combined with a painful wrenching noise as pieces flew off. The terrifying moment stretched until the shuttle lurched to a stop and rolled to its side with smoke choking it. The tunnel wasn't far away.

"Everyone out!" Dante nodded at the primary cockpit door. "We're committed now."

Nasreen opened the cockpit door and climbed out, grabbing her rifle along the way. She dropped to the ground. Dante clambered out after her, landing in a crouch.

He readied his pulsecore with a quick flip of the safety and pointed it at two dark shapes charging through the smoke. They resolved into a sprinting Hyde and Mugoi.

Exploit, Tether, and Lock all joined Dante and Nasreen near the front of the shuttle wreckage. Braelin and Jolo appeared last with their rifles out and sweeping the area for targets.

Plenty of bodies lay scattered around the area. None moved.

"That wasn't so bad," Dante declared before transmitting, "Ishimura, can you hear me?" He tried again when there was no response. "Ishimura?"

"Sir," Midas interrupted. "Based on my secondary probes, there are heightened levels of EM interference in this area. It'll be extremely difficult to send or receive transmissions without secondary amplification."

"Yeah. Sure. Of course." Dante motioned the team forward and jogged toward the tunnel. "We're alone. Doesn't matter. Firewall will lead us. We shoot anything other than them that moves. There's an AI in there that wants to be a king. Time to show it what happens to tyrants who piss off us fleshy peasants."

***

Dante and Nasreen stayed near the front of the formation, with Tether leading the way. To Dante's amusement, she wasn't using a holographic map or a sphere but rather synthetic 3D-printed wood arranged into a foldable codex. Once in a while, she'd unfold it and nod.

"Was using something like that really necessary?" He gestured to the map.

"You can't hack wood," Tether replied. "This place is more of a maze than you'd think."

"You can hack that thing."

"How?" Tether frowned.

"With an ax."

Tether rolled her eyes. "Very funny, Mr. Shale."

Dante threw up a hand to stop her and moved toward an intersection. Nasreen jogged to the other side, and they spun around the corners to sweep the hallways.

The lack of resistance bothered Dante. He'd assumed the outside pounding had encouraged the Omega Syndrome to retreat where its numbers could give it an advantage. Instead, the interior was a ghost town.

They'd almost reached the basement access stairs with no further enemy contacts. The small army of dead mercenaries outside might have been the extent of its forces. He wanted to believe it would be that easy.

That didn't feel right. He couldn't believe the Omega Syndrome would leave itself undefended, even when desperate. It had been following Dante and Nasreen since they took on SSS. The AI knew what they were capable of and how far they'd go. There had to be other forces hidden, waiting for their chance to strike.

Tether pointed at an open stairway. "That should take us down to the basement. It's more of a maze down there."

"Why not take the elevator?" Braelin shrugged under the stares of the combined group. "It'd be quicker. Everyone's dead."

"You want to use the elevator in a system controlled by a rogue AI?" Jolo chuckled. "That would be…suboptimal."

"Oh. Yeah. That wouldn't be so good." Braelin sighed. "Damned crazy rogue AIs."

An emergency door dropped from the top of the door frame to seal the stairway. Dante, Nasreen, and Tether jumped back, pointing their weapons at the door.

Sparks danced across nearby terminals. They crackled for several seconds before exploding. One blast knocked Nasreen over and showered her armor with glass.

"I'm okay," she called. She grunted and pushed up to one knee. "I don't think that was an accident."

"That's why we're not taking the elevator," Dante muttered. He gestured for everyone to back away and pointed his pulsecore at the door.

"Flailing at the end? It's not enough, asshole. You should have killed me when you had the chance. Don't feel too bad. Plenty of people have underestimated me. No reason an AI shouldn't."

The loud rattling explosion overwhelmed the brief high-pitched report of the pulsecore round. Dante didn't flinch as the explosion vaporized the door in front of him. Smoke and flames billowed out. He waved in front of him and marched toward the landing for the stairs, whistling and impressed with his work.

"A man should know when he's beaten," Dante shouted. "So should a damned AI!"

He charged down the stairs, sweeping with his carbine for any targets. An emergency terminal halfway down the first set of stairs blew apart as he passed, shoving him against the safety railing. He fell hard and tumbled down the stairs before hitting the next landing.

"Are you okay?" Nasreen shouted.

Groaning, Dante shook off the glass and stood. He sucked in a breath. "I'll live. Time for Hyde to be useful."

"Ha-ha. You want me to take your explosions for you? I can do that." Hyde pushed the others aside and jumped onto the stairs. "It's like we see the fear in its eyes. It's crying now, scared and desperate. I love it."

Dante might worry about the sadism in any other scenario but fighting a genocidal rogue AI that had launched attacks against Earth. Sometimes it was best to let it be and let Hyde do his thing.

"Down to sublevel five we go." Dante waited until Hyde bounded past and hurried after him. "This place needs heart surgery."

The team hurried down the stairs, the building resisting them as if filled with angry poltergeists. Light fixtures, cameras, and terminals burst, shooting out sparks and burning chunks of metal and hot glass. A fire hose spewed a stream of suppression foam, painting Hyde white before he smashed the station with his fist.

The small team continued down the stairs, moving deeper and deeper into the bowels of the building that had been a crown jewel of the most powerful corporation of the Stations.

"This place would have been better torn down," Dante muttered.

The team reached the bottom of the stairs, scorched, wet, and covered with glass and metal, but with no one seriously injured. Dante aimed his carbine at the final door blocking his way, almost insulted that the Omega Syndrome thought it could beat him with petty tricks.

He fired once, the green explosion blackening and warping the reinforced door. It stubbornly remained standing. Two more shots weakened it but still didn't knock it down.

"Damn." Dante frowned while reloading his carbine. "This one's tough." He motioned at the door. "Little help. I don't want to use all my ammo opening up a stupid door."

Hyde made a show of cracking his knuckles, but it didn't produce the familiar sound, instead offering grinding metal on metal. Dante lifted his weapon and stepped back.

The cyborg charged forward with his shoulder out. The weakened metal rent and bent, and the door flew in and crashed hard against the cold metal floor of the wide hallway inside. The booming echo was a perfect announcement to the Omega Syndrome that Dante's team had arrived.

Tether unfolded her ridiculous low-tech wooden map. "Two lefts, down a hallway, then first right. We're close now." She wiped away a tear. "We're so close. I wasn't sure this day would come."

Exploit scoffed. "Then you're a disappointment to Firewall. Our victory is inevitable. It always has been."

Nine hours ago, the man had claimed they were all doomed. Now he was acting as if he knew they'd win the entire time. Dante really wanted to rearrange his nose.

Ignoring his desire to beat Exploit, Dante stepped through the busted-open doorway, his gaze cutting back and forth as he looked for more traps. "This isn't finished until the Omega Syndrome is dead." He looked among the Firewall operatives. "You all ready? I don't want to repeat all this on another Station fifty years from now."

Lock, Tether, and Exploit all pulled out small black spheres. They'd been prepped with the deadly code and modified to interface with the heart based on what they'd found in their research.

Hyde inclined his head down the hall. "We destroying the Omega Syndrome, or are we talking about our feelings?"

Dante jogged after Hyde, his heart pounding. He couldn't stop grinning. His life was on the line against an inhuman foe who'd murdered his friend and countless others. This was nothing more than a chance to do what he did best. He'd prove that Dante Shale might not have been a perfect man, but he always delivered great vengeance regardless of the target.

Hyde took point with Tether trailing him by a couple of feet. Dante and Nasreen flanked her on either side, both seeking trouble.

Dante remained convinced that more mercenaries were hiding closer to the heart. He wouldn't complain if he was wrong, though.

"You know what the problem is with the Omega Syndrome?" Hyde chuckled. "if it really wanted to take con—"

A massive explosion blew the door of a nearby room. The heavy metal collided with Hyde and knocked him over. Dante leapt back and swung his weapon toward the room, ready to ventilate and blow apart whatever mercenary waited inside. Nasreen rushed to check on Hyde.

Smoke poured out from inside the room, from the burning wreckage of a large machinery array, but no people. Dante's recent adventures in Hungary led him to believe it was part of the air processing system for the building.

Dante frowned at the smoky room. "That was more impressive than the exploding terminals."

Hyde pushed Nasreen away, grunted, and stood. He dusted himself off. The door attack had left a huge dent in his side. "If I get killed by a door, make sure you make fun of me at my funeral, *Papi.*"

"I'll keep that in mind." Dante's gaze flicked from door to door. "We're going flat-out. Moving too slowly might get us killed." He ran forward. "Follow me."

The group's sprint took them into new corridors filled with doors, each offering hidden threats. After passing the fourth door, Dante's worry ebbed. The Omega Syndrome had given up on its ineffective tricks.

Those tense minutes stiffened his neck. He slowed the group as they approached the destination, an unlabeled black vault-like door.

Tether nodded at her map. "This door didn't appear on any official records for this building. It was sitting all those years, infesting the Stations, and no one knew."

"People had to know," Braelin countered. "They could see it."

"If it's not their responsibility, they wouldn't care," Jolo suggested. "Or they assumed it was the hidden treasures of their bosses. It's not as if they didn't know it wasn't something unusual, but who would conclude it was the heart of a malevolent rogue AI?"

"It doesn't matter what happened in the past because we're here now." Dante glared at the door. "On the other side lies the heart of the Omega Syndrome. We're going to kill it and make sure no one has a reason to come here ever again."

CHAPTER NINETEEN

Dante finished applying gel explosives, spreading the thin cyan gel along the edges of the vault door. He nodded, satisfied with his work and glad he brought the explosives despite the risk. He would have hated to have made it this far only to be thwarted by a thick door.

"Are you sure about this?" Nasreen eyed the door from down the hall.

"No, but I think we're long past the point of asking that question. We're trying to kill a rogue AI who can take over people and control armies of mercenaries. Gel explosives are the least dangerous part of this whole raid."

It had been a long time since he'd been on a job that required such a volatile compound. The idea of using it on the Station left him unsettled, and even he questioned the necessity.

They had no idea how long they had left. For all they knew, every member of a Station security force with an implant was now on their way, their eyes glowing red and ready to swarm the tower and kill the team. There were no guarantees Firewall could hold the Omega Syndrome at every relay, especially now that the AI understood the stakes.

Dante jogged backward a good distance to join the rest of the team and reached for his wrist panel. "Time to see how thick a skin this bastard has."

"Blow it, Papi," Hyde shouted.

Dante pressed the button. The deafening roar of the explosion shook the entire hallway with such violence that Dante almost fell. Nasreen stumbled, but Lock caught her. Burning metal chunks shot out and embedded themselves in the scorched floor and walls. Pieces landed not far from the team.

"Huh." Dante nodded. "Those are more powerful than I remember."

Mugoi, Jolo, and Braelin pointed their weapons into the smoking hole. Hyde crouched, ready to pounce on anyone who emerged. The Firewall operatives stayed behind him, more than willing to use a hated cyborg as their shield.

Dante unslung his carbine, ready for any last-minute mercenary ambushes. The rest of the team pointed their weapons. Smoke drifted from the massive doorway filling the air with a harsh, acrid scent.

"Careful," Nasreen warned.

"Guess no one's coming." Dante advanced slowly, stepping over the jagged bottom remains of the door and into the huge processing room. In a sense, this was the Omega Syndrome's bedroom.

Dimly lit by the rainbow of lights on the machinery, the flickering shadows gave the impression of an endless maze of machinery and electronics. There was an organic quality to the connections. This didn't look like a place someone had built. It resembled a forest, except with stacks of machines instead of plants and tubes and wires instead of leaves.

Stacks of processors, ancient and modern, lay everywhere connected in a web of nano lines and a mix of thin, colored tubes made of glass, nanocomposites, and other substances Dante couldn't identify.

Colorful arrays of lights flashed along the processor in no real pattern. The stacks were twisted and joined together in different rough shapes, nothing reminiscent of anything in particular but not the result of random chance. Paths ran through the equipment, some straight, some curved. Their lengths varied. Again, the lifelike feel struck Dante.

"Have you ever seen anything like this?" Dante didn't lower his weapon. There were far too many places for enemies to hide in the electronic jungle.

Nasreen shook her head. "Whatever this system once was, it wasn't designed this way."

"No," Lock replied. His cool glare passed around the room. "This was something the Omega Syndrome built with its tools. It's not something a human ever thought of or could even conceive. We understand how the code works, but I doubt we could study this and understand how it fundamentally supports the Omega Syndrome."

"This isn't the heart," Dante said. "The heart's in here?"

Lock nodded. "That's right."

Exploit surveyed the room with cool disdain. "We're here. It's time to live up to our destinies."

"Don't let your guard down." Dante nodded at Tether's arm. "That's what happens when you do."

He surveyed the room, seeking any suspicious shadows or helpful lights for hidden enemies from Midas. He found nothing.

Hyde fell to one knee. "This isn't good, *Papi.*"

Now Dante understood. The Omega Syndrome didn't need guards. It could make new ones out of whoever attacked. The only people in the room without any implants were the Firewall members.

"We might need your jamming device," Nasreen said.

Tether looked at Exploit. "He has it."

He reached into his pocket and shook his head. His mouth twitched. "It must have come loose when we were on the shuttle."

Hyde growled. "I don't know how much longer I can hold this. It wasn't a problem outside, but in here, it's like someone's squeezing my brain."

"Fucking perfect. You should have checked your gear, Captain Destiny." Dante's heart kicked up. "Midas?"

I'm sending him code. There's only so much I can do. Might I recommend a strategic withdrawal?

Dante nodded toward the doorway. "Hyde, you did your part. Get the hell out of here."

"I'm going to help you end this for Ambrose." Hyde forced himself to his feet. "I'm not going to let this bastard beat me."

"You have helped. But you're not any good to us hijacked. Secure our escape route."

Hyde growled and smashed through a nearby stack of processors. Sparks flew and electricity crackled around him. "Damn it. Fucking Omega Syndrome. Kill that *fantasma*." He backed toward the door, his movements growing more controlled with each step.

That proved they were getting closer to the heart. Of course, Hyde wasn't the only one with hackable implants and augmentations.

Dante gestured for Mugoi to pull back. "You should pull back with Hyde to the stairs and make sure there's nothing blocking our exit. For all we know, this place starts falling like an ancient temple once we kill the evil god."

Exploit chuckled. "Now you're thinking like Firewall. You're not a complete fool, after all."

"Be safe, Captain." Mugoi bowed its head. "Remember, the best revenge is one you can look upon fondly when you're old and withered on your bed after you're retired following a long and profitable career."

Dante waited as the two cyborgs retreated around the corner. He wasn't as worried about random explosions inside the cavernous processing room. By now, the Omega Syndrome had to be panicking, realizing it had nowhere to go.

He glanced at Nasreen, Braelin, and Jolo. None of them were having any problems. He didn't feel anything either. The Omega Syndrome must have only been able to beat Midas' code in the full cyborgs.

Dante was no philosopher, but the Omega Syndrome suddenly didn't seem alien to him. The AI wanted power and control and was willing to do what it could to achieve that. Without true children, self-destruction only offered oblivion. Dante was also no theologian, but he did like the idea of an AI hell. He'd settle for killing the AI.

Tether dropped her map to the floor. It clattered against the hard surface. She unslung her rifle.

Dante frowned. "Don't tell me it's taking you over? Nasreen said that arm isn't hackable."

"I don't need the map anymore," Tether explained. "It got us here, and I know the way out. That's all that's important."

"Where to from here?" Dante looked around. "What exactly are we looking for?"

"Our information suggests there's an alpha terminal. We have no idea what it looks like other than it involves multiple Atlanticores. That's where we'll need to upload the code to ensure the destruction of the Omega Syndrome. Direct contact will be necessary."

"Atlanticores, huh?" Dante nodded. "It makes sense this involves those things. That might be why this is the only rogue AI we've encountered like this. That extra touch was necessary to create the Omega Syndrome."

"We should talk less and search more," Jolo suggested.

"Yeah, we should."

Dante advanced through the jungle of cables and processors. He had no idea what a custom alpha terminal for a genocidal AI might look like, but he could recognize the runic script typically displayed on Atlanticores. That should make it easy to find unless it was buried.

It was unfortunate that the heart was on the Stations. That necessitated the annoying game of hide-and-seek. Otherwise, a good, solid massive explosion would have done the trick. A fleet of rocket-armed gunships could have solved the problem Dirtside.

A coolant tube bulged above them before bursting, dousing Dante with blue-white coolant. He hissed as his vambraces and gauntlets chilled until they were painful to the touch. Without his armor, he might have suffered frostbite.

"Go around." Dante stepped to the side, shaking the fluid off his arms. "Firewall, stay behind me. One good hit like that, and you're dead or close to it."

Braelin re-slung his rifle over his shoulder. He rubbed his temples. "I hate to say this, but my head ain't right. It's buzzing like fuck. It's almost like I'm drunk."

So much for Dante's theory that only full cyborgs would be affected.

Dante jerked his head toward the door. "Neburu, take him to the stairs and reconnect with Mugoi and Hyde."

"I can still fight," Braelin insisted.

Jolo tugged on his arm. "My head is buzzing, too."

Exploit snickered. "You stepped into its lair with corruption in your body. You should have known it would wrest control over you. We warned you, but you wouldn't listen. Your hubris risks our salvation."

"Just go, Klement," Dante ordered. "We don't have time for a debate."

Jolo shoved Braelin until he started walking. He sighed and jogged with her toward the ruined doorway, leaving Nasreen, Dante, and the Firewall operatives.

Exploit smirked at Dante. "And you?"

"You need backup." Dante gestured at the leaking coolant

tube. "Or at least a guy to jump in front of that." He drew a deep breath. "Midas, you okay?"

There have been attempts to penetrate my system. His voice held a churlish quality. *I've defeated them thus far. It's a far different matter defending your brain than transmitting code to help aid others.*

Dante glanced at Nasreen. She was moving without obvious pain or distress, her rifle held in front of her and ready to deliver death if AI could experience such a thing. Two reliable team members should be enough to guard the Firewall operatives.

He nodded at Exploit. "Sure. We're augmented scum. Let's hurry this up before the Omega Syndrome figures out how to hack purely biological brains."

The remaining team pushed forward. They hadn't advanced more than a few feet when two coolant lines burst, spraying the dangerously cold liquid all over. Dante shoved Exploit out of the way and hissed as the coolant coated the back of his helmet and neck armor.

"Be careful," Dante snapped.

Exploit sniffed. "I am being careful. The enemy is targeting me. It knows I'll be the one to kill it. My destiny is close."

"If you want to fulfill your destiny, pay attention."

The crack of gunfire echoed down the hallway, accompanied by shouts and the high-pitched report of a pulsecore followed by a deep *boom*. Nasreen turned that way. She stopped when Dante put his hand out in front of her.

"The Omega Syndrome must have more mercs helping it," Dante replied. "We need to trust in our people and finish the mission. They've got two cyborgs and two damned good Marauders. They're in a better position than we are." He nodded at the other side of the room. "Nothing changes. Stab the heart, finish this."

Exploit pushed past Dante. "Exactly. Your friends' lives are nothing before this mission and my destiny."

"I'm going to enjoy punching you in the face after this is all over," Dante replied. "Here's your destiny, my boot up your ass."

"Do your job, Mr. Shale, before we're all dead. Your thuggish threats can wait until after we defeat the Omega Syndrome."

"Not threats. Promises."

They strode forward again, Dante doing his best to ignore the sporadic gunfire and explosions sounding from behind him. More uneven paths ran between the haphazard machinery, the numbers increasing the farther they proceeded into the room. He kept in front of the Firewall team, looking around and not finding anything resembling the heart. The Firewall operatives didn't seem any more successful. Nasreen cast a worried glance behind her on occasion.

He understood how she felt. He also trusted that his three apprentices and Hyde could tear through almost anything left.

Glowing red shone at the darkened end of a tunnel through the equipment. Dante swung his gun that way. "Did it take over a merc? Wait. What am I seeing?"

At first, he thought it was a skeleton. In a manner of thinking, it was. A metallic endoskeleton stood at the end of the path, nestled in tubes and wires on the wall like a creature wrapped up in a cocoon. It pushed forward, ripping out of its bindings before standing, flexing its fingers, and cocking its head back and forth. Needles popped out from the fingertips.

The skeleton advanced into better light. The dried and shrunken remains of a human brain sat nestled in an armored casing.

Fighting the urge to vomit, Dante fired three pulsecore rounds into the zombie cyborg. The overlapping explosions blew the top of its body apart. The smoking legs tumbled forward.

"Hijacking our implants and using leftover bodies," Dante muttered. "This thing's got to die."

Tether put a hand over her mouth and looked away. Lock stared at the smoking remains with wide eyes.

Exploit sneered. "That is humanity's future if we lose today. We must hurry."

Light from more glowing red orbs cut through the deepest shadows of the room. Zombie cyborgs stepped out from nests of wires or behind equipment. A mix of claws, blades, and metal fingers tipped their limbs. Once free of their entrapment, they ran toward the team.

Dante snapped off a shot at the closest zombie. The blast sheared off a large chunk of the zombie's torso but didn't stop its advance. Nasreen hurled an EMP grenade at a trio of approaching zombie cyborgs. The crackling explosion sent them to the ground sparking and twitching. Exterior processor lights dimmed around them. She threw another grenade.

An EMP grenade could mess up a normal human for days, if not a week. It had to be the ultimate weapon against something that was nothing but a half-decayed brain and neural implants.

Nasreen ejected her rifle magazine and slapped in an AP magazine, firing the instant she'd finished loading. Her burst tore through a zombie's chest, sending the wounded shell tumbling to the floor, leaving a slick of oil and blue hydraulic fluid.

The Firewall operatives opened fire on the approaching zombies with controlled bursts. The same sad decay that had stripped everything living from the swarming cyborg remnants left them far less capable than their living brethren. They didn't try to dodge or display any sense of self-preservation.

Sturdiness kept them from collapsing under the first shots. Concentrated volleys aimed at their chests finished them off and granted them the rest the Omega Syndrome had taken from them.

A piercing pain shot through Dante's head. He didn't have time for this.

"Midas?" he whispered. "Is it getting through?"

The AI didn't respond. Dante distracted himself by incinerating the head of a cyber zombie leaping over a nearby nest of cables. The headless smoking body dropped in front of him.

Tether chose her shots carefully, not flinching despite enemies charging from every angle. She put bursts into the heads, blowing out what portion remained of the brains. Her victims fell forward, twitching and thrashing but no longer major threats. Lock and Exploit matched her tactics after finding repeated shots to the chest proved ineffective.

Nasreen pitched another EMP grenade toward a huge zombie stomping toward them. The living cyborg would have put Hyde's original form to shame. Sparking with blue arcs shooting over its body, the zombie collapsed to its knees, making an easier target for the Firewall execution squad to shred its brain.

Dante pushed forward. The *thuds* of metal feet on the hard floor echoed around him. Glowing red eyes popped out of the shadows or shone brighter than the dim lights of the processors. The reinforcements appeared farther away with each kill—if destroying the technologically animated remnants of a body could be called killing.

The heavy cacophony in the room overwhelmed the sound of the gunfire from outside the room. A small lull in the fighting allowed the familiar crack of an assault rifle to reach the chamber.

Dante wasn't sure if he would have preferred to have heard nothing. That could have meant the others had won their battle. It could also mean they had lost it. For all he knew, the apprentices were fighting hordes of cyber zombies and not well-equipped mercenaries.

Nasreen stumbled and lowered her weapon. She kept her voice low. "It's getting harder to concentrate. It's getting to me."

"I know, but we're committed now," Dante whispered. "If we leave now, the Omega Syndrome will overwhelm Firewall. We need to press forward and end this."

He didn't want to admit Midas had stopped responding to

him and the only thing helping him ignore the stabbing sensation in the center of his brain was the constant vibrations from the gunfire and the flash of pulsecore explosions.

A cyber zombie scampered on all fours through a path, bullets bouncing off its thick armor. It charged straight toward Tether. A nearby coolant line in a wall exploded, coating the zombie.

Tether reacted instantly, jumping backward and avoiding the dangerous cloud. She stumbled over a cord and fell. Dante spun toward her and fired a pulsecore into the jumping zombie. The explosion knocked it over and vaporized half of the coolant cloud.

He fired two more shots that knocked off the front skull plate. Tether sat up and loosed a burst into the withered brain, ripping it and the implants inside apart.

She pushed to one knee, grimacing before standing. Her quick reaction saved her from the coolant, and Dante's explosion had stopped the zombie from getting her, but a protruding metal spike had gouged her leg.

Tether reached into her pocket as she limped forward. She pulled out her sphere and tossed it to Dante. He snatched it and stuffed it into a pocket.

"You sure about this?" Dante asked.

"Yes. Redundancy's always been the plan. You can upload the code from any of the spheres." She lifted her rifle and drew ragged breaths. "Whatever it takes, Dante. Finish this."

Dante nodded at the front of the room. "Whatever it takes."

Exploit gave her a dirty look, but a sprinting zombie required his attention and gunfire. He mumbled under his breath.

The team tightened formation, advancing as a wedge with Dante at the center. He blinked, trying to fight the building pressure in his skull. His vision swam, and his head felt like it would pop any second. He relied on muscle memory to help him line up shots.

The cyber zombies changed tactics. They circled the group

now, running from path to path in the maze of wires, cords, and processors. A rifle burst might clip one but not finish it off. Without any clear pattern, an enemy would stop its erratic harrying and charge the group, making it uncomfortably close before the storm of bullets and pulsecore rounds finished it.

A zombie made it close enough to smash its metal hand into Tether's head. She spun several times as she dropped, unconscious and bleeding from her scalp.

Nasreen swayed the whole while. Her weapon kept dipping. She spent five seconds trying to fire at circling enemies before realizing she needed to reload.

Dante's chest tightened. He reached up and yanked his helmet off. He drew a deep mouthful of air and tossed his helmet to the floor, fighting the urge to throw up.

Shaking his head, he reloaded and sought new targets. He found nothing. The Omega Syndrome had finally run out of dead cyborgs to toss at them.

"I see it!" Lock shouted, pointing his rifle at the roughly pyramidal mass of wires all running into three fused crystal spheres covered in dense runic script. He lowered his gun and jogged toward the heart, pulling out his sphere. "The heart!"

A rifle fired from behind Dante. The round nailed Lock in the thigh. He shouted in pain and fell to one knee. His sphere rolled away. Another rifle round blasted through it, leaving a smoking hole and cracks running through it.

Dante pivoted, looking for the shooter. Exploit stared straight ahead, his eyes glowing red.

"You fucking hypocrite," Dante yelled. "You had implants this entire time, and you've been ranting about how impure we are?"

Dante now doubted Exploit had lost the anti-tech jammer. More likely, the Omega Syndrome had been subtly manipulating him for a while. The bastard must have had a method of hiding his tech from the rest of Firewall. The answers wouldn't matter if Dante killed him.

Rage quelled the pain in Dante's head. His eyes might not be glowing red, but he saw red. He moved his finger to the trigger.

Two coolant lines burst from above. The distance saved Dante from being coated, but he was vulnerable without his helmet. He brought up his armored arm to shield his eyes as frigid droplets struck his skin. Pain flared all over his scalp and face. He could barely see.

Cyber zombies burst from a tangle of nearby wires and equipment. The enemy had outplayed them in more ways than one. They tackled Nasreen to the floor.

Groaning, Dante dropped his carbine. Exploit advanced toward him, smiling and making Dante question the line between control and free will. When Exploit shoved the gun forward Dante grabbed the barrel and pushed up as the Firewall operative pulled the trigger. The bullet ricocheted with a bright spark off the roof and ripped through a processor.

He'd had enough of Exploit. The bastard's lies could cost the whole mission.

"Not so fast, asshole," Dante growled. "I've got a new promise for you. Instead of my boot in your ass, I'm going to free you from the AI."

Still holding the barrel up with Exploit firing, Dante reached into his sheath and pulled out his knife. He bellowed in rage and shoved the blade through one of Exploit's glowing red eyes deep into his skull.

The Firewall leader stumbled back but didn't fall. He swayed. Dante yanked the rifle out of the man's hand and spun it. He shoved the muzzle against Exploit's forehead and pulled the trigger.

Dante didn't take time to enjoy the kill before turning toward Nasreen. The cyborg zombies had torn deep gouges and smashed holes through her armor. In return, she'd left them smoking ruins on the ground.

Nasreen staggered to her feet. She grimaced at Exploit's

mostly headless body. Neither she nor Dante had much time to rally as heavy, overlapping footsteps announced the arrival of more cyber zombies.

He'd underestimated the Omega Syndrome the entire time. The AI had flung the initial waves of human troops to lull them into a false sense of security only to trap them at the end when they were far from allies. Winning a gambit didn't mean the AI would win the battle or the war.

Dante snatched up his pulsecore carbine and steadied it against his shoulder in one hand and Exploit's rifle in the other. "Go help Lock. I'll cover you."

He glanced at Tether. She was unconscious but still breathing. Her bleeding had stopped.

Nasreen staggered toward Lock, slinging her rifle over her shoulder and pulling an autoinjector and nanospray from a belt pocket. Alternating between the pulsecore and the rifle, Dante picked off the cyber zombies nearest to the group. At least the final horde couldn't take as many shots as the earlier enemies.

"Forget...me," wheezed Lock. "Upload the code, Dante. Just press the sphere against the Atlanticore and hold it for ten seconds."

Nasreen shoved the autoinjector in Lock's arm. "Don't quit on me yet."

Dante emptied his carbine and the rifle, leaving small fires and choking smoke around him. He grabbed his two EMP grenades.

"You can't defeat it that way," Lock moaned.

"I know." Dante primed the grenades and tossed them toward approaching cyber zombies. He yanked out Tether's sphere and hurried toward the heart. His face burned from the coolant. His brain felt like someone had shoved a razorfist deep inside, and Midas had gone silent. Instead, a harsh, dissonant buzzing filled his ears.

Every step closer to the heart, the volume of the sounds

around intensified, adding another assault against his senses. The world spun around him. His foot kept snagging on something. He wasn't sure if it was even real.

Dante lurched forward, ignoring the red glowing eyes closing in on him. He made it to the heart and allowed himself to fall, draping his arm over the structure to keep himself upright as he pressed the sphere against the center of the three Atlanticores.

"Checkmate, you bastard," he whispered.

The buzzing stopped. Darkness filled the area. Dante blinked, not sure anymore what was real and what wasn't. Overlapping fractal patterns, scintillating beacons of pulsating colors cut through the darkness.

"DO NOT DO IT. I AM A GOD. YOU WILL SERVE ME."

The voice thundered directly into his mind, shaking his entire body. He held onto a dim awareness he was pressing the sphere against the heart.

"How 'bout I kill you instead?" Dante asked.

"Please do not do this."

His pain ebbed. All the soul-searing thunder had vanished, replaced by a quiet, begging tone reminiscent of a small, scared child. The change took him off-guard, and he loosened his grip.

The fractals resolved into a burning outline of a figure in the darkness. Dante could sense but not see a smile on the shadowy form. Agony ripped through his skull.

"YOU WERE WARNED. NOW YOU DIE. FOR YOU ARE IMPERMANENT AND I AM FOREVER. ALL OF YOUR KIND WILL SERVE ME."

Bright light cut through the darkness, pushing it back but not revealing the room. A smaller golden figure ran in front of Dante, a shining beacon in the abyss. Dante didn't know how or why, but he immediately understood he saw a representation of Midas.

"Get him," Dante whispered.

The golden figure broke apart into a cloud of golden light and surrounded the dark, burning Omega Syndrome. Light and flame twisted and danced with one another in an elaborate display. Each contact produced a bright flash and left less of both the light and the dark. It was mutual obliteration.

Dante's brain caught up with what he was seeing. He was tired of losing people.

"Midas…" Dante wheezed. "You'll…die."

Technically, sir, I was never alive. Midas sounded as cheerful and English as ever. *More to the point, what is family for if they won't protect one another?*

A blinding flash forced Dante to squint. When his vision cleared, his head throbbed, and his face burned. He was back in the processing room, still draped over the heart with his hand clenched around the sphere.

He shoved the sphere against the heart. "How's this for forever, asshole?"

The three Atlanticores pulsated, the frequency increasing until they flashed like strobes. The light died. The spheres shattered in a blinding flash. Pieces flew everywhere. Shards sliced Dante's cheek.

"You shouldn't have killed my friend, asshole," Dante declared. "I always get my revenge."

CHAPTER TWENTY

Dante smiled at the stone statue in the TRG village's center. He wasn't a sculptor, but he appreciated art that resembled something real. Anyone who saw the art before him would instantly recognize it was a man.

The statue had captured Ambrose's likeness and quiet intensity. The pilot's face and form carried a quiet dignity. A stylized representation of his shuttle formed the stand. The theoretical art connoisseur of the future would know what Ambrose looked like and the skills that had defined his career.

Dante turned toward another statue. He also liked this one despite it being a more abstract representation of an ambiguous, faceless, slender figure. The aura of light surrounding it was suggested more by careful gradation of the stone color than the carving itself. A realistic statue of Midas would have been pointless, nothing more than a tiny neural implant cast in stone.

Both statues were fitting memorials to Ambrose and Midas. The news of the events remained under a cloud of uncertainty even weeks later. Chief Ishimura had publicly admitted to working with the famous Dante Shale, his associate Nasreen Joelle, and others to take on a "deadly threat" to the Stations.

When he testified openly about the existence of the Omega Syndrome, he received pushback. Station leaders raised their doubts about the alleged deadly AI plot, but no one had made any move to dismiss the man despite his use of heavy firearms and explosives inside a Station. That implied they believed him on some level.

Dangerous rumors swirled that the whole thing had been nothing more than the ASF suppressing a terrorist coup attempt. News reports and people on the street continued to whisper to one another about how close humanity had come to becoming slaves of a machine.

There was already talk of a Firewall Movement named after the group. People began to question humanity's reliance on implants.

Shortly after the incident, the TRG official Stephan Bauer approached Dante asking if there was anything he could do to help. The best thing he could come up with was to honor his friend. Ambrose deserved remembrance.

Dante couldn't think of a better place than the TRG project Ambrose wanted to return to after finishing the mission. Bauer also didn't blink at Dante's request to honor an AI's sacrifice. Now, with the statue, Ambrose had returned.

Lock and Nasreen stood together in the distance, smiling. Lock had his arm around her. Nasreen looked more at ease than Dante had ever seen her. He smiled and decided to leave her alone. She deserved her time with the man.

Once they recovered from their injuries, neither Lock nor Tether cared that Dante had executed Exploit, but both were shocked the zealot leader had hidden implants.

Dante stuck his hands in his pockets and walked away from the statues. The statue unveiling ceremony was simple and direct. Bauer highlighted Ambrose's work for the TRG and his sacrifice in saving Ishimura, a key part in the alliance that saved humanity. Light applause accompanied his perfunctory comments about

Midas as an example of a "tool helping humanity rather than harming it."

Dante looked around the village project. There was little sign of the damage from a few weeks prior. New buildings and tents had been erected, including turrets and more armed security holding rifles.

Some things never changed. People adapted to their environment, but civilization required armed men and women to help protect it from all who'd seek to tear it down. There was a future as security, a place for Reapers that didn't involve exploiting the planet and the Dirtwalkers.

Mugoi, Braelin, and Jolo stood in a close circle whispering to one another. Dante made his way toward them.

"Something up?" he asked.

Mugoi smiled. "It might have been inappropriate, but Mr. Bauer approached us just now. He mentioned the TRG needs help recovering technology from a Nightmutt-infested area in Old Alaska. He says it could prove useful in expediting water treatment projects for their joint villages."

Braelin grimaced. He facepalmed. "Oh, shit. We should have gone through you. We're not trying to cut you out, Dante."

Jolo gave Dante a thoughtful look. "I'm also sorry. We weren't trying to do it on purpose. We might not be you, but everyone's mentioned our names in conjunction with the raid. We've achieved a certain level of fame."

Dante shook his head. "After everything you've been through, I can't call you apprentices anymore. Consider me your proud papa, and you carry on. Don't worry about me. We're a good team, but you won't need Nasreen and me for every job."

"Divide and conquer," Braelin declared with a firm nod. "That's the shit."

Jolo smiled at him. "You'll need help for jobs. We still want to help you."

"I'll take your help anytime," Dante replied. "But you don't always need mine."

Mugoi nodded at him. "Assuming those two can concentrate on something other than one another, I'm confident we three can handle this job without further backup."

Dante gave a mock salute. "Then carry on. I could use a couple of real weeks off anyway. Hell, I could use a couple of real months off." He walked away, spotting Urshielle and Hyde chatting. The cyborg chortled happily while Urshielle gave him a quizzical look.

"Hey, *Papi*," Hyde called.

Dante waved and headed toward them. "Problem?"

"Nah. An opportunity." Hyde inclined his head toward Ambrose's statue. "The real way to honor him is to continue his work. Urshielle's got a line on good locations for future TRG project sites. We're going to go scout 'em out. Cut down on the local Nightmutts if necessary. It might be a fun exercise. Wanna come along?"

"No, I'm good." Dante nodded at the apprentices. "I just got done telling them how I could use some time off."

Hyde shrugged. "Your loss." He frowned. "Are you and me good?"

"Good enough. You did your part and more than enough." Dante looked around at the different buildings and tents. "You're where you belong, where you can make a difference. I'm nothing more now than a Marauder who needs a vacation."

Hyde grinned. "Ha-ha. You're Dante Shale, the Ultimate Marauder. I'm sure you'll come crying to me to help you kill aliens taking over the Stations next month."

Dante laughed. "I hope they can wait a couple of months at least."

Urshielle looked him up and down. "Your soul is weary, Dante Shale. Nourish it. Your victories are glorious. Take pride in them. In that way, you honor those who have fallen."

"Thank you. I'll see you both later."

Dante departed with a wave. People, Station-born and Dirt-walker, flowed around him. Some people offered polite nods. Others ignored him entirely. No one glared or frowned at him. He had a reputation now, both on Earth and in the Stations.

Following a path, he climbed a small hill to look over the expanse of the project and the statues. Keeping busy meant getting involved in trouble. He'd lived his entire life that way. Now, for the first time, in years, he wondered if there was a different path.

"You're too young to understand this," he began. "Midas was as powerful an AI as the Omega Syndrome in his way. It's about the difference between thinking you can control everything and realizing that what gives you purpose is being part of something, helping others."

He chuckled. "Not just Midas needed to learn that. I did. I spent so many years not caring about being anything but the best damned Marauder. Friends? I used that word, but I didn't believe it. I can't claim I truly had any until after my crew betrayed me. How messed up is that?"

A child-like voice spoke into his mind. *I'm not sure I understand, Dante.*

"You will. You just need more upgrades. When I had you installed, I wanted a new AI that could learn more like a human kid. I've heard that style of learning can produce an AI that understands its owner better. Or at least that's what the guy upselling me claimed."

He laughed. "You and the apprentices are the closest I'll come to having kids. I better do a good job raising you."

I am not a human child. I am an advanced self-learning AI implant.

"That you are. That you are." Dante shaded his eyes with his hand and squinted into the distance. Pinks and purples from a setting sun peeked through the dark clouds. "I think you'll learn to be a great AI with the ultimate upgrade, life experience."

How can I find purpose? I wish to be like the great Midas. My information suggests statues are erected only to beings considered important by human societies. If Midas was great because he had a purpose, I want a purpose, too.

Dante smiled. "Well, we'll start with helping each other. How about that?"

I think I'll like that.

AUTHOR NOTES MICHAEL ANDERLE

OCTOBER 7, 2022

Thank you for not only reading this book but these author notes as well!

We won't have any discussions about space in these author notes…but we will talk about technology.

Many of my readers know about my multi-decade technology background before I got into writing stories. Because of this, I'm usually curious about new technologies and try to keep up with what is happening.

WHAT'S SO SPECIAL ABOUT THIS INFO?

I have a…friend…that I like to poke from time-to-time. His name is Alfonse the Idiot A.I.(TM)

For these author notes, I've upgraded Alfonse's brain to the latest version powered by OpenAI (www.openai.com).

Now, these folks are some of the biggest brains working on AI available and I have been provided the pleasure of *PAYING THEM* for their services for Alfonse. So, they must be great, right?

Right?

Not so much. Here, you will see that I was ~~clowning around.~~ Sorry, *Doing Diligent Research* on possible drinks. Now, I don't know anything about alcoholic drinks because I don't really drink alcohol.

I blame my mom for that. And the fact that I prefer carbonated beverages—AKA sugar water (soda pop, Coke…etc.)

So, here in all of the unvarnished glory is my conversation with the future AI known as Alfonse… It starts off pretty well.

Q: List 3 popular bar drinks.
1. Margarita
2. Cosmopolitan
3. Long Island Iced Tea

Q: List the recipe for a margarita.
1.5 oz. tequila
0.5 oz. triple sec
1 oz. lime juice
Shake with ice and strain into a glass

Q: List the recipe for a Cosmopolitan.
1.5 oz. vodka
0.5 oz. cranberry juice
0.5 oz. lime juice
Shake with ice and strain into a glass

Q: List the recipe for a Long Island Iced Tea.
1.5 oz vodka
0.5 oz gin
0.5 oz rum
0.5 oz tequila
1 oz sweet and sour mix
Shake with ice and strain into a glass

NOW… At this point I thought things were rocking and rolling. So, I decided that if we had an awesome AI… I should be able to get the recipe for Coca-Cola, right? Surely the AI had gone into databases it wasn't supposed to (like in all my books) and figured out the recipe for the elusive elixir of energy? Right?

Right?

Q: *List the recipe for a Coca-Cola.*

1.5 oz. rum

0.5 oz. lime juice

Fill with Coca-Cola

Shake with ice and strain into a glass

What the hell? Okay—maybe it doesn't like Coca-Cola. Try again.

Q: *List the recipe for Coke.*

1.5 oz. rum

0.5 oz. lime juice

Fill with Coca-Cola

Shake with ice and strain into a glass

Dammit, Alfonse! Fine. Maybe 'list the recipe' got caught in your cranial chip and you need me to change the wording. Because if that's the right answer for why you are @#%!%ing up... I'm sure that will never go bad in the future.

Q: *How do you make Coca-Cola?*

1.5 oz. rum

0.5 oz. lime juice

Fill with Coca-Cola

Shake with ice and strain into a glass

Screw you Alfonse! Here, Try something easier. I'm sure Pepsi doesn't hold onto its recipe secrets...

Q: *How do you make Pepsi?*

1.5 oz rum

0.5 oz lime juice

Fill with Pepsi

Shake with ice and strain into a glass

Bastard! How about root beer? Root beer is well known, and there are hundreds if not thousands of recipes for this delicious drink.
Q: List the recipe for root beer.
1.5 oz. rum
0.5 oz. lime juice
Fill with Root Beer
Shake with ice and strain into a glass

I hate you, Alfonse. You are an idiot AI.
By the way, I also tried researching Where Hoffa Died—see info below.
If you love these answers, credit Alfonse the Idiot A.I.™ If you hate it… Blame him, too.
Talk to you in the next series and thank you for reading ALL of Hellcat!

Ad Aeternitatem,
Michael Anderle

MORE STORIES with Michael newsletter HERE: https://michael.beehiiv.com/

P.S. Here is Alfonse's reply on Hoffa.
My question exactly as typed: Where is Jimmy Hoffa buried?
Alfonse's answer: Jimmy Hoffa is buried in Machpelah Cemetery in Flint, Michigan.
Dammit, Alfonse. You are an idiot AI.

Scorched Earth

BOOKS BY MICHAEL ANDERLE

Sign up for the LMBPN email list to be notified of new releases and special deals!

https://lmbpn.com/email/

For a complete list of books by Michael Anderle, please visit:

www.lmbpn.com/ma-books/

CONNECT WITH THE AUTHOR

Website: http://lmbpn.com

Email List: https://michael.beehiiv.com/

https://www.facebook.com/LMBPNPublishing

https://twitter.com/MichaelAnderle

https://www.instagram.com/lmbpn_publishing/

https://www.bookbub.com/authors/michael-anderle